Selected for Your Library
by Delegate

John Williams

WVLA Library Appreciation Day
February 4, 2019

THE TALENT THIEF

THE TALENT THIEF

an extraordinary tale of an ordinary boy

Alex Williams

PHILOMEL BOOKS
AN IMPRINT OF PENGUIN GROUP (USA) INC.

PHILOMEL BOOKS

A division of Penguin Young Readers Group.
Published by The Penguin Group.
Penguin Group (USA) Inc., 375 Hudson Street, New York, NY 10014, U.S.A.
Penguin Group (Canada), 90 Eglinton Avenue East, Suite 700, Toronto, Ontario M4P 2Y3,
Canada (a division of Pearson Penguin Canada Inc.).
Penguin Books Ltd, 80 Strand, London WC2R 0RL, England.
Penguin Ireland, 25 St. Stephen's Green, Dublin 2, Ireland (a division of Penguin Books Ltd).
Penguin Group (Australia), 250 Camberwell Road, Camberwell, Victoria 3124, Australia
(a division of Pearson Australia Group Pty Ltd).
Penguin Books India Pvt Ltd, 11 Community Center, Panchsheel Park,
New Delhi—110 017, India.
Penguin Group (NZ), 67 Apollo Drive, Rosedale, North Shore 0632, New Zealand
(a division of Pearson New Zealand Ltd).
Penguin Books (South Africa) (Pty) Ltd, 24 Sturdee Avenue, Rosebank,
Johannesburg 2196, South Africa.
Penguin Books Ltd, Registered Offices: 80 Strand, London WC2R 0RL, England.

Originally published in 2006 in Great Britain by Macmillan Publishers Ltd.

Published simultaneously in Canada.
Printed in the United States of America.
Design by Ryan Thomann.
Text set in Apolline.

Library of Congress Cataloging-in-Publication Data
Williams, Alex, 1969–
The talent thief : an extraordinary tale of an ordinary boy / Alex Williams.
p. cm.
Summary: Orphaned Cressida, a magnificent singer, and
her twelve-year-old brother Adam attend the by-invitation-only Festival of Youthful Genius,
where they join forces with a former race car driver to try to stop a bizarre creature
from stealing the talents of the young prodigies.
[1. Ability—Fiction.   2. Adventure and adventurers—Fiction.   3. Individuality—Fiction.
4. Orphans—Fiction.]   I. Title.   PZ7.W65573Tal 2010
[Fic]—dc22
2009024989
ISBN 978-0-399-25278-5
1 3 5 7 9 10 8 6 4 2

To Hendrika and Harry

• • • • • • • • • • • •

"Talent is nice but kindness is everything."

—Professor Ernst Applebaum

CONTENTS

THE TALENT THIEF

PROLOGUE

· · · · · · · · · · · · · ·

The sleek silver race car with the lucky number seven on the side screamed through the twisting countryside. The talented driver had overtaken the rest of the pack long ago and was still pushing the car to its limits.

The Bluewood Hills racing circuit includes a long and narrow stretch through a dark forest and as car number seven hurtled in among the trees, the driver was too busy trying to stay on the road to notice a shadowy figure sliding along a wire, high above the car. The figure was tall and thin but muscular. Its tattered cloak billowed out behind it. With a thud the figure landed on the car roof. It reached through the window with a long, vein-covered claw. The car started to swerve.

CHAPTER ONE

THE INVITATION

· · · · · · · · · · · · ·

With the ring of a bell and a lazy sigh, the elevator doors opened and Cressida Bloom, gathering in her evening dress, stormed out and swept across the landing. Her younger brother, Adam, followed her, his shiny shoes clacking on the polished wooden floor.

"Cress, what exactly did I do?" he said.

"I'm not talking to you," she fumed as she pulled a key from her tiny handbag and opened the door to the apartment. She pushed her way in and let the door swing back into Adam's face.

Cressida was sixteen and pretty in an unusual way. She was of average height, slim and trying her best to progress from gangly to graceful. Her eyes were a remarkable pale green and framed by small, black spectacles. Her hair was dark and thick, and now she pushed it back from her shoulders and pulled two teardrop-shaped earrings from her ears and let them clatter down on a glass-topped table. She ignored the ornate envelope that lay there unopened.

The apartment was spread over the entire top floor of the building like a luxurious yawn. Elegant furniture, grand paintings and bookshelves groaning with books were all perfectly placed and beautiful lamps glowed their approval in every room. Cressida wandered through to one of the living areas, flopped down into the warm embrace of a leather armchair and closed her eyes. Adam clattered in.

"Was it because I cheered?" he asked.

Adam Bloom was twelve and looked very uncomfortable in the dinner suit he was wearing. He fumbled to undo his bow tie and kicked his shiny shoes off so they skidded under a sofa. He had scruffy fair hair that grew in all directions like a pineapple top and he was almost as tall as his sister. His dark brown eyes seemed always to be asking questions. He was the kind of boy who stayed on roller coasters and went around again. Adam annoyed Cressida endlessly.

"No, it wasn't because you cheered," Cressida replied wearily.

"Was it because I yelled out that stuff about you being the best singer in the world?" Adam persisted.

"No," Cressida answered, sinking further into her chair and clamping her fists to cheeks glowing with embarrassment.

"Was it because I stood on my seat at the end and

accidentally knocked that lady's hat off while I was waving at you?"

"No," Cressida muttered.

"What was it, then? Hmm?" Adam asked, blinking at his sister with confusion.

"All those things!" Cressida said. "The cheering, the yelling, the standing on the chair! I'm singing in a concert at the Wireless Union Music Hall for the people of Riverfork City and you're goofing around like you're an exhibit at the zoo!" Cressida felt her cheeks grow hotter. "The lady whose hat you knocked off was the wife of the mayor, for goodness' sake!"

"Ah, she didn't mind," Adam said.

"I minded!" Cressida said, her eyes white-hot and angry behind her spectacles.

"I was being supportive. I thought you'd like it," Adam mumbled.

"I didn't! I hated it!" Cressida cried.

Adam fell silent and dropped onto a sofa. He gazed down gloomily at his socks. There was a pattern on them of jumping sheep. He suddenly felt silly. He hated it when his sister was mad at him. And it happened so often.

Cressida breathed in deeply and tried to calm herself. She looked at Adam's sad face and felt the familiar feelings of guilt creep into her stomach. She pushed her spectacles back onto the bridge of her nose (they were always slipping down).

"I'm sorry. I'm not feeling so great about things at the moment," she said. Just then Uncle Brody, a large, wheezing man of about sixty, waddled into the room puffing on a cigar. He had a round, salmon-pink face with podgy cheeks that made his beady eyes look even smaller than they were. His mouth was like two thin, wet strips of rubber. It was the kind of face that could never look kind or happy. He seemed surprised to see Cressida and Adam. He frowned.

"I thought you two were in bed," he said, his fleshy jowls wobbling. He moved over to a cabinet and poured himself a large glass of brandy.

"We went to Cressida's concert, Uncle Brody," Adam said.

"A *concert*?" Uncle Brody retorted, as though he had never heard the word before. He swigged his brandy and licked his toadlike lips.

"Yes, Uncle," Cressida sighed. "I sang in a concert tonight."

"She was great! She *is* great. When she hits the high notes, she can shatter glass," Adam added, and Cressida shot a warning look in his direction.

Uncle Brody looked at Adam and Cressida's evening wear with a mixture of annoyance and bemusement.

"Why can't you just be like normal children? Hmm?" he asked. "When I was forced to become your guardian, I didn't think I'd have all this staying up till all hours and fancy-dressing. Children should—"

"I am sixteen years old!" Cressida blurted out.

"Don't you take that tone with me!" Uncle Brody cried. "If your parents were here, they'd be mortified!"

"Well, it's a good thing they're not here, then, isn't it?" Cressida blurted. She felt a wave of sadness and anger wash over her.

Uncle Brody glared at her, his tiny eyes shining and his wet lips quivering with fury.

"Get out of my sight!" he hissed.

"Gladly," Cressida replied, and with that she flicked off her high-heeled shoes, walked out of the living area and padded down the hall.

She stepped out onto a wide balcony that boasted a heart-stopping view of the entire city. The cool night air felt soothing on Cressida's face. She took a deep breath and looked down at the thousands of twinkling lights below. Cars honked as they made their way in steady streams along the grid of roads that crisscrossed Riverfork City. In the big park to the west, people were taking horse-drawn carriage rides, and in the bay, boats small and large blared friendly high and low foghorn notes to avoid running into each other in the evening mist. So many people, yet Cressida felt very much alone. She started to cry.

"Uncle Brody's not happy with you," Adam said quietly as he joined her.

"I don't care," Cressida replied, stifling her sobs. "He's a hideous creature only loosely disguised as a human being."

"Sorry I showed you up. . . . I think maybe I'm trying too hard to stand in for our parents."

"You don't need to do that."

"We're probably in shock," Adam said. "You know, since the incident. It's only been fourteen months, after all."

Cressida said nothing at this. She took a gulp of evening air and tried to compose herself because she had something important to say.

"I'm not sure I want to carry on singing."

For a moment, Adam looked stunned, teetering on his heels. Then he slapped his hand down hard on the wooden balcony railing. "You must!" he shouted. "You have a beautiful, rare talent!"

"Don't talk to me about talent. Look what it did to our parents," Cressida said. Her voice cracked and she gave a little cough.

"The way they died didn't have anything to do with their talent. It had to do with thin ice," Adam said.

"Yes, but they wouldn't have *been* on thin ice if they weren't trying to win their millionth stupid ice-skating contest," Cressida said. "They had everything. Why didn't they just stop?"

"Because they had to share their talent with the world. Because they *wanted* to. It would have been a waste not to," Adam said.

"How come you're such an expert anyway, Adam?" Cressida asked, her eyes taking on a steely look. "It's not as if you have any talent of your own, now, is it?"

Adam bit his lip. His sister's words stung and he felt a lump rising in his throat, which prevented him from speaking. He knew he did not have any talent of his own, unlike the rest of his immediate family. But that hadn't seemed to matter to him when his parents were alive. Sure, they had encouraged Cress's singing, but above all they had wanted him and Cress to be happy. They had always said he was special anyway—he and Cressida both were, in their own ways—even if Adam could never see exactly how himself. His eyes brimmed with tears.

Cressida felt the guilt churning in her stomach again, but she fought the urge to apologize. Her parents were stupid to leave her and Adam the way they did and Adam was even more stupid for continuing to cheer them on.

"I'm going to bed," Cressida said, and she headed inside. Adam nodded. He understood she was upset. He just wished he didn't always have to take the brunt of it.

Next morning, Cressida was sitting at a small table on the balcony, lost in thought, munching toast and watching the sunlight twinkle on the water in the bay. Adam came out and stretched and yawned with gusto. He grinned at his sister. Any bad feelings he had felt toward her the night before were gone. He did not hold grudges and, anyway, since his parents had died he had decided that it was his responsibility to keep himself and his "artistic" sister on an even keel. It was what his parents would have wanted, he was sure. And she was his sister, after all! Uncle Brody certainly could not care less.

"Morning, Cress!" Adam said.

Cressida grunted in response. Adam sat down and grabbed a slice of toast from the rack and began to butter it with enthusiasm. Cressida tried to ignore the louder-than-necessary scraping noise. As Adam took a hearty bite, he remembered something and reached into his pants pocket. He dropped the ornate envelope, which had been on the glass hall table, in front of Cressida.

"Aren't you going to open it?" he asked. "It's been sitting there for days now."

"It'll be a tedious invite to sing at some dreary function," Cressida muttered, pushing the envelope away.

Adam picked it up and tore it open. He pulled out a silver card with beautiful swirly writing on it and read it aloud.

Cressida Bloom is cordially invited to attend

The Festival of Youthful Genius,

a celebration of the world's most brilliant
people aged ten to sixteen,
which will take place in the superb Hotel Peritus
in the stunning City of Paralin.
Please telegram to confirm.
—Your humble servant, Fortescue.

"Those people should write travel brochures," Cressida said. "'Brilliant,' 'superb,' 'stunning.' Give me a break."

"You gonna go?" Adam asked, his eyes shining. "It sounds great!"

"Didn't I say last night that I am giving up singing?" Cressida said.

Suddenly, cigar-stained fingers grabbed the card from Adam's hand, and Uncle Brody dropped down heavily into a chair and started to read it to himself, making disgusting little snuffling noises as he did so.

"What's this?" he mumbled. "Why would anyone invite either of you to anything?" And with that he threw the card down on the table, where it landed in the butter.

"Because she's amazingly talented," Adam answered.

"There's no such thing as 'talent,'" Uncle Brody said. "There's only luck."

"Your brother was talented," Cressida said. She could feel herself getting irritable again. Uncle Brody always made her get like that.

"Your father had a lucky break," Uncle Brody said. "It should have been me with all that ice-skating glory."

Adam cast his gaze over Uncle Brody's enormous bulk. "You were an ice-skater?" he asked, trying to keep the amazement out of his voice.

"Could have been," Uncle Brody replied, "if it weren't for my ankles. Your father had the good luck of having strong ankles. All there is to it."

And with that Uncle Brody rummaged in his jacket

pocket and pulled out a half-smoked cigar and a box of matches. He lit the cigar and started puffing, retreating into a little world of his own.

Cressida watched him and decided not to remind her uncle of his own extreme good "luck"—how his brother's gift had enabled the rich and very lazy lifestyle Uncle Brody currently enjoyed, without Uncle Brody having to lift a finger, or ankle, of his own.

"Talent does exist and my sister has it," Adam suddenly declared. "And she needs support to make it grow."

"Shh, Adam," Cressida said. She did not want support. She did not want to make her "talent" grow. She just wanted a safe, quiet, happy life.

"You two talk too much," Uncle Brody said, his face now hidden by a cloud of smoke. "I want some changes around here. I want you in your rooms a lot more often. I certainly don't want to see or hear you after eight o'clock in the evening, and there'll be no more, you know, frivolity with dressing up and going out. I don't want young, noisy lives disrupting mine."

Cressida felt her spirits sink further. Living with Uncle Brody was already bad enough, even though she spent a lot of time out of the apartment at various events. Without those chinks of freedom she could see herself becoming truly miserable in a very short period of time. She plucked the card from the butter and, with a huge effort, smiled at Uncle Brody.

"Uncle, do you think I may go to this?" she asked. "I'd be out of your way. Maybe for a long time, and . . ."

Adam looked at his sister with rising panic. She might not want to sing, but she certainly wanted to get away from their uncle, maybe forever, and Adam did not relish the idea of being left alone with him.

"And . . . and you'll have the apartment all to yourself," Adam stuttered, "and you can wander around smoking cigars and drinking brandy all day and all night in peace. Please let us go."

Cressida frowned at Adam, but he just shrugged and grinned. She decided to say nothing. Adam was not her favorite person in the world at the moment. Even so, she could not sentence him to life alone with Uncle Brody.

Their uncle mulled the request over.

"Yep, you can go. But take the trash out first," he said.

Introductory Note to
"Project Golden Harvest" Notebook

Myths and legends do not just appear out of thin air. There is always some spark of truth that starts them off. Of course, the years might expand the truth like the snowball gaining in size as it rolls down the mountain, but what if that initial spark were enough to ignite a dream?
My dream. I have spent many years now in libraries and museums translating ancient parchments and reading reports from explorers and locals. This mysterious, wonderful, shadowy entity must exist. And I shall find it, escape this ordinary life and make my dream a reality—whatever the cost.

CHAPTER TWO
THE HOTEL PERITUS

• • • • • • • • • • • • •

The seaplane thundered through the stormy night, its engines working hard against the powerful wind that was throwing it around like a toy. Adam looked out the window at the dark ocean churning below. The heavy rain made it difficult to see anything, but suddenly a large mass broke the surface and a waterspout shot up into the air. Adam gasped and turned to Cressida sitting next to him, her fingers gripping the armrest of her seat so tightly, her knuckles were white.

"I think I just saw a whale, Cress," he said.

At that moment Cressida had no interest whatsoever in sea life.

"I wish we'd stayed with Uncle Brody," she muttered. "Anything is better than this."

The seaplane gave a lurch and Cressida fought the urge to be sick.

"Are you kidding?" Adam said. "This is great!"

He turned his attention back to the window and looked out at the huge propeller, which was hacking its way through the damp air.

"I think the propeller's stopped," Adam said. He paused. "No, it's okay."

Cressida closed her eyes and tried her best to ignore her brother.

As dawn broke, Cressida was relieved to get off the seaplane and board a train. She and Adam slept through the day as the train rumbled across endless green fields punctuated with woods and winding rivers. They awoke as it was getting dark. It took them both a moment to remember that they were on a train crossing an unfamiliar country. The rain lashing against the window made Cressida feel weary to her bones. Was this storm following them? And she had had no idea Paralin was so far away. As she listened to the rumble of the wheels on the track and swayed this way and that with the movement of the carriage, she thought being still and quiet was a luxury she would embrace like a long-lost friend. She looked across the cramped compartment at Adam peering out the window into the gloom beyond, an excited look on his face. He always seemed to be lost in the moment, taking everything in gladly. Now he turned to her and paused for a second before speaking.

"I'm not sure I'm going to be very welcome at this festival."

"Why's that?" Cressida asked.

"Well, when I sent the telegram telling the organizers we were both coming, they sent one back saying only you were invited. Strictly no family."

Cressida felt the stirrings of trouble. Her brother was like the fountain of all woe.

"So what did you say?" she asked.

"I said I had to come because you were . . ." Adam turned his face to the window and mumbled, ". . . afraid of the dark."

"You said what?!" Cressida exclaimed.

"I said you had Goldminer's syndrome," Adam said.

"And what, pray tell, is 'Goldminer's syndrome'?" Cressida asked, trying to keep herself calm.

"Actually, I made it up, but I said you needed a buddy to calm you down when the darkness got to you. I said you would not be able to make this long journey through the night without me."

"And they believed it?" Cressida asked.

"Not at first," Adam replied. "But I said it was both of us or nothing, and they *really* want you at this festival."

"Couldn't you have said something else? Something less ridiculous?" Cressida asked with a hint of despair in her voice. "And all this must have cost a fortune in telegrams," she added.

"It was the best I could do," Adam replied. "And there's no way I was going to stay behind with Uncle Brody, that brandy-swilling, cigar-chomping slug!"

Cressida rolled her eyes and let out a long sigh.

"When we get there, Adam, I want you to stay well away from me. Got that?"

"That's fine," said Adam, trying to sound cheerful, "because they said my accommodation will be separate from all the festival people, anyway."

Adam turned back to the window again. The train was leaving the inky darkness of the countryside and entering a big city. Gas-powered streetlights threw a soft yellow hue over cobbled roads. This must be Paralin, the City of Wonder, Adam thought to himself. He marveled at the beautiful buildings and, as they steamed farther into the heart of the city, he marveled even more as the buildings got bigger and more dramatic. It was a wonderful, sparkling place and it seemed fitting that they should be holding the Festival of Youthful Genius here. He glanced across at his pouting sister and had to remind himself that she was a genius, a musical one. But also a grumpy one. Perhaps you had to be grumpy to be a true genius. How would he know? He was, after all, so very, very average.

The train was slowing and Adam could see that they were pulling into a magnificent railway station with high stained-glass ceilings. A large sign on the platform read: WELCOME TO PARALIN.

"We're here. Paralin," offered Adam breezily as he stood and pulled his suitcase down from the rack above his head.

"Do you think so?" responded Cressida with sarcasm.

Outside the station was a dapper-looking man in a smart uniform holding a board with CRESSIDA BLOOM written on it in large, tidy letters. He stood in front of an enormous car with curving black bodywork perched on large golden wheels. Cressida approached the man and said that *she* was Cressida Bloom. The man smiled broadly and introduced himself as Castor, the chauffeur for the Hotel Peritus.

"It is indeed an honor to be in the presence of such luminous talent," he gushed as he took Cressida's luggage and stowed it in the trunk. Adam noted that, despite her current disdain for the notion of talent, this piece of flattery improved Cressida's mood instantly and she smiled and jumped into the back of the car without so much as a glance at Adam. Adam rolled his eyes and felt a slight sinking feeling in his stomach. He was a long way from home, if you could really call it home, and the only person he knew in this place was acting as though he wasn't there. He quickly shrugged off any thoughts of self-pity.

"I'm Adam, Cressida's brother," he said, stepping forward and extending a hand to Castor. Castor shook the hand without much real interest and got into the driving seat. Adam realized he would be receiving no special treatment, so he hurriedly piled his own luggage into the trunk, clambered into the car and reclined in its deep leather seats.

"Ah, this is the life," he sighed.

Cressida shot him a menacing look and hissed under her breath, "Do not embarrass me, Adam Bloom. I mean it."

"Hey, I'm invisible," he replied.

And he meant it too.

The car swept through the shiny, wet streets and pulled up outside an incredible-looking building, the Hotel Peritus. Tall, thin windows with elaborate patterns in colored glass were dotted like exclamation marks all the way up to its large domed roof that caressed the clouds. Adam thought it was the most impressive building he had ever seen. Castor switched off the engine and opened the car door for Cressida. She stepped out and Castor busied himself getting her luggage and giving it to a groveling porter who had appeared from the brilliance of the lobby. Cressida, carrying nothing, walked up the regal front steps and into the hotel while Adam wrestled his suitcase from the car.

The lobby was no less grand than the exterior, and Adam let out a low whistle as he looked up at the swirling gold ceiling decorations and admired the glass sculptures that were dotted around. He noticed a couple of indoor water fountains over by the elevators and fought the urge to jump in them. He didn't think Cressida would approve if he did. A big banner strung across the entire lobby read, WELCOME, TALENTED CHILDREN OF THE WORLD!

"What about a welcome for us average ones?" muttered Adam as he caught up with his sister.

"This trip isn't about you, Adam," Cressida whispered fiercely. "Come on, let's find our rooms."

• • •

As they rode up in the elegant mirrored elevator, Adam wondered why Cressida's key was so much bigger and shinier than his. Maybe it was linked to the fact that a smart porter stood silently behind her, holding her luggage, while Adam's arm was aching with the effort of holding his own. But he didn't have time to dwell on these thoughts, as the elevator stopped abruptly at the seventh floor.

"Madam, this is your floor," the porter chimed with cheery respect. The elevator doors slid open with a sigh. The corridor beyond was beautifully decorated with rich cream carpets and mirrored panels with chrome fittings. This hotel was buffed and polished to perfection. Adam watched as Cressida and the porter got out of the elevator.

"Cress, see you downstairs in about an hour for the welcome dinner?"

"Not sure I'm hungry," Cressida replied.

His sister could certainly hold a grudge, thought Adam. He turned to the porter and cleared his throat.

"Um, which floor is my room on?" he asked, holding out the small, grimy key he had been given at reception.

"Top of the world," muttered the porter from the corner of his mouth as he leaned back into the elevator and jammed a finger onto the top button on the floor panel. The porter moved clear as the doors slid shut and Adam felt the elevator surge upward.

• • •

When the doors opened again, the surroundings were very different: a dank, smelly corridor leading to a metal staircase. Adam walked out of the elevator and clattered up the stairs with his luggage. He pushed open the door at the top and stumbled out onto . . . the hotel roof. He was on a flat section at the top of the dome, about a hundred meters across. The view was amazing. A million twinkling lights spread out below him and, in response, a million stars shone back at them from the sky. Adam was impressed—but then he became a little worried. Where was his room? He turned and saw what looked like a tin shed over by a chimney stack. Surely *that* wasn't it. He walked over and, as he pushed the small key into the lock of the battered door and turned it, his suspicions were confirmed. The door opened and he stepped inside. When his eyes adjusted to the gloom, he saw damp walls with buckets of paint stacked against them. At least there was a mattress to sleep on, though it wasn't the cleanest one he'd ever seen. He breathed deeply. The place smelled as bad as it looked.

As Adam dropped his suitcase on the floor, he looked out of the shed's grimy window. Loneliness crept into his heart. He missed his parents and he wished Cressida would be nicer to him. Here he was in a tin shed in a strange country at a festival he was not invited to because he had no talent. He fought back the urge to cry. He took a deep breath and tried to think positively: at least he had this fantastic view of the city. In many ways he had the best spot in the whole hotel.

Suddenly he saw something move on the far edge of the flat section of the domed roof—a figure maybe. A chill went through Adam's bones. He rubbed his eyes and looked again, but this time there was nothing. He must be tired. It had been a long journey. However, his grumbling stomach told him that before he could sleep he must have something to eat.

CHAPTER THREE
DINNER WITH GENIUSES

· · · · · · · · · · · · ·

Cressida flopped down onto the bed. Her head was spinning from the journey. She had a strange feeling that she was still on the move, a kind of to-and-fro movement in her bones. It made her feel a little unsettled. As she sank into the glorious soft comfort of the bed, she realized she could not complain about her room. It was large and decorated with impeccable taste. There had been a personal handwritten note awaiting her in the room, welcoming her to the Festival of Youthful Genius, and a gift-wrapped box containing a necklace with a silver musical note hanging from it. Just right for a singer. She had put it on straightaway and she touched her hand to it now. Her emotions were mixed. Being pampered felt good. She hadn't felt this looked after and safe in a long time. But she knew she was only being treated this way because people wanted to use her talent. It was an exchange she resented.

Her thoughts drifted to Adam. She refused to feel responsible for him. It wasn't her fault her parents were gone. He could have dinner on his own downstairs with the other guests while she perused the rather delicious-sounding room-service menu. He would be all right. Adam always made the best of situations. He would probably be entertaining everyone in no time. He would start by describing their dramatic journey in exaggerated, exciting terms, and then he would talk about other things. Cressida wondered what other things. Well, he would almost certainly talk about his sister. Cressida sat bolt upright. Maybe she would go down to dinner after all.

Adam wandered into the grand, busy dining room and looked around. So this was what a room full of geniuses looked like. The soft ambient light thrown from half a dozen pendulous chandeliers lit up a sea of animated faces. The noise of the chatter excited Adam but also made him feel a little uneasy. Chatter meant all these people were getting along and Adam was still very much a stranger.

At least a dozen long tables, covered with thick white tablecloths, were packed with children. They ranged in age from ten to sixteen, and as Adam's eyes flicked from face to face, he tried to guess each one's talent. The frowning boy with the glasses, maybe science. The girl with the purple scarf and the faraway look, maybe poetry. He could not imagine what the boy with soup down his chin could be good at.

Adam scanned the room for Cressida and saw her sitting near the end of a table, looking a little lost. She had come down after all. She had an empty chair next to her and Adam bounded over.

"Hi." Cressida smiled, looking up at her brother. She almost looked pleased to see him. Almost.

"What's your room like?" asked Adam as he sat down.

"Lovely," she replied. "Leather armchairs, a marble fireplace, an enormous four-poster bed. Oh, and fresh flowers. How's yours?"

"Um, similar. But they must have forgotten my flowers today," said Adam.

Just then, a rather curious-looking gentleman with a neat white mustache stepped onto a raised platform at the end of the room. His hair was carefully slicked back and a strange mix of bright red with the odd gray stripe. He wore a smart dark suit with brass buttons and trousers tucked into tall leather explorer's boots. Even more bizarrely, he was wearing round sunglasses. The effect was of someone trying to appear more interesting than perhaps they really were.

"Welcome, brilliant young people of the world!" he boomed with a deep, velvet-like voice. "My name is Fortescue, and I have taken over a large part of this hotel so that we can all celebrate your astounding talents!"

Fortescue glanced around the room, and for a split second, Adam felt Fortescue's eyes land on him and was sure he saw a confused, almost worried look flash across the man's face. Then Fortescue's gaze moved on and he smiled broadly.

"Enjoy your meal and please do get to know each other. Dazzle one another with your achievements! The feats, displays and performances shall begin tomorrow!"

With that, Fortescue stepped down and left through a small door next to a big painting of a shepherd shearing a sheep.

Adam looked across the table at a robust, square-jawed boy of around fifteen. He had thick blond hair and extremely pale blue eyes, which were framed by white eyelashes. The boy stared hard at Adam with a half smile on his face, and then he spoke.

"I am Hans Fortissimo!" he stated with pride. That can't be his *real* name, thought Adam. "And I play the piano like a god!"

Hans laughed and slapped the table hard with strong fingers. But this outrageous boast seemed to break the ice and started a domino effect around the table.

"My name is Sophia de Graf," said the pretty but frail girl next to Hans. She looked about thirteen. "I do mathematics."

"Six times five!" blurted Hans.

"No, I really *do* mathematics," said Sophia with more confidence. Her dark ruler-straight bangs reached almost down to her eyes, and they shook as she said *do*.

"Okay, four thousand seven hundred and fifty-eight times nine thousand four hundred and twenty-two," chattered Hans.

Sophia looked to the ceiling and with barely a pause said, "Forty-four million eight hundred and twenty-nine thousand eight hundred and seventy-six."

Everyone looked impressed except Hans. He was too busy scribbling numbers on a piece of paper. After a couple of minutes he looked up.

"She is right!"

"I always am," Sophia said. "Gets kind of boring sometimes."

After this feat the introductions continued. Carl, a thin, pale boy with freckles on his nose and a smell of turps about him, was a genius at painting. Sasha, a tall, willowy girl with long arms and curly hair, was skilled at hockey. Apparently she never missed the goal no matter how far away she was. And so on, until everyone's attention came to rest on Cressida. She looked shy. Adam was surprised. He had seen her sulk a hundred times; however, he had never really seen her bashful. He quite liked it. It made him feel closer to her.

"Naturally I know I'm good at what I do, but I'm not so good at boasting," she said eventually.

"Then learn!" enthused Hans.

Cressida smiled at this. "I'm Cressida Bloom and I sing."

"And she's *really* good," added Adam. "She may look like a wet weekend, but she sounds like an angel."

Adam cringed. That hadn't come out quite the way he had intended. Cressida scowled.

"Thank you, Adam," she hissed through gritted teeth.

Hans turned to Adam. "And what is your name and what do you do?"

"I'm Adam, Cress's brother, and, um, I don't really do anything."

"But what is your talent? Your gift?" Hans urged.

"I really just came to keep Cress company," said Adam cautiously.

He shot Cressida a look. Couldn't she help him out here? But his sister carefully avoided eye contact.

"Who is paying for your stay?" asked Hans, his disbelief growing as he scrutinized with distaste the average boy exposed before him.

"Um, I get the feeling I'm kind of being *tolerated* by the organizers," Adam answered.

This comment seemed to bear some weight as, in the next moment, groaning silver plates heaped high with the most delicious-looking food were placed in front of everyone at the table. Everyone, that is, except Adam—who had a small sardine on a cracked tea plate slammed down in front of him. By the look of the pathetic fish, a cat had already had a nibble at it. Adam tried to smile bravely.

"My favorite," he muttered.

Although her brother was irritating Cressida as usual, she did feel this was a little unfair, so she lifted her plate toward his, intending to scrape some golden, sticky roast potatoes onto Adam's. But Hans seemed to read her thoughts and held up a hand, shaking his head slowly.

"No. Not for him. He should not really be here. Let him stick with his fish."

Cressida put her plate back down sheepishly, and Adam felt a twinge of hurt at his sister's weakness.

As the children at the table dug in to their glorious food, Adam prodded his sorry-looking sardine and tried to tell himself he was special because he was the only one with a sardine. But it was no good. The sardine was a final slap in the face. He felt sorry for himself. He couldn't help it. Who did these kids think they were? Was being good at something an excuse to treat other people badly? Suddenly he wanted to be alone, and he got up abruptly from the table. Cressida looked at him quizzically.

"I'm going to bed," Adam mumbled.

"Okay, sleep well," Cressida answered cheerily, but Adam was sure that there was guilt nestled underneath her words.

Adam walked unseen through the hubbub of the dining room and wandered into the lobby. He was so lost in thought, he bumped straight into the tall figure waiting there. Adam lifted his gaze until he saw his own reflection doubled up in the lenses of a pair of dark glasses. Fortescue removed the sunglasses to reveal two squinty little eyes, one a murky blue, the other a dull brown.

"Leaving so early?" Fortescue asked with a hint of menace.

"Been a long day," Adam replied, a touch of fear creeping into his voice. Fortescue was the kind of man who made Adam feel as though he had just done something wrong, even if he hadn't. "Thought I'd hit the sack."

"I would suggest over the next few days you keep yourself to yourself," hissed Fortescue. "We are delighted to have your sister with us, but from your telegrams we understood she was unlikely to come alone. So we had to invite the both of you. However, she is here now and she will be looked after."

Adam nodded and edged away toward the elevators. Fortescue turned and watched Adam suspiciously until the elevator doors closed.

Adam let out a sigh of relief as the elevator ascended. What a strange man. What a strange day. He would be glad to get to his room. Then he remembered. Not a room—the shed on the roof.

CHAPTER FOUR
THE DREAM

. . . .

As Adam stepped out onto the roof, he once again had the feeling that there was someone there. He heard a sudden clattering noise and, turning swiftly, thought he saw, momentarily, tattered silk flapping in the night air on the edge of the roof. Then, nothing. Adam shivered and told himself it must have been something perfectly harmless and ordinary. Perhaps a stray kite tugged loose from a child's fingers by a strong gust of wind. Nevertheless, once he was inside his shed he decided to lock the door, though he opened the window a crack, hoping to dispel the rancid smell a little. He thought he would sleep in his clothes as it was cold in the shed. He opened his suitcase and pulled out a woolen scarf and wrapped it around his neck. As he closed the suitcase again, he gave the handle a little polish with the end of his scarf. In such a tatty place, his shiny leather suitcase was the only reminder he had of comfort and nice things. Adam could tell the mattress had seen better days as soon as he lay back onto it. He would have to avoid that spring on the left-hand side that was peeking out, hoping to poke awake a sleeping victim.

Adam went over the events of the day in his mind as he tried to drop off. Traveling on the plane and train had been fun, but things had certainly taken a turn for the worse since arriving at the Hotel Peritus. The terrible "room," the awful dinner and, worst of all, his sister treating him so badly. And Fortescue. He was odd. One brown eye, one blue. The words sounded like the noise the train had made as it had crossed the country to bring them here. One brown eye, one blue, one brown eye, one blue, one brown eye, one blue. And as his thoughts became even more muddled, Adam fell into a deep sleep.

As he slept, Adam tumbled into a most peculiar dream. All of the talented children from the dinner were in a cavern-ous dark room, standing in a circle. In the center was a tall, shadowy figure, turning on the spot, long arms outstretched. The children seemed to be in a trance, their eyes glazed. In his dream Adam felt apart, like an observer. But suddenly the tall figure saw Adam and stopped. It stepped forward into the light to reveal . . . Fortescue, his face twisted with anger. He glared at Adam, the fury glowing in his eyes, one brown, one blue.

"You have no business here," he hissed.

Even though Fortescue looked frightening, Adam felt at the same time that Fortescue was frightened of him.

Adam awoke with a start. At first he thought he'd rolled onto the spring that poked out of his mattress, but in the next moment he saw why he had really woken up. Someone, something, hunched, thin and bony was climbing out of his window. Adam gasped. At full height, he reckoned the figure must be at least eight feet tall, and it wore an oily-looking tattered silk cloak and hood, which enshrouded it completely in shadow. Then the intruder was gone, the window left creaking. For a moment Adam lay still, his heart pounding and pounding. This was crazy. Who was that? *What* was that? A thief? Adam checked that his suitcase was still there and unopened. Fear made him lie still, his eyes flicking about anxiously. But then curiosity got the better of him and he stood up slowly and unlocked the door.

As he left the shed, he saw movement over where the flat part of the roof curved downward. Adam paused for a moment. Was this a good idea? Probably not, but he ran over anyway. As he reached the edge of the roof, he saw the peculiar cloaked stranger grab hold of a wooden handle hanging from a cable. The cable stretched from the hotel's dome down to a roof window on a house on a street a long way off. The intruder pushed off and the tattered cloak billowed outward as the gangly figure sped through the night sky. The sound was like a zipper being undone quickly. At the bottom the stranger let go of the handle, landing on the balcony below it, and disappeared inside the attic of the house like a shadow seeking the comfort of darkness. It was an amazing sight and Adam was spellbound. He felt both afraid and fascinated at the same time. Most of all he felt intrigued.

Adam's desire to know more about his bizarre visitor was rapidly overcoming any sensible ideas he had about staying put. So, with impulse winning out over careful thought (as usual), Adam pulled his belt from his trousers and threw it over the cable. He grasped both ends with knuckle-white fists and pushed himself off the domed roof of the Hotel Peritus. A reckless boy in flight over a city of light. Luckily he did not fall, but as he watched the traffic moving far, far below, he clung tighter and did wonder whether he had lost his marbles.

He approached the house with alarming speed, the wind whistling in his ears and the redbrick wall rushing toward him. Just in time, he let go of the belt with one hand and dropped heavily onto the balcony, where he rolled into a ball. He stood up and cursed his rash behavior. If the stranger was inside and intended to harm him, he had no escape. He glanced down at the street at least twelve stories below. Or perhaps whoever it was was just shy, Adam tried to reassure himself. Maybe they would like a friend. Adam took a deep breath. He hoped this was the case. He decided to find out and climbed through the window into the attic.

It was dark inside and it took a moment for Adam's eyes to adjust. But as they did, he became aware that the room was large and full of gleaming objects. He blinked a few times and stepped farther into it. They were trophies. Hundreds of them. He picked one up. It featured a bronze boy running. Adam strained to read the inscription—"Awarded to Giles August for the fastest mile." He put it down and picked up a miniature golden pumpkin on a marble base. The inscription read—"For Mr. Clarion Pepper, Best in Show." Adam looked around in awe. Amid the trophies were other glittering objects—bright costumes, jewelry, watches, gilt-edged mirrors. Was this a thief's hideout? A thief who only stole trophies and shiny trinkets? A dry scuttling noise in the corner made Adam turn quickly, and he thought he saw two shining yellow eyes staring at him from the shadows. Adam swallowed hard, his heart racing again. He stepped back, but in the next moment he felt a presence next to him, around him, above him. There was a feeling of immense physical power that he couldn't explain. His head began to swim. The dark figure now at his side started to make a curiously soothing noise. Adam grew faint and dizzy, his thoughts thrown into turmoil. Was that a bony hand or a . . . claw hovering over his head? And what was that revolting musty smell? But nothing else happened. Next, whoever—or whatever—it was made another peculiar noise. It sounded like a hiss of disappointment. Then, with a swish of the cloak and a dry clatter, the towering, bony stranger bolted for the door and was gone.

Adam waited for a while, frozen among the glinting trophies, concentrating on making himself calm by breathing slowly and deeply. The encounter had left him shaken, yet feeling curiously empty. He felt as though the stranger had wanted to take something from him but Adam did not have whatever it was to give. And because the stranger had had such an incredible presence, Adam felt he had somehow let it down by not helping. Adam tried to push these nonsensical thoughts out of his mind. He had to focus if he wanted to get back to the relative safety of the hotel. After a few more deep breaths, Adam opened the door and looked out into the corridor beyond. It was dimly lit by a single lamp hanging from the ceiling. The lamp was swaying slightly, casting splashes of silken shadow into corners. There didn't seem to be anybody around. A bare wooden staircase led downward to Adam's right. Adam tiptoed across the corridor to the top of the stairs, his palms moist. Then he had a sudden, overwhelming desire to be out of the house as quickly as possible. He flung himself down the dilapidated stairs, flight after flight, until finally he reached the bottom and pushed through a large, creaky double door to step out breathlessly onto the street. He looked up and down it. It was empty. Now all he had to do was get back to the hotel, and as luck would have it, a sign at the end of the street pointed the way.

CHAPTER FIVE
THE PIANO CONCERT
· · · · · · · · · · · · · ·

The pale light of dawn crept across Adam's face and he flicked open his eyes with a groan. What extraordinary things he had dreamed. As he awoke fully, he sat up and remembered. The attic room full of trophies and the chilling visitor—they were real. Adam unlocked the door of the shed and walked out onto the roof. Despite the fact that his head was full of such strange thoughts, he could not help but be amazed at the sight that greeted him. The rising sun peeking over the horizon was throwing a blanket of soft pink light over beautiful Paralin. Adam looked around and took in the mile upon mile of rooftops, the towers, the domes, the lush parks and the many ornate bridges spanning the two wide rivers that ran through the city. In the distance, mountains loomed like misty, hulking sentries. A city of dreams. But a city of strange happenings too.

Adam went over to the edge of the flat part of the roof

where the cable had been attached. It was no longer there! His spirits sank. With the cable removed, any way of telling where it had led was gone. As was any proof. Now no one would believe his tale or help him to unravel it. He looked across at the streets opposite. Pretty as they were, all the buildings in them looked the same. Adam laughed at himself as he knew others would when he tried to tell them of his nighttime encounter with an eight-foot-tall thief. It felt like a dream, but Adam's memories of those shining eyes, the hunched posture and the tatty cloak were clear and vivid in the cold light of day.

Adam knocked on his sister's door. He was still feeling a bit light-headed and peculiar and wanted the comfort of a familiar person to talk to. Cressida opened the door and Adam saw that she was not alone. Hans and Sophia were lounging in her two large leather chairs. Adam felt a pang of loneliness. He didn't really want to bare his soul to his sister with these two here. But he had no choice. He went into the room and tried to adopt a friendly expression as he spoke.

"Morning." His voice sounded flat even to himself.

"Morning," replied Hans with good cheer.

Sophia just smiled in a distracted way. She was probably counting the tulips on Cressida's quilt and multiplying them by the amount of roses on the wallpaper, mused Adam.

"Did you sleep well?" asked Cressida.

Adam thought she seemed unusually polite. Perhaps she wanted to make a good impression on her new friends.

"Yes, apart from a curious tall, cloaked visitor waking me up in the middle of the night," said Adam matter-of-factly. He couldn't see how else to start the conversation.

"Okay," Cressida said, trying to halt whatever flight of fancy Adam was about to embark on. She was just starting to make friends with Hans and Sophia and the last thing she needed was Adam talking childish rubbish at them.

"I followed the intruder down a cable from the roof to an attic room in an abandoned house nearby," Adam continued, his brown eyes blinking at his sister.

Cressida sighed. "Adam, it's really too early for this," she said.

"No, no, let us hear more!" Hans exclaimed.

Fired up by Hans's interest, Adam continued in a rush. "Well, the room was full of trophies. The stranger must be a thief, a thief who likes trophies. Then whoever, well, whatever it was leaped out of the shadows at me. It was hidden by a cloak but really, really tall, with very odd eyes, glowing, hypnotic almost. Next, a hand—well, it looked more like a kind of leathery claw—was hovering over my head and there was this singing, humming noise, which tingled all through my bones. Um, then it left." As Adam heard himself speak the words, he felt foolish. It did indeed sound like the mixed-up muddle of a dream. Perhaps that was really all it was.

"And to think we thought you had no talent!" exclaimed Hans. "Listen to him! Making things up is a *great* talent!" Hans was starting to enjoy himself, and, cupping his chin in his hand in a mock show of anticipation, he said, "Tell us more!"

Adam did not know what to make of this request. He shuffled awkwardly.

"That's pretty much it," he said, with a shrug. "There is no more."

He glanced at Cressida, who looked away.

Hans gloated at his little victory. "Oh, shame! The spark of talent has gone out," he said, and with that he leaped up and flexed his fingers. "I should go and prepare." He gave a little bow to Cressida and Sophia and sneered at Adam as he left the room. "A singing thief with leathery claws that steals only cheap trophies—priceless," he muttered with a snort.

Sophia looked at Adam with something approaching pity. "Adam, do you feel you need to multiply your personality because you don't feel equal? Is that it?" she asked, squinting at him intensely.

Adam did not know what to say to this. He wasn't sure the question even deserved an answer. He stared at Sophia for a long moment until Cressida broke the silence.

"The two of us should go and get breakfast. We don't want to miss any of Hans's recital," she said to Sophia almost in a whisper. Sophia nodded. "What are you going to do?" Cressida said, turning to Adam, her question sounding like a challenge.

"Obviously not the same thing you're doing," answered Adam, feeling well and truly left out. With that, he turned and slammed out of the room.

Adam mooched around the lobby, not really knowing what to do with himself. He was deliberately avoiding the breakfasting geniuses in the dining room. He felt he deserved a break from making a fool of himself.

People in hats, suits and pearls looked at him over their newspapers and tutted. They were probably here for Hans's piano recital. Adam glanced at the poster on the easel that stood next to the large double doors leading into the Hotel Peritus Theater. HANS FORTISSIMO—CHILD GENIUS! it read, and above the words was a picture of Hans, beaming, winking and thundering away on a grand piano.

Adam thought the image captured Hans perfectly— brash, bold and frozen in a glorious little world of his own. Smiling to himself, Adam drifted across the lobby and hovered by the main entrance to the hotel. It was raining again and he watched people scurry by on the street outside clutching umbrellas or holding newspapers over their heads. They all seemed to know where they were going. They were important. How come he felt like a piece of chewing gum that's stuck to a shoe and has to be scraped off?

Just then a bell sounded and Adam turned to see a red light flashing above the theater doors. A voice boomed out from a loudspeaker: "Ladies and gentlemen, please take your seats for the performance."

All the people who had been sitting in the lobby jostled for position as they fed into the theater. It was like watching toothpaste being squeezed back into the tube. The dining room emptied too and dozens and dozens of children filed across the lobby into the theater. Adam saw Cressida and Sophia, but they didn't see him. Or at least they pretended not to.

Minutes later the doors were closed. Adam wandered over to look through the small frosted windows in the doors. But rather eerily, Fortescue appeared from nowhere and blocked his way. Fortescue removed his sunglasses to reveal those unsettling eyes once more, one brown, one blue. Adam wondered if this was an honor reserved only for him.

"Not you again. Now, shoo, boy. You are nothing. You have no use. This is all *way* over your head," Fortescue snarled through gritted teeth. "I am making history here, and I'm afraid you won't even be a footnote."

"Fine. I'm not welcome. I get it," Adam said. Recent events had given him an angry edge, which at this moment overrode his fear of Fortescue. "But now that I *am* here, do you think I could sneak in and see Hans play?"

"Do you have a ticket?" Fortescue asked.

"No."

"Are you a young talent?"

43

"No. We've already agreed I'm 'nothing' and 'have no use,'" Adam retorted.

"Then you have your answer, don't you?" Fortescue said with a cruel grin.

"I guess so," Adam said, looking down at his shoes now. He felt deflated.

"Funny thing is, Adam Bloom," Fortescue continued, with a new mysterious tone to his voice, "I know what it's like to be you. Talentless, wondering where you belong, stumbling blandly through an insipid wasteland, wallowing in mediocrity. Invisible and unremarkable."

"You do?" Adam asked. He felt cheered for a moment.

"Oh yes, and I didn't like it one little bit," Fortescue snapped. "So get out of my sight, you . . . you tedious echo of my past. You make me feel strangely uneasy, as if I've just eaten a moldy sandwich and I'm waiting for the ill effects to kick in."

Fortescue shuddered, clicked the heels of his explorer's boots together, put his sunglasses back on and opened the theater doors. He marched inside and locked the doors behind him.

Adam felt a little shocked and extremely hurt by what Fortescue had said. He also felt angry. He decided he *would* see the concert. All he needed to do was find another way into the theater. So he walked out of the main entrance and made his way around to the side of the hotel. It was still raining and the streets had taken on a silky sheen. Brightly colored, jaunty cars burbled along, their little windshield wipers flicking back and forth busily.

Adam peered down the narrow alleyway at the side of the hotel and saw a number of drainpipes gurgling water into large puddles. A couple of soggy-looking rats were rummaging in a pile of rubbish. Adam could practically see the fleas jumping around on them. Giving the gnawing rodents a wide berth, he headed to the end of the alleyway and noticed a small blue door at the bottom of a short flight of stairs. He tried the rusty handle and the door creaked open. Already he could hear the distant tinkling of a piano. Adam went inside and found himself in a labyrinth of twisting corridors, each more gloomy than the last. It would have been easy to get lost, but Adam followed the sound of the music until finally he came to a steep staircase. He walked up the wooden steps, pushed open a door and found himself standing among ropes and pulleys. He was in the wings at the edge of a stage, on which he could clearly see Hans, hunched over an impressive, shiny black piano, hammering away skillfully on the keys.

CHAPTER SIX
THE TANTRUM

· · · · · · · · · · · · · ·

Adam shifted his attention from Hans to the audience. Rows and rows of ecstatic faces showed that they were deeply enjoying the recital, especially Fortescue. Standing to one side of the stalls, lit by the creepy red glow of the exit signs, Fortescue seemed to be in utter rapture. A strange smile was stretched across his face under his clipped white mustache, and the veins stood out on his neck. His sunglasses glowed crimson. Adam looked back at Hans. The boy was certainly gifted. His fingers glided over the keys at incredible speed and the music flooded out like a force of nature.

Adam noticed a small table next to the piano on which there was a piece of wood balanced on two bricks. What was that for? He would soon find out. With a final flourish, Hans came to the end of his piece. The audience erupted into enthusiastic applause, but Hans hushed them with a wave. Flushed and sweaty, he leaped up, stepped over to the small table and, with a swift, sharp downward sweep of his hand, chopped the wood in half. Then he threw both his arms up in the air—a signal to the audience. This time they went wild, standing, clapping and hollering.

"Part two will come after a short, well-deserved interval," panted Hans. His eyes were wild and he bounded offstage. Adam barely had time to duck down out of sight. He watched Hans weave through the ropes and old bits of scenery backstage and slip through a dimly lit door with a gold star stuck to it. The audience stayed in their seats and chattered excitedly. The words "inspired," "brilliant" and "sublime" were being bandied about freely. Adam turned and saw Cressida and Sophia talking and laughing in the third row. They were obviously having a good time, and Adam felt pleased that he too had found a way to watch Hans play. In fact, he had managed to get the best view in the theater. He smiled at this little victory. He knew he was not welcome—both Cressida and Fortescue had made that painfully clear. But, like a rat at a feast, he would try to enjoy as much as possible anyway, without drawing attention to himself.

Just then Adam's train of thought was derailed suddenly as he saw someone approach Hans's dressing-room door and go through it, closing it quietly behind them. Adam could not make out who it was in the darkness, but, once again, his curiosity got the better of him and he tiptoed over to the star's door and pressed his ear to it.

He could make out an odd trilling noise like that of an exotic bird. Adam pressed his ear closer to the door. The noise sounded soothing, hypnotic even, and vaguely familiar. Adam's heart started to race with excitement and fear. He heard Hans say, "Won't you come closer? You are in shadow there. I am aware my brilliance is overpowering, but I do like to see my fans."

Then, though he could not be sure, Adam thought he heard Hans gasp, and a bright reddish-purple light lit up the edges of the door for a few seconds. Whatever was in there with Hans let out a high-pitched gargling sound that sent a shiver along Adam's spine.

"What happened?" Adam heard Hans ask eventually. He sounded confused.

His question was answered by a deep, satisfied growl.

Adam felt compelled to hide, and he scuttled back to his original position in the wings. His instincts were right—as soon as he ducked down out of sight, the mysterious visitor opened Hans's door again and melted away into the darkness. A heartbeat later, a stunned-looking Hans came out and stumbled over toward the stage.

He stood briefly in the wings as if in a trance, then he seemed to shake himself out of it. He blew on his hands and charged back into the spotlight. The audience gave Hans a rapturous round of applause before simmering down to enjoy the second part of their divine musical treat. Hans nodded knowingly at the broken piece of wood and got a giggle from the audience. He edged around the piano stool, flipped his jacket tails out behind him with a dramatic flourish, sat down and cracked his knuckles over the keys. Like a tiger pouncing, he brought his hands down hard on the keyboard.

And the sound was awful and jarring. The audience shifted in its seats as one. Hans frowned, raised his fingers and brought them down once more. Again they produced a terrible, jangling din. Hans plowed on. Although there was some kind of tune emerging, it was masked by wrong notes and clashing chords, and chords that were not even chords. Hans stopped and the audience held its breath. He looked at his hands. He flexed his fingers, then knitted them together. He could remember the basics of how to play, but that sweet feeling of musical flow and flourish was suddenly gone. He stared at the keys. They were no longer his friends. His black-and-white colleagues mocked him.

"Is it possible you damaged your hands . . . ?" asked a large, pompous woman with a stylish hat and dangly earrings, sitting in the front row.

When you stupidly chopped that bit of wood in half, thought Adam, finishing the implied question for her.

"No, they are fine," replied Hans.

He struck the keys again and the noise was so bad that the whole front row winced. In the third row, Sophia frowned as she tried to solve Hans's problem.

"The way you played before was following a complicated but strict algorithmic pattern," she called out. "But now your playing is mathematically random. Did you know that?"

Hans stared at his hands before looking out at Sophia almost blankly.

"What?" he snapped, and then suddenly a volcanic rage seemed to grip him. "Well, that's the end of the concert!" he exclaimed, slamming his fists down onto the keys. "You enjoyed yourselves. Now you can all leave! Go! Get out!"

There was a short pause and then, like scolded dogs, the audience got up and began to shuffle out. Sophia and Cressida looked at each other and thought better of going over to Hans. They headed for the exit too.

As the theater emptied in hushed silence, Adam watched Hans rock back and forth on his stool. Suddenly he kicked out at the piano, and Adam couldn't help noticing that the resulting din still sounded better than Hans's formal efforts. Adam leaned out from his hiding place to look into the auditorium. It was empty, save for one man—Fortescue. He had a curious expression on his face. Adam could not quite work it out. Was it satisfaction? It couldn't be, Adam thought. Why would Fortescue be pleased that a concert of talent he had arranged had flopped? Then Fortescue turned and walked briskly out of the theater.

At last, believing he was alone, Hans gave in to the full force of his temper. He stood up and, with a grunt, he flung the stool across the stage. He picked up one piece of the wood he had broken earlier and started to smash the piano keyboard with it, sending jagged sequences of random notes reverberating through the theater. And they *still* sounded better than his atrocious playing.

"Why, why, why?!" cried Hans as he threw open the piano lid and started tearing at its strings. This really was the most impressive tantrum Adam had ever seen. "This"—twang!—"can't happen"—twang!—"to me! I am Hans"—twang!—"Fortissimo!"

And with that, Hans leaped from the stage, stormed up the center aisle and barged his way back through the doors into the lobby. Silence.

Adam didn't like being alone in the gloomy wings, so, with one last look at the wrecked piano, he backtracked along the twisting corridors and out the side exit. He noticed that another rat had joined the trash party in the alleyway, and, skirting around them, he emerged onto the busy street in front of the hotel. Hurriedly climbing the steps back up to the main entrance, he weaved around a stream of concertgoers who were leaving huffily and strolled into the lobby, deep in thought.

CHAPTER SEVEN
THE AMAZING AMY SWIFT

· · · · · · · · · · · ·

Adam was surprised by what he saw in the lobby. Everyone has embarrassing things happen to them. It's all part of being alive. Most people like to go somewhere quiet afterward to lick their wounds. Not Hans Fortissimo. He wanted to hold a public debate on his dreadful performance. At least a dozen of the child geniuses were gathered around Hans, who was seated in a red leather armchair in the middle of the lobby. Adam made his way over and hovered behind an ornate pillar. He did not feel he could join the talented group, but he wanted to hear Hans's version of events. Cressida and Sophia sat down next to Hans as he began to rant.

"It was not my fault!" he bellowed. "Someone else *must* be to blame! My family will take this hotel to court!"

Cressida cleared her throat and spoke shyly. "Um, I'm

52

probably being silly, but what was the chopping of the wood all about?"

Good question, Cress, thought Adam.

"I always do that," replied Hans, exasperation in his voice. "It's my trademark."

A stocky-looking boy of about fourteen with cauliflower ears and quite a few missing teeth was squatting on the floor near Hans. He leaned forward.

"I am Foster Barrel, world-champion wrestler, and I thought the wood-chopping was the best bit. I used to do that in martial arts. Broke planks with my head too, hundreds of times. But then I discovered wrestling. Rolling around on the floor is where I truly belong." Foster gave everyone a toothless grin. Nobody could think of anything to say to this, and after an awkward pause, Cressida turned back to Hans.

"But, um, why is it your trademark?"

"It's to say I do not care if I can play or not. I can break my hands. I do not care," Hans answered.

"How come you're so upset, you know, if you don't care?" Cressida asked.

Adam nodded—another good question.

"Of course I care, you stupid girl!" Hans shrieked, and suddenly all his brashness left him and he slumped down in his chair and looked miserable. Cressida did not like the way Hans had yelled at her, but she understood that he was very upset, so she took his hand anyway.

"I'm sorry, Hans," she said, and Hans gave a sad little nod to return the apology.

Adam knew he was meant to be staying invisible. However, he felt he should say something because he was the only witness to the curious events during the interval. Perhaps they were related to Hans's misfortune. He stepped out from behind the pillar and took a deep breath.

"Er, did you have any visitors during the interval, Hans?" Adam asked softly.

For once, Hans did not have the energy to dismiss Adam with a put-down.

"Oh, just a fan. I have a lot of fans."

Adam did not want to give away that he had been spying, but he suddenly wondered how much Hans remembered of the encounter at all.

"What did the fan say to you?" Adam asked.

"The usual," replied Hans. "I'm brilliant—lah-dee-dah."

"What did this fan look like?" Adam continued eagerly, just stopping himself from adding that he was only asking because he himself had not been able to see the visitor properly in the gloom of the wings.

"I don't know," Hans answered. "Tall, I think. I can't remember."

"It's just, I can't have been dreaming last night, because I'm sure my strange cloaked visitor on a wire was also your . . . fan," Adam blurted, "tall, hugging the shadows, and furthermore, I heard that peculiar humming noise again. When—"

"Ah!" Hans interrupted with a groan. "He's starting with the 'leathery claws' again! I'm going to my room to pack. I'm getting out of this madhouse!"

"You're leaving?" Cressida asked. She was surprised at the disappointment she suddenly felt. Hans was rude and full of himself, but in a strange kind of way, she liked him. He had seemed comfortable with his talent and she admired that, since she sometimes found it so hard to be that way herself. Also, it had to be said, he was strikingly handsome.

"There does not seem much reason to hang around if I cannot play," Hans grunted. "I shall return home and consult with my tutor. With luck this is merely a blip before I move on to another level of brilliance."

And with that, Hans stomped over to the elevator and pressed the call button.

Cressida watched him go with a hint of sadness. "Bye," she whispered under her breath.

A few of the talented children looked at Adam curiously as they dispersed to get on with their own practicing and preparation work. Adam stopped his sister. She gave him a pitiful look.

"You know, you're starting to sound just a little bit weird, Adam. Pull yourself together," she said as she stalked off with Sophia.

Adam sighed and slumped down in the chair that Hans had been sitting in.

It was then that he noticed someone looking at him over the top of a newspaper. The someone was a woman

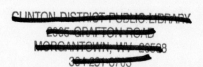

wearing a sheepskin jacket, and she had the most striking piercing blue eyes. Adam could not tell how old she was. Most adults seemed very old to him. But she had an air of intrepid elegance and a kind face. He wondered how long she had been there, staring at him. To his surprise, she now put down her paper and approached him.

"Good way to get yourself laughed at, talking about strange humming cloaked figures zipping down wires and suchlike," she said with a strong, yet friendly voice. "My name is Amy Swift. Call me Amy. Wanna grab a hot chocolate? They put those little marshmallows in."

It had been a long time since anyone had spoken so warmly to Adam. He smiled and nodded.

"I'm Adam Bloom, by the way," he added.

"Pleased to know ya, Adam Bloom by the way. Let's go someplace quiet and talk," Amy said, walking briskly away.

The snug was a small room that led off the hotel dining room. It had half a dozen leather armchairs, a fireplace, some shelves full of dusty books and a large painting of snow-covered mountains on the wall. Adam looked at Amy Swift more closely while she examined the painting. She was certainly interesting. She had a scar down one cheek and wore what looked like racing goggles around her neck. And she sported the most amazing stopwatch on her wrist. Her blond hair was tied back and she had a strange eagerness about her, as though she was waiting for something to happen.

A waiter approached with two steaming mugs of hot chocolate on a silver tray. He put the mugs down on a small table between Amy and Adam. Amy sat, picked up a mug and drank deeply.

"Ah, delectable!" She smiled at the waiter and he nodded and left.

Adam took a swig of his chocolate and it was indeed fantastic. Then he plucked one of the marshmallows out of the mug, and that was wonderfully gooey and sweet.

"So, tell me more about your mysterious stranger, Adam," Amy said, looking Adam square in the eyes.

Adam was taken aback for a moment at her no-nonsense way of talking, but then he felt grateful that someone was finally taking him seriously.

"I don't know, really, Amy. I saw something. On the roof," he replied.

"Tall, gangly, clawed, cloak and hood, not . . . human? And so scary it made you wanna pee?" she asked.

Adam was surprised. "That does sound like what I thought I saw," he said slowly.

Amy suddenly adopted a faraway look. "I thought I'd imagined it," she muttered.

"I almost thought it was a dream," Adam echoed.

"Did it take anything from you, kid?" Amy asked, leaning forward.

"Um, no," Adam replied. "But I think it tried to do something to me, after I followed it to a room stuffed full of trophies. Is that what it does, then—steal? Steal trophies?

Did it take one from Hans? Is that what's upset his playing so much?"

"Let me put it to ya this way—what do you do?" Amy asked.

"You mean what's my talent?" Adam replied.

"Yeah, if you wanna call it that."

"I don't have one," Adam admitted.

"Ha! Then you're lucky. You may never need to know what that . . . creature does or how or why." Amy settled back and gazed into space once more. "Something deeply sinister is going on, Adam. Spark plugs are failing to spark, wheels are turning slower and slower and the finish line is nowhere to be seen."

Adam didn't have any idea what she was talking about, but it didn't sound good.

"Are we all in danger?" he asked.

Amy ignored Adam's question and asked one of her own to nobody in particular.

"Have I tracked it down, then? Is this how that oil-rag Fortescue is emptying our fuel tanks?" she muttered. With that, she drained her mug, slapped it down on the table and jumped up.

"Catch ya later," she said with vigor, and bounded out of the room.

Adam frowned. If he had felt confused before, he felt even more so now.

CHAPTER EIGHT

FEAR MULTIPLIES

· · · · · · · · · · · · · ·

That afternoon, there seemed to be a large amount of people heading up to the roof of the Hotel Peritus. The elevators were full of mathematics professors from universities in and around Paralin, all gabbling with fevered excitement. Because of the crush, the talented children had to use the stairs and as they climbed they moaned about their aching legs and feet (all, that is, except the brilliant runners, jumpers and other sporty ones, who raced up as fast as they could). Giving in to curiosity, Adam trudged up the fifty-something flights with the stragglers and wondered what on earth could be so fascinating up on the roof.

The first thing he noticed when he stepped out onto it, apart from the great many people, was that there was now a large hook in the top of his shed. Attached to this hook were dozens of ropes dangling from an enormous golden hot-air balloon in the shape of a plus sign. The rain clouds from earlier had cleared and the balloon looked strange and impressive as the sunlight caressed its angular surfaces. Nevertheless Adam felt annoyed that his room was being used for this event. Okay, it wasn't much of a room, being a tin shed after all, but he had started to see it as home.

In front of the shed door stood Fortescue, and next to him, looking excited but nervous, was Sophia de Graf. Cressida stood nearby supportively.

"There she is! The mathematical genius!" cried one gray, bespectacled professor, clutching his head with excitement and pointing at Sophia.

"She's five percent smaller than I thought she'd be," said another.

Adam found a chimney pot to stand on, and as he looked out over the people, he noticed Amy on the far side of the crowd, near the edge of the roof. She nodded in his direction.

Before Adam could think what her presence might mean, Fortescue stepped forward and addressed the gathered throng.

"This afternoon, we celebrate the genius of Sophia de Graf!" He waited for the roar of applause that had been triggered by the mention of her name to subside before continuing. "To start, Miss de Graf will astound us with a truly staggering display of counting. Last week, a few thousand—and there's a clue—citizens of the city of Paralin were chosen to take part in this event. They were all given a green flag, which this afternoon they will place in a pot and put in the middle of their gardens."

Fortescue opened the shed door and nodded to Sophia, who stepped inside. He then closed it.

"Sophia has twenty seconds to count them all," Fortescue declared, and with that he threw a lever. The ten small brackets that had been pinning the shed to the roof were released, and the shed shot into the sky. It went up and up until it was at least three hundred feet above them. Then a cable attached to the underside of the shed snapped taut and stopped it from climbing any higher. Fortescue turned over a small hourglass.

Some of the professors had rushed to the edge of the flat section of the roof and were looking out at the many green flags in the gardens below.

"I can see hundreds of those flags just from here!" declared one professor.

"She'll be able to see the whole city from up there!" called another professor.

Sure enough, through one of the shed windows, Sophia was looking down on the maze of streets and the countless wet rooftops reflecting the afternoon sun. It was truly an amazing sight. However the splendor of the city was of no interest to her as she scanned the thousands upon thousands of green flags she could see dotted all over Paralin. Her eyes flicked restlessly from one flag to the next, the numbers stacking up at an incredible rate in her brilliant mind.

"What an awesome event!" said one of the children, craning his neck to get a glimpse of Sophia at the shed window.

I wonder what they did with my luggage, thought Adam. He feared the shed had probably been emptied for this spectacle.

"Time's up!" cried Fortescue as the last grain in the sand timer ran through. The shed was quickly winched back down onto the roof and the brackets clamped back into place. Sophia, looking very intense, stepped out.

"And the man who knows the official number of green flags is none other than the owner of the Hotel Peritus, Mr. Otto Bellette!" declared Fortescue.

A twittery, plump man in a suit that was too tight for him stepped forward from the crowd, clutching a golden envelope. He was wearing a monocle and a floppy bow tie—an appearance that was ridiculous rather than distinguished. He turned to address everyone.

"Firstly, may I just say what a pleasure it is to be staging the Festival of Youthful Genius here at the Hotel Peritus." Mr. Bellette smiled at Fortescue, who tried to smile back but did not quite manage it. "We weren't sure at first about the whole thing, but Fortescue is a very determined and persuasive man, and now—"

"Get on with it!" interrupted an impatient professor.

"Yes, how many green flags?" added another through teeth clamped around a foul-smelling pipe.

Mr. Bellette raised a hand of surrender and gave the envelope to Fortescue. Sophia looked as though she were about to burst, as though the flags themselves wanted to fly out of her mouth and ears. Fortescue opened the envelope and looked at the number printed on a piece of card inside. He nodded.

"Sophia de Graf, how many green flags were displayed today in the gardens of Paralin?"

Sophia took a deep breath.

"Four thousand two hundred and seven," she said.

Adam thought Fortescue looked almost angry for a moment, but he soon changed his expression to one of deep disappointment.

"Four thousand two hundred and eight, it says on the card," he said.

Sophia looked confused and then like she was going to cry. A murmur started up in the crowd—phrases like "so close" and "no such thing as 'close' in mathematics" were bandied about. Cressida tried to make eye contact with Sophia; she wanted to show her support despite her new friend's failure. However, Sophia was looking at the floor, her hands clenched, full of dislike for herself. Cressida sighed. Did talent lock so many who possessed it into a lonely, isolated prison?

At that moment a harried porter emerged breathlessly onto the roof, holding a message. He pushed his way through the disappointed crowd to Fortescue's side.

"Just had a phone call," he gasped out. "Mrs. Swallow from Riverside is very apologetic, but she forgot to put her flag out. She was, er, shampooing her poodle, apparently."

"Then Sophia was one hundred percent right!" cried a professor, clutching joyfully at his gray goatee.

Sophia gave a sigh of relief and looked up with a smile as the crowd cheered. Now Adam noticed that Fortescue had the same expression on his face as he had when he was watching Hans play—a kind of quivering excitement, like a cat tensing before its lethal leap on a unsuspecting mouse. It was chilling.

"Now, for the next part, things get a bit trickier," Fortescue announced with relish, his voice rising over the calls from the crowd. "Sophia will count all the blue doors in Paralin. So we do not expect any difficulties with poodles this time—"

This caused a titter. Mr. Bellette suddenly chipped in.

"And there are a *lot* of blue doors. Thousands probably. Paralin blue is a *very* popular color."

Fortescue talked on over Mr. Bellette, ignoring this rather boring remark.

"The answer we want from Sophia when she steps out of the observation booth"—Adam smiled to himself. "Observation booth" indeed—"is the number of blue doors *multiplied* by the number of green flags."

Sophia raised her eyebrows at this and took a deep breath as Fortescue opened the shed door for her with a flourish. She stepped inside. Fortescue pulled the lever that released the brackets, and the golden balloon and tin shed shot back into the sky. He turned the hourglass over once more.

Adam looked up at the shed hovering high in the sky. Sunlight was reflecting off the windows, which made it practically impossible to see inside. But every now and again Adam wondered whether it was a trick of the light or if he could see another figure in the shed with Sophia? Could he see a thin but powerful arm? A glimpse of a tattered cloak? A flash of glowing, violet-colored light? Adam glanced across at Amy, who was peering up and frowning. Had she seen it too?

CHAPTER NINE
RACING AROUND THE HAYSTACKS

· · · · · · · · · · · · ·

And that's time!" cried Fortescue as the last grain in the hourglass dropped.

The shed was reeled back down onto the roof and the brackets clamped into place. Again Sophia stepped out. She looked dazed and confused, as though she had just emerged from a long hibernation in a dark cave. She shook her head and smiled vacantly. Fortescue consulted the card in the golden envelope once more.

"Sophia, what figure do you reach when you multiply the number of blue doors in Paralin by the number of green flags?" Fortescue asked.

Sophia looked blank and merely said, "It's pretty up there."

There it was again, Adam noted, as the strange satisfied look flashed across Fortescue's face. But it was swiftly replaced with an expression of concern.

"Yes, but what is the answer, Sophia?" Fortescue prompted.

Sophia thought hard. She could faintly remember what numbers were. She just could *not* remember how she used to shuffle them around with such ease.

"I don't know." Sophia shrugged eventually. "There are oodles of doors. Oodles."

"The altitude must have got to her!" exclaimed one worried-looking professor.

"Child, what's the square root of four hundred and twenty-eight?" asked another.

Sophia continued to look befuddled.

"Fourteen times seven?" yet another professor ventured gently.

"Um, does anyone have a piece of paper and a pen?" Sophia replied.

The crowd gasped with shock. Adam looked across at Amy, who looked back with a grim recognition dancing in her blue eyes. They both looked at Fortescue, and Adam thought he could see a faint smug smile hiding at the corners of his mouth, yearning to spread.

"She's lost it," one boy said, his eyes wide with surprise.

And with that remark the crowd broke up and muttered their way back down into the hotel. Awkwardly, Cressida put her arm around Sophia, who was just now starting to register her loss.

"You all right?" Cressida asked.

"I feel sort of empty," Sophia replied.

"What happened up there?" Cressida went on.

"I saw the light," Sophia replied in a hollow, distant voice.

Cressida did not know what to make of this, but Sophia obviously did not want to talk anymore. For a moment Cressida wondered about Hans's and Sophia's sudden loss of their talents, on the same day. It was certainly a strange coincidence. She pushed these thoughts to the back of her mind as she led a weak Sophia back down the stairs.

Clearly, Amy had very strong ideas about what was going on, and she stormed over to Fortescue and looked him square in the sunglasses. Adam stayed where he was and strained to hear. Mr. Bellette lingered by Fortescue's side, finding himself strangely captivated by Amy's dynamism.

"What in the name of eternal pit stops did you do to that girl?" she asked with mounting fury.

Fortescue did his best to look taken aback. He glanced at Mr. Bellette and pulled a face that said: Where did this madwoman come from?

"I don't know *what* you mean," he answered out loud.

"You remember me! I've been tailing you these last few months, ever since our last encounter—the one where you punctured my tires forever," Amy said. "You're up to something, and I don't think you're working alone either . . ."

"Why, I have never seen you before in my life. Have you, perhaps, run out of your madness medication?" Fortescue lowered his voice, stepped back and leaned close to Mr. Bellette. "Is this really the sort of clientele you want in your hotel, Mr. Bellette?" he whispered.

Mr. Bellette looked into Amy's piercing blue eyes. "I quite like her," he said.

"No, no, no, Mr. Bellette. Listen to me," said Fortescue with force, a sheen of sweat breaking out on his forehead. "A hotel can self-destruct swiftly and so easily when it takes in rude, abusive guests such as this."

Mr. Bellette thought about this. A cloud of doubt passed across his face.

"Why, I'm gonna—" began Amy as Adam leaped down from his chimney pot and dashed to Amy's side. In the last few days she was the only person to have offered him even the slightest glimmer of friendship, so he did not want her thrown out of the hotel. Adam addressed Mr. Bellette.

"My friend is sorry for any disturbance, and she will be amazingly and *so* quietly well behaved for the rest of her stay," Adam said.

Fortescue looked at Adam with anger before flickering his gaze back to Amy's defiant countenance. Individually these two people unsettled Fortescue, but teamed together they made him feel distinctly rattled. However, the weak and simpering Mr. Bellette smiled and shrugged— Amy was off the hook. As she went to speak again, Adam shot her a warning look. Then he practically dragged her away from Mr. Bellette and the fuming Fortescue, down to the hotel.

• • •

In her room, Amy quietly paced up and down. Only the elegant clock on the dresser broke the silence with its robust ticking. She was still angry. Adam was sitting by the window, deep in thought, watching Amy walk backward and forward over his elongated shadow. He noticed her jaw was clenched, her fists were clenched. Even her hair looked clenched. What a remarkably bizarre day it was turning out to be. Adam felt he had a number of pieces to a curious puzzle, but he had no idea how they fit together or, indeed, whether he actually wanted to solve it at all. However, he was glad that Amy was still there to talk it through with him.

"You think Fortescue had something to do with Hans losing the ability to play and Sophia losing her mathematical skills?" Adam asked, finally breaking the silence.

"Yes. And I now believe he has an accomplice who must have got in through a trapdoor in the bottom of that shed," Amy replied. She rubbed her temples.

"The cloaked creature?" Adam asked.

"I reckon so. I didn't really believe it until you said you'd seen something similar," Amy replied.

"But how do you know Fortescue and the stranger are linked?"

"Oh, they're connected all right. Fortescue organized the last race I drove in. The Fortescue Grand Prix, would you believe?"

"You're a race car driver?" asked Adam with both surprise and admiration in his voice.

"*Was* a race car driver," Amy replied. "I grew up on the plains of North Cornolia. My pappy was a mechanic, so there were always automobiles parked here and there. When I was small, I used to drive them around dirt tracks with blocks of wood on my feet to reach the pedals." Amy smiled to herself. "It reached the point where a day wasn't complete without a spin around the haystacks. And then when I got to the age where most girls were trying to kiss boys in those haystacks, instead of smooching 'em, I was racing them. My pappy said I was born with racing in my soul. I believe he was right."

Amy looked at Adam's spellbound face and gave a hearty chuckle. She had made a fan. She went over to a large battered suitcase on her bed and pulled out a worn bulky scrapbook. She threw it to Adam, who caught it with a grunt. He opened it to find page after page of photographs and clippings—all of them featuring Amy. Amy racing and Amy holding up trophies, a long, gleaming silver coupe car with large wire wheels and big round headlights always in the pictures with her.

"Wow. I like your car," said Adam.

Amy smiled sadly and nodded. "She's unique, built by Hank Sorensen—total genius and speed freak."

"Tell me more about the last race you drove in," Adam implored.

"Well, as I was about to win the *Fortescue* Grand Prix"—Amy put as much contempt into the name *Fortescue* as she could—"something landed on the roof of my car. Everything became a blur after that. When clarity returned, I had crashed into a barrier . . . and all my driving flair was gone. I came last in the Fortescue Grand Prix and haven't been able to race since." Amy winced and clicked her fingers with frustration. "I drifted about for a few weeks, wondering what to do, and then I happened to read about a fantastic chess player, Farley T. Knight, who lost his skill at an event organized by—"

"Fortescue?" Adam interrupted.

"You got it," Amy replied. "So I figured I'd follow Fortescue on his travels. Try to somehow ratchet up some answers. Get proof—and get my talent back! And now, since speaking to you, Adam, I've been getting clearer flashbacks about that Grand Prix day. Whatever you saw the other night, the same thing reached a claw in through my car window. There was a glow and a humming sound too."

Amy took the scrapbook from Adam and flicked wistfully through the pages. "Oh yeah, and one of my favorite trophies went missing around the time of the race. Wonder if it ended up in that trophy room you saw?" Amy added bitterly. "Wonder why it wants them . . . ?"

Adam suddenly had an idea. "I'm going to talk to my sister, Cress," he said. "She's performing tonight, and Fortescue's shadowy stranger is bound to strike during the interval like it did with Hans. Maybe with Cress's help we can catch it!"

"I'm not sure I want you to get involved, kid," Amy said. "This is personal and it could get real dangerous."

"I have to warn her anyway! She could help you and you could help her and I could help both of you," Adam pleaded. He really wanted to be involved. He wanted to know what was going on.

Amy put the scrapbook down. She looked at Adam for a long moment. She was used to being on her own and doing everything for herself. However, this boy seemed fairly smart and maybe his sister could help her too. Amy punched Adam playfully on the shoulder.

"Okay, you're on. Max revs, buster. Max revs!"

Adam knocked on Cressida's door. She answered, saw it was Adam and rolled her eyes.

"Can I talk to you?" he said.

Cressida said nothing, but she left the door open and retreated inside her room. Adam followed and closed the door behind him. Cressida was wearing the same dress she had worn to the concert in Riverfork City. Around her neck she had the necklace with the silver musical note charm.

"How's Sophia?" he asked.

"She's gone home," replied Cressida. "She said things just didn't add up anymore. Besides, this is a place for talents . . ."

"Know the feeling," said Adam.

"I'd like to preserve my voice, if you don't mind, Adam," said Cressida, sitting down on her bed and staring gloomily out the window.

Adam looked at his sister. She always seemed sad nowadays.

"Doesn't the singing make you happy, Cress?" he asked.

Cressida shrugged. "I have expressed an interest in giving it up. Or had you forgotten?" she said wearily.

Adam thought about this for a second. Perhaps it was best if his sister did not sing tonight. Maybe it would save her from a visit by the mysterious, sinister creature. Even if *she* didn't want her talent, Adam would protect it for her.

"Well, you don't *have* to sing," he suggested.

"I know that. But I'm here now and I have my pride," she replied. "Besides, Fortescue has found a special venue for me to sing in. Sounds interesting."

"I wouldn't trust Fortescue too much," Adam mumbled.

"Is there a reason you are here?" Cressida asked, irritation rising in her voice.

"Look, I know you think this leathery-claw-stranger stuff is a load of rubbish," he went on. Cressida snorted. "But I don't think it's a coincidence that two people have lost their talents today. Please, will you let me wait with a friend in your dressing room during the interval?"

"A friend? *You* have a friend *here*?" Cressida asked, barely disguising the shock in her voice.

"Yes, Amy Swift. She's a race car driver. Is that all right, then?" Adam asked again.

"Amy Swift, a race car driver," Cressida repeated with disbelief. "And is she friends with your cloaked monster?"

"Oh no. Like me, she wants to catch it."

"I see."

"So can we wait in your dressing room?" Adam urged again.

Cressida let out a sigh of surrender. Her brother was getting crazier by the moment, but she could not be bothered to argue. Her thoughts were on her singing, not on the vivid fantasy life of Adam.

"If you must," she said. "Now I have to go and warm up. I'm singing in the hotel aviary, whatever and wherever that is."

And with that, Cressida got up and left the room. Adam watched her go with concern. He did not want to use his sister as bait, but he couldn't think of a better plan—he was, after all, very, very average. So how could he?

CHAPTER TEN

THE AVIARY

• • • • • • • • • • • • •

Cressida Bloom walked into the hotel aviary and looked around with awe. The place was bathed in a golden glow from the setting sun, and the first thing to strike her was how big it was. Towering walls made entirely of glass led up to an elaborate glass roof with a narrow metal walkway suspended underneath it. A very rickety-looking staircase reached up to the walkway. Must be for the window cleaners, thought Cressida. They certainly had their work cut out.

All around Cressida were enormous tropical plants and hundreds upon hundreds of exotic birds. Of course, Cressida realized, an aviary is a place where birds are kept. And what spectacular birds they were—all shapes and sizes, with lush and brightly colored plumage, and in this huge place they had plenty of room to stretch their wings. They flashed to and fro like darting rainbows, their many distinct calls echoing back, sharp and shrill, off the expanse of glass.

Cressida lowered her gaze and took in the raised platform where she would be singing and the couple of hundred chairs arranged in neat lines in front of it. She started to feel the usual fluttering in her stomach. It irritated her. She had a theory that the bigger the talent, the bigger the butterflies. She often thought that she would be happy as a mediocre, by-the-numbers backup singer if that would banish those annoying butterflies forever.

Suddenly she felt something brush briefly against her neck. She spun around.

"Do you like it?" asked Fortescue. Cressida had no idea how long he had been there. He gestured around at the aviary.

"Oh, very much," she replied, pushing her spectacles back up onto the bridge of her nose.

"The acoustics are superb, apparently, so we shall take our chances with the bird droppings," said Fortescue with a smile.

Cressida couldn't help noticing that he did not look directly at her. His eyes flicked about restlessly as though his mind were on other things. Aside from this, Fortescue seemed to be a very pleasant man.

"I am so glad you could come, Cressida. I have heard such wonderful things about your voice," he continued. Cressida glowed a little at this—if against her own will. "And I thought the aviary would be good for you because it's so filled with light. No need to worry about the dark in here," he said.

Cressida cringed inside. "Um, I'm not really afraid of the dark. That was my brother being . . ." She paused while she searched for a word. "Creative."

"I see. Well, we must all try to break free from the dreary constraints of our family, mustn't we?" Fortescue said, a dark frown creasing his brow. Then he laughed suddenly. "Still, it's a marvelous place to sing! I shall leave you alone now to warm up. The audience will arrive in around twenty minutes. Your dressing room is just over there, behind the orchids." Giving Cressida one last tight-lipped smile, he turned sharply and walked out of the aviary.

Cressida went over to the platform and walked up the steps onto it. It was an astounding venue, and for a moment all her doubts about the joys of being talented left her. She wanted to fill this place with music. Her music. She took a few deep breaths and began to sing. It was an old song about a shepherd. The words didn't really matter—Cressida's beautiful voice would have made a dictionary sound wonderful. In fact, her voice was so pure that even the birds stopped their own singing to listen.

As Cressida closed her eyes and lost herself completely in her song, she failed to notice a very large bird drop down onto the walkway underneath the glass roof. Then it swooped through the air and landed quietly just behind Cressida. Except this wasn't a bird, and it hadn't swooped. It had slid down on a wire.

Cressida stopped suddenly. Had she heard something? She turned around quickly and gasped.

The hunched visitor clenched its cloak tight around its gangly form—advancing toward her with swift, bloodcurdling movements. Cressida wanted to move, to run, but there was something mesmerizing about the creature's hooded yellow eyes that kept her fixed to the spot. Her heart was beating hard. Adam was right after all, she found herself thinking. But he had not seen the cloaked being fully. Now, with a hesitant awkwardness, it slowly pushed back its hood to get a better view of this human who was capable of making such a stirring sound. At the same time it let its cloak fall loose. As the evening sun lit the towering figure, Cressida could see it in its entirety. It was the most frightful creature she had ever seen, and she let out a gasp. Such a peculiar mixture of sinister features. Its skin was thick and leathery and of a strange dark, mottled blue. The legs and arms were thin but sinewy and obviously very strong. Cressida shuddered as she observed the creature's face. Fearsome yet strangely fascinating, the wide mouth contained sharp yellow teeth, and there were scars across its cheeks and forehead, the consequence, perhaps, of many terrible battles. Tufts of light blue hair sprouted from its bony chin. It was a wild face, and yet the yellowish eyes seemed to glow with a fierce wisdom. Something else too— was it innocence? Sadness? Somehow she found the longer she looked at it, the less afraid she felt. It had more straggly blue hair growing from its scalp, and two small ears laced with pink veins poked through. For a moment it regarded her, head to one side, nostrils quivering sensitively, squinting in the low sunlight. Then it pulled its hood back up and made a curious trilling noise. The effect on Cressida was instantaneous. The remaining fear she felt left and a warm glow spread all over her, as if someone were heaping praise on her. She felt flattered and safe, lulled into a state of peaceful surrender. The creature swept closer to Cressida and a long gnarly claw hovered above her head. Cressida grew weak. She closed her eyes. She felt as though she were far away, lost in a wilderness where everything familiar to her had vanished. The creature threw back its head and let out a short, high-pitched gargling sound. In the next moment, a glowing pinkish sphere about the size of an orange and covered in swirling golden patterns emerged from the top of Cressida's head.

The creature gazed lovingly at the sphere and relished the familiar powerful feeling it experienced whenever it took from another living thing. But beyond that it felt something else. Something it had not felt before. It could see this sphere was special. It was an orb of exceptional purity, aglow with stardust. The vibrating, shimmering patterns that shifted and changed on its surface were exquisite. Perhaps it was perfect. The creature let out a melancholy growl. It felt a tugging, restless feeling in its gut. This human is special. This human *was* special.

The creature hovered anxiously for a moment, but then it seemed to make a decision. Tenderly it tucked the sphere into its cloak and was gone, hurtling up the wire. . . .

• • •

Cressida opened her eyes. What had just happened? Her thoughts were a turmoil of words and images that felt as though they had been dumped into a bucket of water and were now being stirred wildly with a stick. She felt short of breath. She needed to lie down. Behind the throng of orchid flowers Cressida found a small door into a tiny room with stained-glass windows. There was an armchair in the corner and she flopped down into it and fell asleep instantly. She was awoken minutes later by Fortescue telling her it was time to sing.

Adam and Amy were safely hidden in some lemon trees at the back of the aviary when Cressida emerged from behind the orchids. A cheer went up from the audience, followed by riotous applause. Music lovers from all over Paralin, wearing hats and outlandish cravats, were aching to hear Cressida. Many of the talented children were there too. Foster Barrel shifted impatiently in his seat and gawped at the birds flying overhead, but the others stared at Cressida, still as statues, spellbound. Adam felt a twinge of pride. He *would* protect his sister and her talent from Fortescue and the creature. He and Amy had it all planned. Adam was going to sneak into Cressida's dressing room just before the interval. When the visitor came, Adam would grab it with Amy's help. Between the two of them they should be able to overpower it, surely. Then they would make it tell them what was going on, even if Fortescue wouldn't. But beneath Adam's lofty optimism was a bass note of fear. He tried to ignore the dread twitching in his limbs and switched his attention to his sister. For now, he and Amy would enjoy the concert.

Cressida walked up onto the platform and gave an awkward little bow. Adam thought her showmanship could do with some work. Good thing she was such an amazing singer. But as Cressida opened her mouth, it became obvious straightaway that something was wrong. Instead of singing a wondrous melody, Cressida made a kind of dry clicking noise. Adam's spirits sank. He looked at Amy, who was shaking her head sadly. The monster had struck already.

Adam's heart went out to his bewildered sister croaking feebly onstage. The audience was confused and shifted in their seats. Cressida knew her music had left her—when? why? how?—and she looked out at the rows of disappointed faces with a growing feeling of helplessness. Failure had her in its cold and clammy grip. Adam glanced to the side and saw Fortescue standing in the shadow of a large palm tree. Adam could not see his face, but he knew that strange satisfied expression would be there. Fury began to build in Adam's chest and then, almost by accident, he saw something moving above them. Up on the walkway below the roof. It must be Fortescue's accomplice.

"I see it!" he shouted.

Without a thought, Adam acted instantly. He leaped up

and pushed his way through some dense shrubbery until he found the base of the staircase. He clattered up the shaky steps, frightening tropical birds from their evening perches. Cressida had stopped trying to sing and now she and the audience watched Adam climb higher and higher into the roof of the aviary. Amy was surprised. The kid certainly has guts, she thought. For a split second she considered racing after Adam, but she figured that the thing, whatever it was, would easily get away now. It had too much of a lead. Cressida was too bemused to think anything. Fortescue stepped out from under the palm tree and glowered as he watched the headstrong boy.

The creature spied Adam when he was about halfway up the stairs. It backed away and rushed for the open panel in the roof. But a large blue bird with a long yellow beak flew into the creature's path, forcing it to swerve, and as it did so, its cloak snagged on a rusty piece of railing. Stuck, the creature started to scream and thrash about. The audience all looked to see where the noise was coming from and recoiled at the sight of something flapping back and forth way up in the roof, though it was too far up for anyone to see what it was.

"What is that? It's quite horrid," asked one woman with disgust.

"Looks like a bird that's got stuck," said another woman.

That's no bird, thought Amy to herself. Adam had

almost reached the top of the staircase. He was trying not to look down. The ground was now a very long way away and the staircase was swaying alarmingly. As Adam closed in on the creature, it suddenly let out a piercing wail and ripped its cloak from the railing. Moving so fast it was nothing more than a blur, it leaped for the open panel in the roof. At the same time, Adam jumped for the creature's cloak. The creature was strong, and as it heaved itself out onto the roof, it dragged Adam up with it.

CHAPTER ELEVEN

THE NIGHT OF MASS EXTRACTION

• • • • • • • • • • • • •

The creature was trying to run, but Adam held on to its cloak with all his might. It was obviously desperate not to be separated from it, so it was as good as having hold of an arm or leg and a lot less scary.

"Tell me what you've done to my sister!" Adam yelled.

The creature turned on Adam and pinned him to the glass of the aviary roof. Adam breathed in its unpleasant musty smell again. He noticed the glint of metal wire looped and attached to the outside of the cloak—that explained how it zipped from one place to another. He tried to peer into the shadows of the creature's hood, but all he could see were the two glowing yellow eyes.

"Why were you hanging around? Did you want to see my sister fail? Is that it?" Adam blurted. He squirmed for a moment in the creature's clutches, but its grip was so firm it was almost . . . sticky. "Well, I hope you feel guilty. Whatever you're doing, it's wrong. Hear me?"

The creature stared at Adam briefly; it seemed to be thinking about what he'd said. Then suddenly, with incredible speed and power, it sprang away from Adam and leaped from the roof of the aviary to a drainpipe on the main building of the hotel. With fast, nimble movements it seemed to scuttle up the wall and out of sight. Adam assumed it actually climbed the drainpipe, if with almost impossible speed.

Adam lay still for a while, his heart hammering and his breath ragged. What *was* that thing? Gradually, Adam became aware that there was still something clutched tightly in his fist. He opened his fingers to reveal a tattered piece of the creature's cloak. There was a label sewn into it. He looked at the blue lettering on the square of gold material.

Later that evening, in Cressida's room, Adam sat down next to his sister and dug her in the ribs with his elbow in a feeble attempt to lift her spirits. It was no good. Cressida was in a very gloomy state of mind. She had changed out of her dress and put on pants and a sweater. She wanted simple warmth at this moment, not the stagnant finery left over from her dismal failed performance.

"We've both been ordered to leave," Adam said. "Seems Fortescue took great pleasure in telling Mr. Bellette that his guests should not be cavorting on the aviary roof with one of the hotel's own exotic birds. That Mr. Bellette will believe anything. And I suppose you've served your purpose, Cress."

Cressida didn't bother replying. Her voice was very croaky and she had developed a nasty cough, for which Adam now gave her his handkerchief.

"Let's go over this again. What do you remember from before the concert, Cress?" Adam asked.

"Not much," Cressida replied huskily, her brow creasing. "I thought it was a dream—there was a presence, soothing for a while, then a tugging, as though something was being taken from me."

Cressida's eyes filled with tears, but Adam decided to push further with his questions while the remnants of the encounter were still fresh.

"But now you know it wasn't a dream. I chased the evil thing myself. Did *you* see its face?"

"No. Er, I can't remember," Cressida replied evasively.

"Probably not. It seems to hide itself in its cloak usually. That's what I tore this from, so I think it's called Nipso," Adam said. "Odd name, huh?"

He showed the piece of cloth to Cressida.

"Yet we don't exactly know why I couldn't sing," Cressida said simply. That part of what had happened still wouldn't come back to her, and Adam couldn't help her because he didn't know either why she couldn't sing. Cressida coughed into Adam's handkerchief and looked out the window. It was getting truly dark. The gracious rooftops of Paralin were silhouetted against a purplish-gray sky.

"It's a mystery, Cress," Adam said. He wanted to tell his sister that everything would be fine, but he had no way to back up such a promise. In fact, he feared Cressida's singing voice had gone for good. Perhaps he could comfort her another way.

"Hey, but you wanted to give up singing anyway, didn't you?" Adam tried.

Cressida turned to him, her face like thunder. "This isn't quite what I had in mind," she croaked loudly, setting off an even more raucous coughing fit that lasted for several minutes. When she eventually composed herself again, she added bleakly, "Well, I assume we go home now, though there doesn't seem a lot to go home for."

Adam knew what she meant. Uncle Brody wouldn't exactly be overjoyed to see them.

"Let's go and talk to Amy first," said Adam firmly, "and quickly, before we are physically thrown out of the hotel. We were supposed to have checked out half an hour ago."

Adam knocked on Amy's door. Moments later it opened a crack and Amy peered out suspiciously. When she saw

Adam, she opened the door wide and ushered him in. She seemed to be excited about something. Her hair was a straggly mess and her eyes looked wild.

"I've brought my sister, Cress," Adam said.

Amy held out her hand and Cressida shook it. Cressida winced at the firm grip. You could always depend on Adam to find "interesting" people, she thought.

"Pleased to meet ya, Cress," Amy said breathlessly. "Sorry about your voice, but I'm doing all I can to get to the bottom of this!" Before Cressida could reply, Amy headed into the small bathroom.

"Come listen to this," she urged.

Adam and Cressida followed her. The bathroom was tastefully decorated with white diamond-shaped tiles and gold taps. An impressive painting of a small plane flying down a valley between two looming mountains hung on the wall. A pair of oily racing gauntlets were soaking in the sink. Amy leaned over the bath and put her ear to a copper pipe that ran down the length of one wall. She held a finger to her lips.

"I've been hearing voices," she said with excitement.

Cressida looked at Adam as if to say, Where did you find this fruitcake?

Adam ignored her and spoke quietly. "Voices?"

"Shh! Yes, Fortescue and some kind of hubbub. Children, I think."

Amy pushed herself away from the pipe and rushed back out of the bathroom to pull a scroll of paper from her suitcase. She rolled it out on the bed, and Adam and Cressida moved closer to see what it was. It looked like a blueprint of the hotel.

"Where'd you get that?" Adam asked.

"A famous race car driver can move mountains at Paralin city hall," Amy answered, poring over the blueprint. "Aha! That pipe leads down into a huge boiler room in the basement, and next to that is what looks like a large wine cellar. *Very* large." Amy rolled up the blueprint and smiled at Adam and Cressida. "I'm going down there."

"Can we come?" Adam asked.

"Rather go solo for speed, if you don't mind," replied Amy, scraping her hair back into a ponytail.

"But I'm nearly fast on my feet, almost above average in a fight, and Cressida would really like her singing voice back."

"I'm not sure I want to go . . ." croaked Cressida, but Adam silenced her with a swift elbow jab to the ribs.

Amy sighed and looked from Adam's eager face to Cressida's forlorn expression. She threw a blue silk scarf around her neck and nodded.

"Okay, but keep up," she said.

They took the back stairs and emerged in a narrow corridor with peeling dark red paint and a scuffed tile floor. Amy consulted the blueprint again and pointed to a faded mural on the wall depicting a jolly fellow swigging from a bottle.

"Seems whoever designed this hotel had a sense of humor," she whispered. She strode toward the mural, with Adam and Cressida following. She ran her fingers over the paint and then pressed hard against the label on the bottle in the mural. With a low rumble, the whole section of wall opened to reveal a stone staircase leading down into darkness.

Amy shrugged. "Seemed logical," she whispered as she started to creep slowly down the staircase, an excited-looking Adam and a bemused-looking Cressida behind her.

Soon they could hear voices, and as they reached the bottom of the staircase, they saw that they were on a balcony overlooking an enormous underground room. The walls were rough, as though they had been carved out of rock, and leading away into darkness there were rows and rows of wine racks full of dusty bottles. In the middle of the cavernous space, all of the remaining talented children were standing in a large circle. There were at least seventy of them. Then Fortescue stepped into the center. Adam gasped.

"It's just like my dream," he said.

"Ssshhh!" hissed Amy, and she dragged him down to her level so that just their eyes peeked over the edge of the balcony. Cressida ducked down too, puzzled and on the verge of getting cranky. What was this strange goose chase her brother had dragged her on?

"I'm sure you are wondering why you've been brought down here," said Fortescue, looking around at the children, who all seemed quite excited about their nighttime adventure.

"A midnight feast?" exclaimed Carl, the freckled boy who was a genius painter.

Fortescue answered with a sneer. "How quaint. Truth is, we're running out of time. Suspicions are being raised. A certain talentless boy is sticking his nose in where it isn't wanted." Amy looked at Adam and raised her eyebrows. Adam smiled. "And although we would rather take your talents when you are using them, because that is when they are most potent, we are going to have to speed things up a bit."

The children looked at each other, puzzled.

"What are you going on about?" asked one bold child.

Then they all gasped as two shining eyes suddenly emerged from the shadows of an alcove.

"What's that?" asked another child with a trembling voice.

The cloaked creature loped into the center of the room and stood behind Fortescue. It towered above him, its face shadowed by the hood but its eyes glowing out from within it. The children looked at each other in fear.

"Nothing to worry about. Nothing to worry about," said Fortescue, raising a hand. "It is a friend. Don't let its . . . unusual appearance discombobulate you."

The creature made a peculiar warbling sound, causing all the wine bottles to rattle.

"The Festival of Youthful Genius is drawing to a close. But, rest assured, it will be a spectacular finale," Fortescue said, turning slowly on the spot, looking from one young genius to the next.

There was danger in the air. Adam could feel it increasing, like a thundercloud gathering mass. He clenched his fists with frustration. What could they do?

"We have to stop this!" Adam whispered fiercely.

"Perhaps we should get the police?" Cressida muttered. She also had a growing sense of dread.

"No time," replied Amy. "And anyway, what would we tell them? They'd never believe us."

"Well, what shall we *do,* then?" Adam asked, his tone urgent.

Amy thought for a moment, then she took a deep breath and stood up.

"Run, children, run!" she shouted. "And cover your ears!"

CHAPTER TWELVE
THE MYSTERIOUS NOTEBOOK
· · · · · · · · · · · · ·

But it was too late. The creature had taken center stage, arms spread, claws pointed, trilling its strange sounds. The children were transfixed, their eyes glazed. Driven by frustration, Adam also jumped up and echoed Amy's words.

"You must get out of here. Go! Now!"

Fortescue shuddered at the sight of the boy. Why wouldn't that tedious, talentless little wretch just go and leave him to his business?

"Who is the wrestling genius again?" Fortescue asked, thinking quickly.

Foster Barrel, the large, toothless, stocky boy, awoke abruptly from his trance and raised a meaty hand.

"Of course you are. Silly me," Fortescue said.

"My name's Foster, wrestling champion of the world and all that," grunted the boy. "I wrestled a grizzly once, and I tell you, that bear had more than a sore head by the time I was finished with him."

"How utterly charming," Fortescue said. "Look, Foster, the 'experiment' we are about to conduct is enormously important, so could you make sure these anarchic trouble-makers are kept at bay for the next few minutes?"

"Sure thing," Foster replied, slapping his hands to-gether. Any excuse to show off his superior strength. He strode up the stone stairs to the balcony and loomed over Adam, Amy and Cressida, his shadow throwing them all into darkness. "Don't try nuffin', you anoraky troublemak-ers," he said with menace.

"You're making a mistake," said Adam. By then the creature was gargling at an almost deafening pitch. Fortes-cue picked up a large sack as, suddenly, a loud crackling noise filled the room and, one by one, bright, glowing spheres started to emerge from the top of the children's heads. The creature was revolving slowly on the spot. Foster looked baffled.

"What they trying to prove with this experiment per-zackly?" he asked.

"Well, they've proved you're as stupid as you look," replied Adam in frustration.

With pained expressions, both Amy and Cressida watched the creature extract the children's talents—in the shape of these delicate orbs. For, they now realized, this was exactly what had already happened to themselves. Amy felt a wave of hatred for the creature. But Cressida was fascinated by it all over again. She was surprised at how solid and tangible the spheres looked. Who would have thought talent itself could glow so brightly?

The shining spheres of talent floated toward the creature, all colors of the spectrum, some spotted, some covered in swirls, some striped—all indescribably beautiful. Fortescue plucked them from the air as they reached him and stuffed them into his sack.

Suddenly Foster turned and stormed back down the stairs. As he reached the floor, his talent sphere began to rise from the top of his head too.

"Hey, what's going on?" he demanded. But even as he spoke, his eyes glazed and a dazed expression spread over his face. Within moments his sphere was floating toward the creature. It was small and mucus green, with black and blue patches. Fortescue looked disappointed as he plucked it from midair and added it to his sack.

And with that, the crackling noise stopped. The room seemed very quiet all of a sudden. The children were rubbing their eyes and stumbling about, bumping into each other. All the spheres together had been so bright that the room, by contrast, now seemed utterly dark. The creature and Fortescue took advantage of this cloak of bafflement and shadow to quietly disappear into an alcove.

"There they go!" Adam cried, spotting their departure through the gloom. He gave chase along with Amy and Cressida. Foster stepped vacantly into Adam's path, but he seemed smaller and clumsier now and Adam pushed him to one side with ease.

"What happened?" Carl, the painting genius, asked Adam as he rushed past. He looked dazed and his fingers were shaking.

"You were robbed," Adam said.

Next to Carl, Tara, a girl of about ten with ginger ringlets, was tapping her feet clumsily on the floor.

"I'm a tap dancer, but my rhythm has gone," she said, close to tears. "The rhythm was my friend."

"Don't worry, we'll help all of you!" Adam said with determination in his voice. He rushed into the alcove just in time to see the doors of a service elevator slam shut. The metal pointer above the doors showed that Fortescue and the creature were heading up to the roof. Fortescue's planned escape appeared in Adam's mind like a vision.

"I know how they're going to get away," he said, and with that, he turned and led Amy and Cressida back the way they had come.

"*Should* we chase them?" Cressida croaked.

"Darn right we should!" Amy declared. "Lead on, Adam!"

Adam clattered out onto the roof at full speed, with Amy and Cressida just behind him. All of them could see instantly that Fortescue and the creature were intending to escape in the "observation booth." The golden balloon in the shape of a plus sign would carry them far away.

The creature and the sack of talent spheres were already inside the tin shed, and Fortescue was pulling on the lever to release the brackets holding it in place. He tugged just enough so that the shed rose into the air about five feet and then stopped. Fortescue hurried underneath it to detach the thick wire cable altogether. There was now a large rudder attached to the rear of the shed for steering. They had obviously planned their escape carefully. But they had not planned on Adam.

"Why?! Why are you doing this?" Adam called as he rushed over and grabbed Fortescue by the arm.

"Give it up, boy. Your sister will get used to her loss in time. Go home," Fortescue snarled.

"You can't keep doing this," said Amy, placing her fists on her hips defiantly.

"Wanna bet?" said Fortescue, throwing the now-detached heavy cable at Amy, who barely ducked in time to avoid it.

The shed started to rise rapidly, and Fortescue banged on the trapdoor in its floor. It opened and a pair of long, sinewy, leathery-clawed arms reached out and pulled him up. Adam lunged and grabbed hold of Fortescue's legs.

"This is getting beyond a joke," said Fortescue, kicking out at Adam.

The shed was rising very fast and Adam was dangling from Fortescue's legs. Fortescue himself was hanging on for dear life to the creature's arms.

"Give back what you both stole!" Adam cried.

"What's it to you?" asked Fortescue, trying to kick Adam off.

"I don't like bullies!" Adam answered.

"That's life. Get over it," Fortescue sneered.

The shed was high above the hotel now, but despite the alarming situation, Adam found himself distracted by Fortescue's explorer's boots—they had very, very thick soles. Fortescue was obviously much shorter than he looked. Then he kicked out at Adam again. Adam tried to get a better handhold by grabbing at a pocket on Fortescue's jacket. But the pocket tore off and a notebook fell down to the roof of the hotel. A moment later Adam fell too. Down, down, down.

Something broke his long fall. It wasn't particularly soft, but it probably saved his life. With a groan Adam stood up and watched the balloon and his shed drift away across the night sky. There was a strong wind blowing and Fortescue, his creature and the sack of talent spheres would soon be a long way away. Adam rubbed his back and looked down at what had cushioned his landing. It was his suitcase. At least it *had* been his suitcase. Now it was just a crumpled mess.

"I saw it lying near that skylight," Amy said. "I moved it under you. It was the only thing I could think of to break your fall, kid."

"Thanks," said Adam. "Wondered where it had got to." He was tired, achy and frustrated, but then he remembered the notebook. He started to search the roof.

"What are you looking for?" asked Cressida, trying not to cough.

"Aha!" Adam exclaimed. He saw the brass corners of the notebook glinting in the moonlight. He picked it up and looked at it. On the battered leather cover were the words PROJECT GOLDEN HARVEST. "This feels important," Adam said, tapping it. He looked at Amy, who smiled. It took a lot to impress Amy Swift, but tonight Adam Bloom had done just that.

Inside the tin shed, Fortescue slapped at his ripped jacket pocket and scowled.

"My notebook! That *tiresome* boy!" he snarled. "If he has it, he and that mad racing woman will know a lot more than I want them to."

Fortescue sat down on a stool and grabbed hold of the lever that led to the rudder. He pulled an elegant compass from the inside pocket of his jacket and turned the rudder until they were pointing eastward. The balloon slowed right down.

"Hmm, wind's against us, anyway," Fortescue mused to himself. "Perhaps we'll hover around the outskirts of Paralin for a while. See if we spot them leaving. I must get that notebook back."

The creature had been sitting quietly in the darkest corner of the shed, carefully stroking Cressida's talent sphere, but now it made a low gargling noise. Fortescue was thinking about all the information in his notebook and wondering what Adam would make of it. The creature made a louder, more insistent noise. Fortescue looked over at it. It was squatting quietly in the gloom, but its eyes were luminous and staring at him expectantly.

"What's got into you?" Fortescue asked. He thought for a moment. "That boy didn't say anything to you up on the roof of the aviary, did he?"

The creature fell silent.

"Don't take heed of anything he said," Fortescue added, a twinge of concern flitting through his mind. "Like I keep telling you, if they don't have any talent, they are of no interest to us. And that boy is distinctly ordinary, though, it has to be said, very annoying. Do you understand?"

The creature did not respond. It sat as still as stone, its eyes not moving from Fortescue. Fortescue felt annoyed. He would have to quash this little rebellion.

"Do you understand?!" Fortescue repeated.

The creature shifted. It shuffled backward, farther into its corner. It gave a low yelp of consent.

"I am your friend, your *only* friend. We've talked about this, the importance of our friendship. How it means that I care about you and want you to be happy. And you do as I ask because you want to please your friend," Fortescue said, and then he attempted a charming smile. "And don't I give you all those special shiny gifts? Only a friend would do that. So no more doubts, hmm? We have much in common. Stick with me, stick to the plan."

Fortescue pulled something that glittered from his

pocket. A necklace with a sparkling silver charm of some sort dangling from it. The creature's eyes lit up and it grunted softly.

"From me, especially for you, my loyal Nipso," Fortescue said. "We are a team without peer, a dream union."

CHAPTER THIRTEEN
THE SILVER SWIFT

· · · · · · · · · · · · ·

The next morning it was clear that the Festival of Youthful Genius was over. The once-talented children were leaving the hotel. They shuffled out in silence. They all knew that their skills were gone, but they were confused about what exactly had happened and they all secretly hoped that the condition was temporary. Many of the children believed that the hotel was somehow to blame, so the general desire was to get away as quickly as possible and hope that their talents would return when they got back home. Mr. Bellette stood on the steps of the Hotel Peritus and tried to cheerily wave the children off. Tara, the tap dancer who now had no rhythm, deliberately stepped on his toe.

"It's all been wonderful!" he said, trying not to wince.

"It's been a weird, freaky disaster," she said.

"But a weird and *wonderful* freaky disaster," Mr. Bellette said, determined to have his jolly send-off.

• • •

In her room, Amy was flipping through the pages of Fortescue's notebook. She, Adam and Cressida all had their coats on because they knew it was very likely they would be thrown out of the hotel at any moment. Amy was finding the notebook fascinating. Adam was trying to look too, as was Cressida—though she wouldn't admit it—but Amy kept flicking the pages over just as they started to read. The notebook was crammed with all manner of information. In the first section there were bits from old maps and parchments, symbols analyzed and what looked like copies of cave paintings. The second section read like a journal describing expeditions to a place called Marscopia. It sounded like a strange, faraway place—a seething mass of rampant jungle interspersed with rocky plateaus and dark, forbidding caves. There were long lists of items needed for these expeditions. In the third section the pages folded out—names and odd circles were dotted across enormous maps covering many continents. The fourth section was virtually indecipherable, being a mass of hasty, excited scribbles.

"What does it all mean?" Adam asked. He could tell the notebook would need to be studied for hours to give up its secrets.

"Beats me," Amy replied.

"Looks like the ramblings of a madman," said Cressida, her voice still raspy.

"All I know is, there are maps—and maps almost always lead you someplace," Amy said. "Somewhere in this notebook there will be clues about where Fortescue is headed next."

Suddenly there was a knock at the door. Amy looked up and shoved the notebook into the pocket of her leather coat, but Adam, thinking quickly, quietly plucked the notebook from her pocket seconds later and tucked it swiftly into his own. Amy went over to the door and opened it. Mr. Bellette was standing there with an awkward smile on his face.

"I believe the Blooms should have left by now," he said, peering over her shoulder to prove he knew they were there. "And, Miss Swift, we'd prefer it if you, um, found alternative accommodation as well," he added, shuffling in an embarrassed manner. "One of the children said you were down in the wine cellar last night, which is strictly out of bounds to guests."

"Don't worry. I'm outta here, buster," replied Amy, gathering her belongings together.

"How much did Fortescue pay you?" Adam asked Mr. Bellette, with a bold stare.

"I don't know what you mean," Mr. Bellette replied, flustered.

"To host the so-called Festival of Youthful Genius," Adam said.

"Yes, a marvelous success," Mr. Bellette answered, but he sounded unsure.

"It was enough for you not to ask any questions, wasn't it?" Adam said.

"I do have a business to run. You should leave," said Mr. Bellette primly, looking at his shoes.

Amy clattered out of the room, pushing roughly past Mr. Bellette. Adam and Cressida came next, Cressida with her suitcase and Adam with a paper bag containing a few items he had saved from his squashed suitcase. Amy walked up to the elevator and pressed the call button. Mr. Bellette headed briskly for the back stairs. The elevator doors opened.

"So what's the plan?" Adam asked Amy eagerly.

"Plan?" replied Amy. "What do you mean?" She wrestled her luggage into the elevator.

Adam looked a little taken aback, but he grabbed Cressida and dragged her into the elevator with them.

"What do we do now?" he persisted.

"Dunno about you, kiddo, but I'm going after Fortescue and that thing again. Still wanna get my racing feet back," Amy answered as she hit the basement button on the elevator panel. "I know a lot more now, so I reckon I'm in pole position. It's time to start the engine and get back on the trail!"

"Great! We'll come with you!" Adam exclaimed.

"No, no, no," said Amy, shaking her head. "I like to travel light."

"Leave it, Adam," said Cressida wearily. "We should go home."

"No, Cress," said Adam. He turned to Amy as the elevator dropped downward. He was getting angry. "Without me you wouldn't have that notebook. Without me you wouldn't know where to go!"

"What is it you really want, Adam?" Amy asked.

"I want to get my sister's singing voice back," he replied, "and I want to know why Fortescue and his . . . and his . . . talent thief are doing what they're doing. Is that too much to ask? Can we come with you? Please. We are three people without talent. We should stick together."

Amy let out a long sigh and made a clicking noise with her tongue.

"No," she said. "It's for your own good. This is a dangerous battle and one I'd rather fight on my own. If I can, I'll get Cressida's talent sphere back. That's my best offer."

Adam pulled Fortescue's notebook from his pocket and held it out.

"Fine. But you won't have this," he said, his eyes shining.

Amy stared. She had to hand it to him, he was smart. She wasn't about to wrestle the notebook from him. Maybe it *would* be helpful to have him along. She could not help but laugh.

"Okay, okay. But cause me any trouble and I'm ditching the both of you like two shredded tires. Got that?"

Adam nodded.

"How will we travel?" Cressida asked.

"Why, in the Silver Swift, of course," Amy replied.

"That beautiful car? The one in your album?" asked Adam, a big smile spreading across his face.

"Yep, but remember, it was an old photo," said Amy, looking a little uncomfortable. The elevator jolted to a halt and the doors opened to reveal the basement.

"Is this it?" asked Adam.

The car in front of them looked nothing like the amazing machine in the photograph. True, she was long and silver like the car in the picture, but she was also completely covered in dents and scratches. The headlights were at strange angles, the hood ornament in the shape of a swift was bent and the black number seven in the white painted circle on the driver's door was streaked with grime. Even the roof had a dent—must have been where the creature landed, Adam mused. The once-grand Silver Swift looked very sorry for herself.

"She could probably do with a bit of a buff and polish," Amy said.

"You think?" Adam replied.

"I tell ya, once that creature takes your talent, you swing way over to the other end of the spectrum. Explains why Cressida's voice is all croaky and why I have the driving coordination of a one-wheeled beer truck. Yes, siree, every bend is a challenge, every stop sign a chance to forget where the brake is," Amy said. "Still, I got here safely and I shall get us where we're going safely—hopefully."

Adam caught Cressida's frown and, sensing she was

about to voice concern about traveling in such a crumpled heap, with such an unreliable chauffeur, gave her a reassuring smile and a playful punch on the shoulder. Cressida, who did not have the energy to argue with Adam, gave a resigned little shrug.

Amy went around to the back of the car, gave the trunk an almighty kick, and it sprung open. She flung her luggage inside. Cressida put her suitcase in and Adam threw his paper bag in as well.

"Where are we going?" Adam asked.

Amy smiled. She could feel the delicious anticipation of an adventure ahead. She had had enough of mooching around the Hotel Peritus and was glad to be moving on.

"Gimme the notebook." She held out her hand. Adam looked doubtful. Amy rolled her eyes. "I'll give it back to you. Sheesh!"

Adam reluctantly handed it over and Amy folded out a map that showed a route through a huge mountain range.

"Look," she said, pointing at the map. "The Kappa-Nage Mountains. They start just a few miles east of here. According to the notes, a man called Shafer lives there. He crops up a lot in the book, especially in the expedition section, but Fortescue doesn't seem to like him much."

"It says here, 'Have no more use for Shafer and he knows too much. Silence him once and for all after festival?'" said Adam, running his finger along the edge of the map.

"Exactly. Perhaps if we race to this Shafer guy, we'll find

Fortescue there and I can get my talent sphere back," said Amy, giving the map an optimistic flick with her finger.

"And Cressida's," Adam added, urgency flooding his voice. "And all the others. We may have a chance to stop Fortescue and the creature from taking any more too!"

Amy looked into Adam's determined eyes and let out a chuckle.

"Get in, mister trailblazer," she said, leaping into the driving seat.

Adam pulled at the passenger door until it sprung open with a twang.

"I'll go in the back. I'm going to sleep for a bit," said Cressida quietly. She had discovered that if she whispered her voice was clearer and she didn't cough. Adam nodded and heaved the front seat forward so Cressida could squeeze her way into the small rear seat.

"Cress, you don't mind coming, do you?" Adam asked.

"I don't know what I think at the moment, Adam," Cressida replied, pushing her spectacles back into place. But despite her lack of clarity she knew the pit of pain caused by the loss of her parents had just become much deeper. Not because her talent had gone—in some ways that was a relief, of course—but because she did not know who or what she was without it.

Adam thought Cressida looked sadder than ever. Her spark was gone—usually she would never let him lead the way like this.

"I know you don't have the energy to feel angry right now, you're probably feeling a bit numb and all that, so until you feel better I'll be angry for you and I'll stay that way until we get your talent back. Okay?" Adam said. He blinked at Cressida, his eyes brimming with a tenacious resolve.

Cressida gave a weak smile. "You're nuts," she mumbled.

"Yeah, but only in an average way," Adam replied.

Cressida found a blanket on the backseat and pulled it over her. Adam pushed the front seat back into place and closed the door. He looked around. The interior of the car spoke of comfort and thrills. The seats were a deep red leather and the dashboard was a dark-colored wood, packed with dials and shiny switches. Amy turned the ignition key and the engine growled into life.

"She may not look as pretty as she once did, but, boy, she still has heart!" she exclaimed with a grin, pushing her foot down gently on the accelerator. The long, silver car purred out of the basement, up into the sunshine.

CHAPTER FOURTEEN

AVALANCHE!

· · · · · · · · · · · · ·

Adam was surprised at the pace they were traveling in this so-called race car. In fact, some people were walking faster than the car was moving. Cars behind were honking and a pigeon had decided to perch on the roof for a leisurely sightseeing tour of Paralin. Adam looked back at Cressida. She was asleep, huddled under the blanket. This speed was obviously good for tired people, even if it wasn't so good for actually getting anywhere.

"Don't you think we're going just a *little* bit slow?" said Adam, switching his gaze to Amy.

An irate motorist drew up alongside them and yelled, "Be careful you don't break the sound barrier, lady!"

"Ah, go milk a cow!" Amy called back. She turned to Adam. "We can't go any faster."

"Why not?"

"I had a speed limiter fitted," said Amy.

"A what?" said Adam.

"Speed limiter. For safety. I have no coordination now, so I had a device fitted to protect me and everyone else on, or off, the road. This is top speed."

"I think you may have been overly cautious," said Adam.

But then a stoplight turned red and Amy suddenly seemed to be all thumbs and no fingers. She pressed the horn, turned on the radio, indicated left and right, heaved on the handbrake and turned the wheel so they scraped the entire length of the car along a lamppost. Adam winced at the noise of metal on metal.

"Yes, the speed limiter's a good idea," he concurred.

"And now it's green and we're good to go!" said Amy as she wrestled the car into first gear with a terrible grinding noise and moved off—slowly.

"I can see this is going to be a *very* long journey," said Adam.

"Hey, I can drop you off here if you like, buster."

"No, no. It's fine."

And in fact it was fine, and once Adam had gotten used to the honking horns and sarcastic comments from other drivers, he realized that it was a great way to see the city. They drove past little parks with attractive fountains and twisty streets with ornate houses. They crossed over bridges that spanned the two rivers of Paralin, and Adam looked down at the beautiful wooden boats that cruised up and down them. By the time they reached the edge of the city, Adam was feeling rested and calm. He looked over at Amy, who was concentrating fiercely on her driving, her fingers gripping the steering wheel so hard, her knuckles were white. Adam smiled to himself and decided to spend some time reading through Fortescue's "Golden Harvest" notebook. He flicked to the intriguing fourth section toward the end and tried to decipher some of the scrawly handwriting.

The creature craves a friend. I will be its friend [...] a gift of a silken cloak and hood, made special to it by my own clever, personal touch. It was a moment of brilliance, what I did was I [...] and then it serves a dual purpose [...] keeps it hidden from others who may take it from me, experiment upon it for their own purposes, then my Golden Harvestplan would be ruined and [...] NEVER!!! I will succeed.

There is evidence that it values beautiful things, shiny things, so what else but to give it great gifts of this sort to prove my friendship. Though, and my ingeniousness astounds even me [...] We will then be bonded to one *another by a generous friendship of giving and taking—we are so alike, this creature and I, are we not, and [...]*

I will begin. If my Golden Harvest project is to work, I need to guide the creature. Soon I shall see what it makes of humans. I shall start with Shafer, that ridiculously dynamic man, how he irritates. Oh, the wielding of such power thrills me!

There was that name again, thought Adam. Shafer. It would be good to find him and hear his side of the story— it looked as if Shafer had been Fortesecue and the talent thief's first victim. Adam closed the notebook.

"Learn anything useful?" Amy asked, being careful not to take her eyes from the road.

"Yes. Fortescue is every bit as crazy as he seems," Adam replied. He yawned. He suddenly felt heavy-limbed and tired. He could not remember the last time he had slept properly, so he tucked the notebook back inside his coat pocket, huddled down farther into the comfortable seat and dozed off. Long dreams of spinning, glowing spheres greeted him.

Adam awoke to an amazing sight. Through the windshield he could see snow-covered mountains. Amy had stopped the car beside a twisty road halfway up the first mountain of the Kappa-Nage range. Adam looked down and saw that there were actually wispy clouds *below* them.

"We've made good progress, considering," he said, stretching.

Amy bristled. She decided to ignore the "considering" and said, "You've been asleep the whole day."

And, sure enough, Adam could see the sun setting in the west, its slow descent turning the clouds below a warm orange color.

"Wow!" said Cressida with a crack in her voice. She too had just awoken and she too was taking in the stunning mountainscape around and below them. She pushed her spectacles up so they were sitting squarely on her nose as she looked about.

"Great, isn't it, Cress?" said Adam as he shouldered open the door to get out. He breathed the crisp mountain air and jiggled some life back into his legs. Amy and Cressida got out of the car too.

"Feels good to be away from that hotel," Cressida said quietly.

"Yep, it's mighty fine to be out of the pits and on the move," Amy said.

Their breath emerged in cool gray cloudy plumes, and they took in the sparkle of frozen plants by the roadside and the jagged array of icicles clinging to the rock face nearby. All three stamped their feet on the ground in an attempt to warm up. Suddenly a strange noise snapped them out of their restful mood, and Adam, Amy and Cressida looked *up* the mountain for the first time. They were met with a remarkable sight.

On the mountain's peak was a very familiar-looking shed with a golden balloon in the shape of a plus sign towering above it. Next to the shed were two figures.

"Can they see us?" asked Cressida.

"I think so," replied Adam. "In fact, I would guess they landed because of us. From the air the car must stand out like a sore thumb."

"Why is he making that infernal din?" asked Amy.

Although the figures were a long way above them, it did indeed look as though the shorter of the two figures, Fortescue, was cupping his hands around his mouth and . . . yodeling. The noise was deep and disturbing.

In an instant, Adam knew what Fortescue was doing and it made his blood run cold. Directly below the creature and Fortescue, and directly above Adam, Amy and Cressida, was a massive shelf of snow, balanced on a rocky overhang. It only needed a maniac with a loud voice to get it on the move.

"He wouldn't be trying to start an avalanche, now would he?" said Adam, the words catching in his throat.

"I've got a horrible feeling the crazy skunk just might be," said Amy, horror building in her voice.

"I suppose they don't want us meddling," whispered Cressida.

The packed snow above them was starting a creaky protest. The powdery snow at the surface was already beginning to drop down onto the road with soft, yet heavy, thuds.

"Let's get back in the Silver Swift," said Amy, her hammering heart evident in her voice.

"We'll never get away in your car the way it is," said Adam.

"Well, we sure as heck can't outrun an avalanche on foot," said Amy.

"Where's the speed limiter?" asked Adam.

"Under the hood," replied Amy. "But—"

"Can you open it?" asked Adam urgently. "Please."

"Hey, nobody messes with my car," warned Amy, her voice rising. More snow dropped onto the road. Okay, so they were in immense and immediate danger, but her car was her paradise island, her flight of fancy, her Sunday rest, her reason for living.

"We are going to perish here if we don't move quickly," said Adam, trying to remain calm.

Amy folded her arms and clenched her jaw.

"Open it!" said Cressida, her voice croaky but surprisingly firm.

Amy jumped. Then she gave a resigned sigh. She looked up at Fortescue, who was yodeling even louder now, and with a grimace she opened the driver's door and pulled a little lever that made the hood spring open. Adam looked swiftly inside the engine.

"Do you know where it is?" he asked Amy.

She shrugged. "Hey, I spend my time behind the wheel, not under the hood."

Adam tried to block out the chilling noise that Fortescue was making and the sickening grumbles of the mass of snow above them. A large drift hit the ground hard next to him, and in that moment he decided to become an instant mechanic. That's the engine, that's the gearbox, the accelerator must be that lever and the "speed limiter" must be the rusty bolt that someone has welded in to prevent the lever from moving fully. Adam looked around and found a large stone. He picked it up and hammered the bolt with all his might.

"Hey! That doesn't look very delicate!" cried Amy.

"The avalanche is coming," whispered Cressida, quivering with fear.

The bolt broke off and Adam threw it away.

"Time to go!" he called as he threw himself into the driving seat. Cressida wondered for a moment if it was a good idea for Adam to drive, but there was really no time to discuss it, so she squeezed her way into the backseat. Amy also had concerns, but she knew she could not drive at high speed anymore, so she jumped into the passenger seat. Adam looked at the controls with confusion. How hard could it be? Steering wheel, pedals, gearshift. Perhaps he would take a moment to get used to everything. But then he glanced into the rearview mirror and saw a massive, white, monstrous wall of suffocating snow bearing down on the car. He snapped on his seat belt, twisted the key in the ignition, pressed the clutch, rammed the gearshift into first and stuffed his foot down on the accelerator as he released the clutch. Luckily, at that moment, Amy remembered to release the handbrake too and the car bellowed and pounced forward. The Silver Swift had been unleashed and Adam would just have to learn to control it on the move.

CHAPTER FIFTEEN

THE BROODING OF SAUL SHAFER

· · · · · · · · · · · · ·

The Silver Swift was very fast but the avalanche was even faster. Adam could feel the back of the car being buffeted by the rumbling force of the tide of snow behind them. He pushed his foot down harder on the accelerator and the car surged and broke free of the leading edge of the avalanche. But that tiny lead was lost in the next moment as the road curved to the left. For the car to stay ahead of the avalanche she would have to leave the road. Driving a car is a big responsibility and Adam did not want to put his passengers in danger, but he saw plummeting straight down the mountain as the safest choice.

"Hang on!" he yelled.

The Silver Swift shot off the road and flew through the air, her wheels spinning wildly. When she landed, Adam had to fight with all his strength to stop the car from plowing straight into a pine tree. Instead it just glanced off it, causing another large dent to the bodywork, and sped on its way.

"Sorry," said Adam, wincing.

"Won't show," replied Amy.

"It's gaining," croaked Cressida. She was looking out of the small oval rear window and her view was taken up entirely with rushing, thundering, terrifying snow. Huge trees were snapping under its weight like matchsticks. It was a dazzling leviathan devouring all before it.

"I'm going as fast I can!" cried Adam, ramming his foot down as far as it would go. The snow was licking at the rear bumper again. The avalanche had such a surging, weighty mass that they would never get out if it swallowed them.

"Hit the overdrive! Won me plenty of races, that has!" yelled Amy over the roar of the avalanche.

Adam scanned the dashboard and saw a small red button covered by a hinged glass panel. Above it was one word in tiny letters: DANGER. Adam reached for it. Amy reacted with alarm.

"Whoa! Not that one!" She exclaimed. "Never, ever press that! That's Sorensen's folly!"

"Sorensen's what?" Adam asked, struggling to keep control.

"Here, this one." Amy pointed at a big switch marked OVERDRIVE—USE WITH CARE. Adam flicked it. The car suddenly screamed like a banshee and the trees on either side of them became a green blur. Adam hung on to the steering wheel with all his strength. He could feel his body being squashed back into his seat by sheer g-force. He felt sick but sort of excited at the same time.

"Surprisingly quick, isn't it?" said Amy, her fingernails digging into the dashboard.

"We're getting away from it," said Cressida, trying to stop herself from being thrown around too much by the fearsome thrashing motion of the car. She paused. "Um, but I think it's gaining again."

"We must get out of its path or we'll be pulverized," said Adam.

From the peak of the mountain Fortescue looked down at his handiwork—his sunglasses glinted with menace. He could see the avalanche rumbling away into the low-lying cloud, but he could no longer see the silver car. He allowed himself a small, satisfied sigh of relief. It was a shame he had lost his notebook, but at least he no longer had to worry about people sticking their noses where they did not belong. He looked across at the creature. It was staring down into the blurry whiteness in the valley and growling to itself in a curious way. Fortescue did not want to allow the creature time to ponder on things.

"Come along. There's a brilliant clockmaker nearby I'd like to drop in on. After we have relieved him of his burden, we should visit Shafer," Fortescue said with a briskness in his voice.

The creature loped back to the tin shed. Fortescue followed.

"All is well," he muttered to himself with a satisfied sneer.

Far below, the incredible weight of the avalanche was still bearing down on the Silver Swift. Adam and Amy were scanning from side to side, desperately trying to find a way out of the path of the white monster. Then, up ahead, Adam saw his chance. A small track led up and away to the next mountain. The track was way off to the left, higher and out of reach of the avalanche—but also out of reach of the car. Adam looked around quickly and saw an old barn with a sloping roof pointing toward the track. The roof sloped all the way down to the ground on the nearest side. Adam spun the wheel hard to the left, and with the engine roaring in defiance at their relentless pursuer, he swerved the Silver Swift so it was now screaming toward the barn.

"Hey, wanna let me in on any flash maneuvers you got planned, kid?" asked Amy, her fingernails digging deeper into the dashboard.

"I'm hoping that barn isn't as old as it looks," replied Adam. His heart was thundering.

"The avalanche is going to swallow us!" cried Cressida, her voice cracking.

The churning snow now flicked at the car's side windows and Adam could feel the left wheels, those nearer the avalanche, becoming heavy and unwieldy. He shoved his foot down hard on the accelerator and the car hit the roof of the barn. The Silver Swift clattered up it at great speed as the avalanche bore down on them still. And then, as the car became airborne again, the avalanche smashed the barn into splinters and continued downward.

The Silver Swift hit the track above fast, skidded across it and, despite Adam straining on the steering wheel and slamming on the brakes, slid sideways into the rock face on the farside and came to a jarring halt. The engine gave a little cough, as though to say "Sorry," and stopped. Smoke rose from the hood. Adam, Amy and Cressida all sat in numbed silence, staring at one another.

"And so we come to the end of your first driving lesson. How'd you find it?" asked Amy.

"Er, yes, I think I need to work on my parking skills a little," replied Adam.

Amy laughed and so did Adam. The relief at having escaped the avalanche was overwhelming. Even Cressida smiled weakly.

Adam tried the ignition key, but all they heard was an unpleasant metallic clicking noise.

"We'll have to scoot on foot from here," said Amy with sadness. She patted the dashboard. "But she did us proud."

They all got out of the car and wrapped themselves in as many warm items as they could find—coats, thick socks, scarves. By the time Adam had finished, only his tufty hair was poking out of the top of his several layers of clothes.

They watched the avalanche continue to rumble its way to the bottom of the valley far below. Finally the snow settled and a silky silence rose up, cloaking the mountains in calm after the ferocious disturbance.

"Least there's no town down there," said Amy.

Adam looked across at the peak where all the trouble had begun. The balloon was no longer there. Amy followed his gaze.

"I'm sure we'll see them again soon enough," she said. "Let's get our luggage out of the car and go and find this Shafer guy."

They walked for a couple of hours up the winding track, their shoes crunching on fresh snow. The sun had set and the stars were coming out in the clear evening sky. The moon, full and low between two mountains, helped to light their way. Pine trees reached out to welcome them with snow-covered limbs. Amy was marching ahead, occasionally glancing at the map in the notebook to get her bearings. Adam looked across at Cressida as she trudged along with her suitcase.

"Want me to take your bag?" he asked.

"No," she replied.

"You all right?" he asked her.

She shrugged.

"Not quite the trip you expected?" he added.

Cressida looked at him with disbelief. "Er, well, actually, Adam, I expected *all* of this. You know, a creature like nothing you've ever seen, talents being stolen left, right and center, and a race down a mountain against an avalanche. Gee, how boring and uneventful it's all been." She coughed—her bitter sarcasm had strained her voice.

"You talk as though it's all my fault," Adam said, feeling hurt.

The familiar wave of guilt swept over Cressida. Maybe she blamed Adam for too much. But noise and chaos seemed to follow him everywhere.

"You think life is a game," she said.

"Perhaps it is," Adam replied.

"Feels like a pointless game with very few rules," Cressida mumbled.

Adam thought for a moment as he trudged along.

"I'm not sure talent and happiness are always connected," he said eventually. "You were miserable when you had talent. Maybe you can learn to be happier without it?"

"Maybe. But how would you know?" Cressida said sharply. "You've never had any talent to lose. Now, just be quiet for a bit. Keep your uninformed philosophies to yourself."

With that, she marched off to catch up with Amy, coughing as she went. Adam felt hurt and small. Did his sister think he was so useless? He tried to ignore the pricking feeling in his eyes. He told himself that Cressida had every right to feel upset, and he was her brother—of course she would take it out on him.

• • •

Half an hour later Amy called out in triumph, "Ha! We're here!"

She pointed up ahead. Adam and Cressida saw a beautiful house made of gray stone and chunky wood nestled on the edge of a large forest. Sweeping meadows lay to the east. The house had a verandah at the front and a massive chimney at one end with a thin wisp of furtive gray smoke curling out of it. Some wooden barns were dotted around behind the house. But nobody spent too long looking at the outbuildings because there, perched on a large rock in front of the house, was a man. He looked weather-beaten and strong and was sitting with his rugged hands resting on a shepherd's crook. There was something about his position that suggested he had been sitting there for quite some time.

"Always nice to see a man deep in thought. Are you Mr. Shafer?" asked Amy.

The man leaned back slowly and squinted through the darkness at the new arrivals.

"What's in a name?" the man replied. "Who are you?"

"Doesn't seem much point in telling you if you're not interested in names," replied Amy sharply. This man was annoying her already.

Adam sighed as he took the notebook from Amy and stepped forward.

"You are mentioned in this notebook. It belonged to someone called Fortescue," he said.

128

At this, the man's manner changed. He jumped down from his rock and looked around.

"Fortescue, you say? Now there's a name I'd happily pay to never hear again. You'd better come inside." And he led Amy, Adam and Cressida up to his house.

CHAPTER SIXTEEN
SHAFER'S TALE
· · · · · · · · · · · · · ·

The inside of the house was tatty, but it boasted a kind of lived-in warmth. There were a number of paintings of sheep on the wall, a selection of shepherd's crooks in a barrel and a large granite fireplace with miniature china sheep on its chunky wooden mantelpiece. The man lit an oil lamp and threw a log on the fire, then dropped into a worn-looking armchair. Amy, Cressida and Adam all found somewhere to sit facing the man, eagerly waiting for him to go on. He had a pleasant face with healthy color in his cheeks and small but sparkly dark green eyes with brown flecks in them. His hair was a mass of tight blond curls with a hint of gray at the temples. Minutes passed in silence before he finally had to laugh at their keen and earnest expressions. He held up his hands.

"Okay, you got me. I'm Saul Shafer. I used to be a shepherd, but my flock went and left me. Now let's see that notebook," he said.

Adam leaned forward and gave the notebook to Saul. He flicked through it, raising his eyebrows at some pages and frowning at others.

"How come you been rubbing side mirrors with Fortescue, Mr. Shafer?" asked Amy.

"Call me Saul. Fortescue needed someone who could track down animals, so he came to me. I used to have over a thousand sheep up here on this mountain and I knew the scent of every single one." Saul's eyes became misty. "If one of my flock was lost, I could find it even if it was a hundred miles away. I could spot bits of its fleece on bracken, or I'd hear it bleating when all anyone else could hear was the wind. I guess it was a gift."

"A talent," whispered Cressida.

Saul nodded. "Fortescue wanted me to go with him to the Marscopian jungle. He had heard tell of some creature there, and he needed someone like me to track it down so he could study it." Saul got up and pulled a small leather-bound book from a bookshelf. He gave it to Adam. "I'm not much of a talker. It's all here in my journal."

Adam opened the journal while Saul took a pipe down from his rack and started to stuff it full of horrible-smelling tobacco. Adam began flicking through and reading out entries from the journal.

19th April

We left the hustle and bustle of Marscopia seaport this morning—thank goodness. It is a strange place, full of strange people who have watched us prepare for our expedition eyes wide, chattering and pointing all the while, as though sharing a secret at our expense. We trudged west all day, traveling deep into the jungle. We have set up camp and our strangely jumpy Marscopian guides have left us. It is just Fortescue and myself now. I must say, Fortescue seems well prepared. Even if we don't particularly get along, we won't go hungry. This jungle is a fascinating place. My senses are alive with all the strange sights, sounds and smells. Though I'm surprised I can smell anything over the stench of the disgusting turnip soup that Fortescue is boiling up.

3rd May

Not sure I like it here. I hope Klaus is looking after my flock carefully. I miss the mountain. I miss my home. The jungle is a living thing in itself, the wildlife strange. There are bugs so big that they soar and dip like birds, and I've seen spiders of a size it makes me gag to write about them. The atmosphere is sticky, uncomfortable and so humid it's like breathing through a warm sponge. Ah, to fill my lungs with mountain air!

"I was a getting a little bit homesick at that point," Saul said, striking a match and lighting his pipe. He started to puff on it.

Amy looked around at the colorful rugs on the floor and the strong yet simple furniture.

"It's a lovely home. I can see why you missed it," she said. "I've been drifting from hotel to hotel recently, but I dream of maybe one day owning my own farm."

"It's shabby but solid," Saul said. "A bit like me."

Amy smiled. "By the way, I'm Amy," she announced.

"Like I said, I'm not big on names," Saul replied with a mischievous twinkle in his eye.

Amy did not know whether to be annoyed or amused. Saul Shafer was certainly an oddball.

Cressida glanced across at Amy. She didn't want Amy and Saul arguing, or wittering about houses all night. She wanted to know more about where the creature came from. She wasn't sure why exactly, but the curiosity was there all the same. There was something about the talent thief that touched her. Why had it pushed its hood back and shown itself to her and nobody else?

"Adam, read on," she urged.

Adam smiled. He wanted to know what happened too. He continued to read.

5th May
Fortescue is really starting to get on my nerves. All I said was that we might be on a bit of a wild-goose

chase and he went berserk. *What am I doing here?*
He won't even tell me what we are looking for. He is
paying me well, but is it enough to make being stuck
in the jungle with a lunatic worthwhile? Not sure
how much more turnip soup I can stomach either.
Fortescue keeps disappearing into his own tent. I
wonder if he has a stash of tastier morsels that he
doesn't want to share.

17th May

Just as I was starting to believe that Fortescue was
completely mad, today I discovered the strangest
footprints. Like a man's but narrower and longer.
There was a distinctive musty smell as well.
Fortescue is pleased with my findings. I am suddenly
his "best friend," but I'm not sure I trust him.

Saul snorted with amusement at this and puffed more
vigorously.

"Now there's an understatement," he muttered.

Adam turned the page and read more.

21st May

We ventured farther south today, and the vegetation
is even denser. High above in the jungle canopy is a
network of vines that crisscross this whole region. I
found unidentifiable tiny marks on a tree, and

Fortescue kept urging me to climb it. I'm a good climber, so I went up. Took me over an hour—I tried not to look down once. The view from the top was incredible, however. I could see over the entire canopy, vibrant in speckled green and teeming with bird life. Suddenly, a flock of colorful parrots took flight, cawing and flapping with alarm. I sought the source of this commotion. At first I could see nothing, then I caught a glimpse of a tall, blue, gangly creature sliding along vines in the middle distance. I had never seen anything like it! But then it saw me and disappeared from sight. When I returned to earth, Fortescue became very excited when I told him what I'd spotted.

If only I could find its lair.

24th May

I decided to try one of these "vine slides" to see if it led me anywhere. I climbed the tree again and using a leather strap I slid down the nearest vine. It was pretty thrilling. When I reached the end of it, there were dozens more vines to choose from, but only one had that musty smell about it, so I took that one. And when I reached the end of that vine, I used my nose to choose the next.

I was traveling great distances across the jungle. The vines were leading me somewhere. Sure enough, I came finally to a cave in the side of a cliff. The vine led right into it. Inside were lots of shiny *objects, instruments from a plane that I guess had crashed nearby, items stolen from lost explorers, watches, silver buttons and buckles, jewels. There were also some beautiful small glowing spheres— I had never seen the like before. I decided to get out before the creature returned. But now I knew I could trap it. How fascinating it would be to see it up close.*

Adam glanced up from the notebook. Amy and Cressida looked spellbound.

"Go on, Adam," said Amy with urgency in her voice. "What happened next?"

25th May
Today I trapped it! A net over the mouth of the cave and a simple trigger system did the trick. Fortescue is beside himself with excitement. We have put the creature in a metal cage. It's extraordinary. I feel strangely sorry for it, yet at the same time it terrifies me. When it looks at me from its crouched position in the corner of the cage it seems to see inside me, to read my every thought. It watches everything with such intensity, as if it is learning

*and remembering all the time! Fortescue is treating
it like a long-lost friend. He spends half his time
muttering to it and the rest with his head buried in
his notebook and a pile of obscure books. The
creature seems to like Fortescue.*

30th May
*Much has happened. Most of which I cannot explain.
I believe Fortescue drugged me, because I awoke in
the creature's cage! Fortescue was outside, his face
pressed against the bars, his eyes gleaming. It's all
very hazy, but I believe the creature made a strange
sound and did something to me, took something, a
bright, shining sphere. I couldn't stop it—it is
stronger than a lion. Fortescue looked ecstatic. He
aimed a dart gun at me and fired. Before I passed
out, I heard him say something . . .*

*"I have found my soul mate. My talent thief.
Let the collecting begin."*

Saul took a long puff on his pipe. "When I came around,
Fortescue and the creature were gone. Everything was gone.
Somehow I managed to stumble back to the seaport and
begged a passage home," Saul said.

"That terrible creature took your talent for tracking,"
said Amy.

Saul nodded. "So I realized. My senses became dull. I

returned here and within a month I had lost all of my sheep," Saul said. "That was over a year ago. I suppose I've been brooding ever since. I do brooding pretty well."

"We're going to catch up with the terrible duo and get Cressida's singing voice and Amy's racing skills back," said Adam with determination.

"Ah, I thought you had the mark of the creature," said Saul, looking from Cressida to Amy. He switched his gaze to Adam. "And what did the creature take from you?"

"My name's Adam, Adam Bloom. Cressida's my sister. Er, I don't have a talent. I'm just . . . average. I think the creature tried to take something from me once, but, um, nothing came out."

Saul narrowed his eyes and nodded slowly. "Hmm, then out of all of us you are probably the one who is thinking most clearly." With that he slapped his hands down on the arms of his chair. "Let's eat," he said.

CHAPTER SEVENTEEN
CALLING FOR BISKIN
• • • • • • • • • • • •

All four of them sat around a chunky oak table. Saul had tried to lend a sense of occasion by lighting a couple of candles and putting a bowl full of pinecones in the center. However, Adam was too hungry to care about decoration. It was only a simple meal, but he thought it was the best he had ever tasted. He had not realized how hungry he was until he had dipped a chunk of crusty bread into his bowl of thick, warm vegetable soup and taken a big bite.

"This is really good," Adam said, dipping his bread into his bowl again.

"The mountain air gets you pretty hungry," Saul said.

Amy was also eating with gusto, ripping bread up and not caring too much when she slurped her soup. Cressida was not accustomed to the rough-and-ready nature of the meal, but at the same time she found it surprisingly agreeable. She sipped slowly and let the warm liquid soothe her throat. Saul was flipping through Fortescue's notebook as he ate.

"What exactly *is* that creature?" asked Amy, helping herself to another chunk of bread.

Saul looked up. "Fortescue used to ramble on about a lot of different theories," he said. "I never really listened to him."

"I think a few of them are in there, in the first part of the notebook," Adam mumbled through a mouthful of bread.

Cressida shot him a look, admonishing him for talking while eating.

Saul flicked through the front pages and nodded. "Ah, yes. Well, it appears his favorite theory was this one."

Saul turned the notebook in the others' direction. He indicated a heavily annotated page with several underlined sentences before taking it back and beginning to read. "'Long ago, when those things that dwelled within this world were very different from what they are today, a group of ancient animals found themselves trapped in an enormous crater. One by one, they all starved, or plummeted to their deaths as they tried desperately to clamber their way up the towering walls. But one of them was different. This strange creature was oddly thoughtful and reserved. It sat quietly in its new habitat, looking around at the steep, smooth walls of the crater and watching with curiosity the bugs, spiders and other creatures scampering, slithering and scuttling around the crater floor. For a while it fed off the broken bodies of its dead crater mates. It was living so simply, it did not need a lot of food.

"'All the time, in its enforced period of contemplation, it considered in detail the life around it—the uniqueness of many living things. It began to be able to pinpoint that which made something special. Suddenly, it could tune into it, feel it, sense it. In time, it even found it could take the essence of what a thing was, extract it—and it came out in the shape of a sphere. The creature grew to love these wondrous objects and it took one from each of the animals it was trapped with. Over the centuries, it took to collecting them whenever it could.' There's something in the margin at the bottom of the page too, some notes about the other ancient animals it might have been trapped with—let me see." Saul turned the notebook sideways and peered closely at the page. "I believe that it says . . . 'the lesser-bearded blue-all-over monkey, famed for its ability to blend into the background against the bright blue skies of the jungle'— that must have been an odd-looking thing—and it says something about a giant reptile." Saul rubbed his chin. "Anyway, I think Fortescue's theory is a bit woolly, but that creature must have learned to do what it does somehow."

"It's not a very scientific explanation, though, is it?" Adam snorted.

"Myth it may seem," Cressida said slowly, "yet a creature to fit a lot of this description exists. . . ."

"For someone who doesn't like to talk, you did pretty good," Amy said now with a wink at Saul, which left him a little flustered. He was relieved when Adam piped up with another question.

"And how did Fortescue find out about it?" Adam asked.

"This bit I know from Fortescue himself. There had been sightings of a strange creature in the jungle for years, but nobody took it seriously. Nobody, that is, except Fortescue. He came across a brief account of it in an old book in his family's extensive, ancient library. It would appear he became more than a little obsessed—read every account he could get his hands on and over the years he interviewed hundreds of natives in the vicinity of the crater. When he thought he had a manageable area in which to search, he came to me," Saul said, drumming his fingers on the tabletop. "And what a happy day that was," he added with heavy sarcasm.

"So let's try and summarize," Amy said briskly. "Our pal Fortescue has tracked down his own twisted, shady soul mate in the shape of an ancient creature who lived in a jungle and likes to steal and collect animals', and now people's, talent spheres, leaving them bereft. Together, they're traveling the world, doing just that."

Cressida frowned. A lot of this didn't seem to fit with the impression the creature had given her when they'd met briefly.

"But what is Fortescue going to do with all the talents?" she asked. She had been quiet most of the evening, but this question had been going round and round in her mind like a trapped bluebottle since she had lost her talent for singing.

Saul shrugged. "Who knows? Who cares?" Hope had left Saul Shafer long ago.

Amy searched Saul's forlorn face. "You know Fortescue is coming. He wants to 'silence' you, it says in his notebook."

Saul's eyes flicked to Amy's. He mulled this over for a moment. "Now there's food for thought," he said. But Saul quickly pushed it to the back of his mind and looked at his guests. A heavy veil of weariness seemed to cover them all. "You're exhausted."

Adam, Cressida and Amy nodded as one. Saul led them to the corner of the room, where he swept aside a heavy curtain with designs of sheep all over it. Behind it was a narrow wooden staircase that led up into the attic.

"Sleep well," he said, gesturing to the staircase with a flourish.

"I'll count sheep if I have any trouble," Adam said with a grin.

Then he, Cressida and Amy trudged up the stairs to discover some straw-filled beds hung from the gnarled rafters hammock-fashion, like giant bird's nests. The beds may have looked unusual, but it became obvious that these were cradles of comfort like no other. Adam, Cressida and Amy were fast asleep before they could mumble their good-nights.

But in his armchair downstairs, Saul stayed awake, restlessly puffing on his pipe and staring into the dying embers of the fire. In the quiet solitude of night, guilt crept up on him. It was his fault all his sheep were gone. Furthermore, in helping Fortescue to find the creature, what had he unleashed on the world? And now it appeared Fortescue would be paying a visit. His brooding might find an end at last. Only question was—when and how would it be?

The next morning, everyone huddled around the table and enjoyed a warming breakfast of porridge with honey. It was snowing and large, lazy flakes could be seen drifting down outside the windows. Saul looked at his guests and smiled to himself. It was good to have people here. It stopped him from getting too lost in his gloomy thoughts. He glanced again at Amy. She had an interesting face. There was determination there, but also a kind of loneliness he recognized. She seemed more tense than the evening before. A frown kept creasing her brow and, in between mouthfuls of porridge, her cheek muscles were clenched.

"You all right, Amy?" he asked.

She looked up, Saul's voice shaking her free from her own thoughts.

"Hmm? Oh, you believe in names today, do you?" she asked with a wry grin.

"Thought I might have to make the effort, in order to break through your reverie," he said. Amy was impressed that he had picked up on her mood.

"It's my car. I know the Silver Swift's only a machine. But we've been through so much together and I just can't bear to think of her lying abandoned in a snowdrift." Amy looked out the window and noticed that the snow was falling more heavily now. "But there's no way—"

"We shall fetch her and put her in one of my barns," Saul interrupted. "I have a good friend called Biskin who'll give us a hand."

"Does Biskin have a tow truck?" Adam asked.

"No, Biskin is a yak," Saul replied.

It took Saul a good half an hour to find Biskin because the obstinate yak had wandered off into the forest behind the house.

"Biskin! Where are you?" Saul yelled, cupping his hands to his mouth. He turned to Amy, Adam and Cressida. "He is out there, and before the whole creature thing I could have pinpointed him in seconds. I could smell old Biskin from a hundred miles away. Now I have no idea where he is."

But Biskin finally responded to Saul's yelling and came shuffling out of the trees and over to the house. He was in no hurry and rocked the snow off his horns with a low grumble. Saul threw a harness on him, grabbed some lengths of strong rope and led everyone back down the track to where the Silver Swift sat looking very sorry for herself. A thick layer of snow had already built up on the hood, but Saul could still see the many dents and scrapes in the bodywork. He gave a low whistle.

"Whoa. This car has seen better days," he said as he lashed the rope to the front bumper.

"Hey, this car has seen glorious days!" Amy exclaimed. "And she will see them again!"

"Righto. Want to tie this end to Biskin?" Saul said, unimpressed.

Amy sighed and took the rope.

"Now, Biskin isn't going to shift this all on his own. So everyone get ready to push!" Saul said.

Amy rolled her eyes. This man had an annoying habit of talking to people as though they were idiots. Saul got behind the car and placed his large, gloved hands on the trunk. Adam and Cressida stood on either side of him and placed their gloved hands next to his.

"I cannot believe I'm pushing a car out of a ditch," Cressida mumbled indignantly to herself.

"We're *all* pushing a car out of a ditch, Cress," Adam responded.

"Yep, it's a fair and democratic process," Saul added.

Cressida fell silent. Amy went around to the driver's side and placed one hand through the open window onto the steering wheel and the other on the leading edge of the door frame.

"And push!" Saul yelled as he shoved with all his might. Adam and Cressida pushed too. Adam could feel the cold of the metal coming through his gloves.

"Pull, Biskin!" Saul added, and the yak gave a low grunt in response and dug its hooves into the freshly fallen snow. Amy heaved and turned the wheel so that slowly, and with a lot of creaking, the car started to move up the track.

It was a long, exhausting haul, but eventually, over several hours, they managed to push the car up the mountain into a large stone barn that sat solidly a little distance away from Saul's house. Everyone stood puffing and panting for a while, and Biskin trudged back into the forest once he was free of the harness.

"Can you fix the car?" Adam asked Saul, when he had finally recovered his breath.

"I'm no expert, but I keep my shearing machine in good condition. Can't be much different, can it?" Saul winked at Adam and looked over at Amy, who was fuming.

"How dare you compare the Silver Swift to a shearing machine!" she cried.

Saul pulled a large hammer from a shelf and waved it at the car. "Now, which end is the engine in?" He grinned.

Amy almost fainted.

For the next few days Saul and Amy worked on the Silver Swift. As it turned out, Saul knew a lot about machinery and Amy was quick to learn. She was pleased to be gaining a greater understanding of her own car. Hour by hour she could see the vehicle that had taken her to so many victories gradually returning to her former glory. Saul was just happy to have something to do that would stop him from brooding about his lost sheep.

Adam kept the wood store full and cooked for Saul and Amy so they always had a hot meal after a long day working on the car. Cressida took regular walks by herself in the forest behind the house, her spirits low. In theory, they both kept a lookout in case Fortescue headed their way, as predicted. But as the days passed, they wondered if he'd changed his plans and gone elsewhere.

In discussions over dinner it became clear that Adam and Amy wanted to move on eastward once the car was repaired. Fortescue's notebook mentioned a great talent he wanted to take from someone in a village about two hundred miles east, so perhaps he had gone that way instead. Adam wanted desperately to stop this talent from being taken too. Amy wanted to follow the trail to her sphere. Saul was not sure he wanted to leave his home and Cressida was resting her voice, her thoughts kept to herself.

One afternoon, Adam was curled up by the fire, flicking through Fortescue's notebook, and Cressida was sitting watching the snow fall slowly outside. The now familiar clinking of metal could be heard from the stone barn. Adam strained to read Fortescue's appalling handwriting . . .

So, I have already verified that the myths and legends are true [...] the cave paintings depict fact! But I always knew there was more to be discovered [...] a key question about this creature that I have asked myself over and over, ever since I

first read its legend so many years ago.
The important question so many have
missed.

I thought I had guessed its answer; my
latest experiment has made me sure at
last! I am truly brilliant. Now I know the
answer, nothing will stop me. Nothing!
Soon I will progress to the next phase of
my terrible plan and once I have found a
way, I will [...]

[...] and the "golden" question, it is—
How did this talent-collecting creature
of legend escape the very crater that
trapped and, therefore, created it?
Its rampage began in the crater, but
it has continued for many years since,
in the dark heart of the jungle—so [. . .]
how did it get out?

Rapidly Adam turned more pages in the hope of finding an answer to the question that Fortescue made such a fuss of, or some indication of what it meant to his grand golden plan. But Fortescue had made no record of it. Adam slapped the notebook shut, his face a picture of frustration.

"Let's just go home, Adam, please," Cressida said suddenly, a wave of emotion catching in her throat. "I don't want to catch up with Fortescue and the creature."

Adam put the notebook down and turned to Cressida. "We can't go home, Cress. We need to get your sphere and the other children's spheres back."

"Are you and Amy going to trap the creature?" Cressida asked, and there was sadness in her husky voice.

"We have to, I suppose," Adam replied. "It will take some doing, though."

"What then?" Cressida croaked.

"I don't know. What difference does it make? Do you feel sorry for it or something?"

"No," Cressida replied. "Maybe."

"Fortescue and his talent thief are traveling around the world taking talent from as many people as they can," Adam said, his voice rising with anger. "It's not right."

"Is that so? If our parents had had no talent, they'd still be alive," Cressida mumbled. Her vision started to swim as salty tears began to well up. She swallowed, pushed her spectacles back into place and tried to blink her eyes clear.

"I'm sorry. They can't be allowed to carry on doing this," Adam said, ignoring his sister's comment.

"Fine!" Cressida yelled. Then she swallowed painfully. Her voice fell to a whisper. "You remain angry. I'm going to get some fresh air. All this hunting talk is getting on my nerves." Her voice cracked and she coughed. Then she got up, threw her coat on and slammed out of the house.

Adam thought about going after her, but then stopped himself. Let her simmer down, he thought.

CHAPTER EIGHTEEN
ENCOUNTER IN THE FOREST
• • • • • • • • • • • •

Cressida strode away from the house into the forest. It was snowing gently and a soft silence embraced her. The frosted trees towered over her head. She felt very much alone and her feeling of loss was almost overwhelming. Her parents were gone, finished by their talent, and now her own talent was gone too. Part of her was grateful to the creature, glad it was gone. It had been a burden. She wished she could have been more like Hans Fortissimo, strong and comfortable with her own abilities. But it hadn't been the case. However, as she walked along, watching the snow-flakes dance to their own music in the breeze, she admitted that being so talented had also been a privilege of sorts. Adam understood that somehow. (Perhaps because he was so average—poor boy.) That was why he wanted to catch up with the creature and get the talents back.

Cressida's thoughts turned to the ancient creature. She was sure it was far more than just the evil freak Fortescue's notebook outlined and Saul's account seemed to suggest. It had a deep and intense understanding of what it was to be alive. It may have been duped into stealing human talents, but from her dim recollection of her time with it, she was sure it had a certain respect for all living things. Fortescue, on the other hand, did not.

In the quiet forest, something moved up ahead— Cressida snapped out of her own thoughts instantly. Her heart started to hammer. Was it a wolf? Cressida had a sudden powerful impulse to head back to the house very fast, but just before she turned, she saw two familiar glowing eyes emerge from the snowy mist. It was the creature.

It stood alone a little way off, as though it had been summoned by her thoughts. Snowflakes glistened on its dark red hood and cloak; the ends of its leathery blue claws were just visible, potent yet still. Cressida could not explain why, but it seemed lonely. Perhaps it was just providing a mirror for her own feelings. A strangely calm sensation swept over her. Those intense, ancient eyes stared at her. She stared back. It trilled hypnotically. An image suddenly leaped into her mind, except it was more of a feeling, an urging—a burning roof, black smoke. And then three words swam into her thoughts like kindly messengers from afar: YOUR CAVE UNSAFE. In the next moment the creature was gone, swallowed by the snow.

• • •

Amy slapped the monkey wrench into Saul's greasy out-stretched hand. He was leaning so far into the engine bay that it looked as though the Silver Swift were eating him. He pushed himself back and stood up. He turned to Amy with a grin.

"I think we're almost there," he said. He pulled a large tarpaulin over the car and slumped down heavily onto a bale of hay. Amy sat next to him. He was so tall and broad, she felt small next to him. But it was not unpleasant.

"Have you lived here all your life?" she asked.

Saul shot a sideways glance at Amy. She was smart and there was something about her that made him feel comfortable and open. For a brooding shepherd that was a rare thing.

"Yes, I've been here all my life," Saul said, scraping away at a spot of grease on his thumbnail. "My parents left for the coastal city of Bonfessa when I was eleven. My mother wanted pearls and my dad wanted a yacht. I never really liked them much. I asked if I could stay here. They agreed and I never saw them again. The mountains, flower meadows, forests and, of course, my sheep became my family. Fortescue had to give me a *lot* of money to get me to take that trip to Marscopia."

"You must miss your flock so much," Amy said.

"I do," Saul replied. "I don't have much in the way of rhyme or reason without them."

"Hey, tag along with us. Get your talent for tracking back and maybe you could have a new flock," Amy suggested.

Saul pondered on this. Amy watched him. She hoped he would come with them. It would be useful to have a car expert along. Furthermore, she realized, gruff as he could be, she liked him.

The door of the barn creaked open and the soft light of afternoon spilled across the stone floor. Cressida stood there with armfuls of blankets and pillows. Adam stepped up behind her, his arms also filled with bedclothes.

"Thought we could sleep in here tonight," Cressida rasped simply. "It'll be fun."

"This has nothing to do with me," Adam added with a bemused shrug, his brown eyes baffled.

The night was so dark that the two figures who approached the house resembled nothing more than shadowy phantoms. Fortescue turned to the creature.

"Let's do this quickly," he whispered. "I should have finished Shafer off ages ago in the jungle."

The creature let out a low, questioning growl.

Fortescue sighed. "I don't know why you can't make the effort and try to speak. You understand me and I do my best to work out what your infernal howls mean, but it would be so much better if—"

The creature interrupted with another series of yelps, its voice rising in pitch slightly.

"Why? Why what?" Fortescue snapped. "Why do we

burn his cave?" Fortescue struggled to control his irritation. With a determined effort he tried to inject a charming warmth into his voice. "We burn his *house* because Shafer is the only one left who knows too much about you. He could stop our plan. And as I keep saying, nothing, repeat *nothing*, must stop our plan. Don't forget, Shafer is a *bad* man. He hunted you down and put you in a cage. I saved you from him, remember? The day I gave you your special cloak that you love so much. Anyway, he could find you again—unlikely as it is now that we have his tracking talent sphere." Fortescue chuckled to himself smugly before continuing. "So we silence him and then we carry on with the great and enormous fun of collecting precious, shiny talent spheres. You like taking them, don't you? And I guide you to the very finest. See how *much* I do for you? I am your *only* friend, Nipso. Never forget that."

The creature trilled affectionately at the sound of its name and dutifully loped off to place large bundles of straw around the house with a silky, muscular ease. Minutes later, Fortescue applied a lit match and the whole house was ablaze almost at once. He and the creature stepped back and watched the flames and smoke pour out of the windows.

"That's that little problem taken care of!" Fortescue yelled over the noise of the fire. But in the next moment he was aware of another noise coming from a little way off. It was a deep growling noise. Like a big cat or maybe—a big car. Fortescue turned, then he and the creature had to leap to one side as the doors of the stone barn were blasted away by the Silver Swift accelerating out, Saul Shafer at the wheel. The car sounded and looked like new. All the dents were gone, its sleek sweeping lines restored to their former glory. The polished silver paintwork reflected the red and orange glow of the fire. Amy was sitting anxiously next to Saul, and Adam and Cressida were squashed together in the back.

"Good to see you again," Saul said to Fortescue, winding his window down and revving the engine, "and thank you so much for the housewarming!"

With that, Saul hit the accelerator and the car screamed away down the track.

"Stop them!" Fortescue bellowed at the creature.

The creature sprinted after the car, its luminous eyes glaring at Adam and Cressida through the rear window. They both gasped and jumped back from the glass. It was a terrifying sight. Even Cressida, who found it hard to believe the creature would really hurt them, felt afraid— Fortescue's hold on the creature was obviously strong. But the Silver Swift's head start was too great. The talent thief soon dropped back.

"I retract my grumble about sleeping in the barn," Saul called over his shoulder to Cressida. "Thanks, Cress."

"I'm sorry about your house, Saul," Cressida said.

"Hey, I was wondering whether or not to come with you. What better way to make my mind up," Saul said. He looked across at Amy with a rueful grin. She smiled back, mindful of his loss.

Adam was looking at Cressida with surprise and confusion in his wide brown eyes.

"How did you know we had to be out of the house, Cress?" he asked.

Cressida shrugged. "It was a hunch."

"A hunch?" Adam repeated. "A hunch that we should all sleep in the barn. Are you kidding? Let me see, I have a hunch we should all dress up as pantomime cows and live in a wigwam."

"Okay, okay. I saw the creature in the forest. Alone. It seemed as though it was warning me. I don't know how," she said.

"Hmm, that's interesting," Saul mused.

"You saw the creature? Why didn't you tell us?" Adam asked, his voice rising.

"Because I don't want you to catch it," she replied. Her voice was almost tender. She looked away from Adam.

Adam chewed his lip. "Let's go back now!" he suddenly blurted in Amy's direction. "The balloon must be nearby, hidden by the trees probably. The sack of spheres will be there."

"This isn't the right time, Adam. We're unprepared. That creature could overpower all of us," Amy replied. She turned to Saul. "Could you drive a little slower?" she added, wincing at how close they were to the edge of the winding track. The valley below was a very long way down.

"Sure. But I'd like to get a little farther away from the fire-starting madman and his bloodcurdling creature first.

That all right?" Saul said, flinging the car around another tight bend.

"Good point," Amy said.

Fortescue tapped a boot heel and scowled as he watched the car disappear into the darkness. He hated it when his plans went awry. He liked to think the world and everything in it were under his control. How dare people defy his wishes? The creature stood quietly next to him. It sensed Fortescue's frustration and shuffled its long, bony feet uneasily.

"The Blooms and that mad racing woman were in the car," Fortescue said. "How did they escape that avalanche? This is turning into a *situation,* a deeply unpleasant situation."

He watched as a large section of Saul Shafer's smoldering roof crashed down inside his house, throwing up a shower of red-hot embers.

"They'll be heading east, following the notes I made about the final talents I wanted to take on this trip," Fortescue said to the creature. "Let's go. We need to be smarter in dealing with these meddlers. There is someone who I believe will help us. Someone we may be able to make a deal with."

CHAPTER NINETEEN
BREAKFAST IN THE CLOUDS

• • • • • • • • • • • •

Although the backseat of the Silver Swift was narrow, there seemed to be a gaping gulf between Adam and Cressida nonetheless. They each looked out of their own window, lost in thought, watching the dark, looming mountains pass. Amy flipped open Fortescue's notebook and traced her finger along the map eastward from Saul's house.

"Let's find this village," Amy said. "Fortescue has marked it out for some reason. There's something or someone there that he wants to find." Amy gripped her seat and looked across at Saul. "And will you please drive more carefully!"

Cressida looked at the back of Saul's curly blond head. He suddenly seemed completely different from the man they had first seen, sitting on that rock.

"Are your brooding days over, Saul?" she asked quietly.

His eyes smiled at her in the rearview mirror. "You

know what, Cressida, I think they are," he said with lightness in his voice.

Cressida wished she felt the same.

The Silver Swift swept along the twisting roads that wound through the mountain range, her powerful headlights lighting the way. The engine rumbled in a contented manner to itself. The heater worked well and the four travelers were safe and warm in their shiny cocoon. At one point Cressida pointed out the plus-shaped balloon and dangling shed passing high overhead, silhouetted against the moon and traveling in the same direction as them. Wherever Fortescue and the creature were headed now, they would get there before the Silver Swift.

"You want them to get ahead of us. You want them to take all the talent from the world," Adam said to Cressida, his usually smooth forehead crinkled.

"You don't understand me at all, Adam," Cressida said, not taking her eyes from the view outside her window.

"No, I don't," he replied.

As the sun started to creep above the peaks of the Kappa-Nage mountain range once more, extinguishing the stars one by one, the Silver Swift crossed a narrow bridge spanning a waterfall and rumbled into a small village nestled high in the clouds. It was a pretty place, with stocky, decorated houses huddled together along winding, roughly paved streets. Snow lay in patches on the rooftops and ground. Colorful flags attached to high poles fluttered in the breeze and almost every red-tiled roof boasted a weather vane. Each one was unique, but they all twirled together, spinning in unison to the changeable winds that whistled through the village. Adam tried to list all the different weather vanes he could see. There was a mountain climber planting a flag, a child riding on a wolf's back, a moose pulling a plow.

"That one's a sheep jumping over a fence," he said.

"Ah, they have good taste here." Saul grinned.

The car purred onward, past traders setting up their market stalls and children on their way to school. Adam waved as the children gawped and applauded the car. Eventually Saul drew up in front of a cafe and switched the engine off. The Silver Swift gave a contented sigh and, after a short tapping sound, fell silent.

"Anyone for breakfast?" Saul asked brightly as he pulled his favorite shepherd's crook from the space beside his seat.

The owner of the cafe was a huge, cheery man with a mustache so thick it looked like the head of a broom. On his large, sloping shoulder sat an eager-looking red squirrel. The man laid a big tray down on the table and started to arrange a most delicious-looking breakfast for his visitors. There were hot buttered crumpets, scrambled eggs, sausages, fried mashed potato, toast, a variety of juices and the most wonderful-smelling fruit tea.

"You can't beat a good breakfast!" the owner bellowed, slapping his enormous belly. "In fact, sometimes I cannot resist and I have another breakfast at lunchtime. On those days I have my lunch at dinnertime. But don't get me wrong, I would never have dinner at breakfast time. Breakfast should always be breakfast."

Adam, Amy and Saul all looked at each other and smiled. They had obviously found the world expert on breakfasts and their grumbling stomachs were grateful. And if the breakfast was a feast for the stomach, the cafe itself was a feast for the eyes. Little brass lamps hung from dark wooden beams with impossibly intricate carvings of flowers on them. All the furniture was also heavily carved with delicate designs, and even the window frames boasted swirling leaf shapes that stretched out across the glass panes.

"My name is Maurice Shaparelli. I came here on vacation twenty-four years ago and never went home," the cafe owner declared, clamping his fist to his chest. "Now this is my home and I love it." He pointed to the squirrel on his shoulder. "This is my friend Tarloff. I raised him from a baby."

"He's cute," Cressida whispered, a reluctant smile forcing itself up unbidden from within. Shaparelli gave a little frown.

"No, no, not cute. He thinks he is tough and handsome like me." Shaparelli tried to look stern, but then he let out a little laugh.

"Oh, okay," Cressida replied. Shaparelli was funny. She liked him.

"So, what goes on around here?" Amy asked, tucking into a large helping of scrambled eggs on toast.

"Oh, not much," Shaparelli said. "We live a simple life up here. That's the beauty of it. Altitudo is like the crossroads of the world. Anyone can live here as long as they respect themselves and everyone else. Those who do not love life and people soon find the air to be too thin and have to leave."

"Would we find the air too thin?" Cressida asked. Her voice was low but her eyes were burning with intensity.

"Oh no," Shaparelli replied. He bent down to look closely at Cressida. "You are all good people. I can tell. The not-very-nice people come and they huff and puff and talk about ways of changing Altitudo, but you cannot change it. It is old and sure of what it is. You wouldn't tie a pink bow on a whale, now would you?"

Saul and Amy swapped glances. This man certainly had a lot of interesting things to say.

"Is this village called Altitudo?" Adam asked.

"Yes. You will have noticed that we are very, very high up. Even the clouds find it hard to get up this high. Most people come here by plane nowadays. You did well to drive it."

"Thank you," Saul said, poking his tongue out at Amy and tapping the end of his crook on the floor in agreement.

Adam laughed at this while Amy fought the urge to respond with a sharp riposte. Instead she looked up at the owner, who had sneaked a large sausage from the table and was pushing it through his huge mustache into his mouth.

"There's an airfield nearby, then?" she asked.

"Well, it's more of a ledge, really. Grace Verdi is the only pilot who can fly a plane onto it. When visitors arrive in Altitudo by air, they always say how brilliant she is." Shaparelli plucked a crumpet from the table. "She is a true genius! Such talent."

At this everyone looked at one another.

"Could you tell us where this airfield is?" Adam asked.

Adam looked down at the napkin that Shaparelli had written directions on. They were all back in the car now, comfortably full and anxious to find Grace Verdi.

"Turn right in front of the cake shop," Adam said, reading from the napkin. "He's written 'sensational cream horns' after that."

Saul turned the steering wheel as he approached the old bakery and the Silver Swift entered a twisty alleyway so narrow, the side mirrors almost grazed the walls.

"Breathe in, everyone," Saul said, concentrating on not scraping the stone.

"Good job you're not driving," Adam said to Amy.

She clicked her tongue and looked back at Adam. "Watch it, buster."

Adam looked down at the napkin again. "Left in front

of the sweet shop with 'the delectable coffee creams and the equally delectable Miss Lorraine,'" Adam said, prodding the napkin. "That's what he wrote."

Saul swerved the car left and he, Amy, Cressida and Adam could not resist craning to see into the sweet shop. A large woman with braided blond hair, rosy cheeks and a wide smile waved at them with a chubby hand. They waved back. Adam looked back down at the napkin.

"Okay, now drive past the pie shop on the left. They have 'mouthwatering sausage rolls,' apparently. And turn right at the end of the street."

"Least we're all clued up on the local cuisine now, if nothing else," Amy quipped.

Saul turned the wheel and drove down a short street and then emerged onto a gently winding grass track that led steeply down from the village to a tiny airfield.

The sight before them was spectacular. Adam, Amy, Cressida and Saul all gasped at once. Like Shaparelli had said, the airfield was really more of a protruding ledge than a landing strip. It was flat but not much longer than Adam could throw a ball. On three sides were sheer drops that fell away for hundreds of feet, and beyond these, in the distance, towering mountains. Clouds nuzzled the edge of the tiny landing strip, making it appear even higher, even smaller and even more dangerous. Four illuminated red balloons were anchored at each of the four corners of the airfield so that it could be seen easily from the air.

Saul parked the car and everyone got out, rapidly pulling on their coats and hunching into them against the crisp, cold air. A thin layer of snow lay on the ground.

"Whoa, check my tire pressure! Can someone really land a plane on this?" Amy said with amazement.

A distant buzzing noise could suddenly be heard and Adam turned to see what looked like a small four-seater plane approaching from the north. It was flying up a narrow, twisting canyon between two sheer rock faces.

"Looks like we're about to find out," he said. This was exciting. He looked at Cressida—even she seemed thrilled at the prospect.

"She must be an amazing pilot," Cressida whispered.

"You're glad you're here, aren't you, Cress?" Adam couldn't help asking. But Cressida did not answer.

Then, as the plane approached, something familiar descended from a large cloud not far from the airfield. Amy groaned and Cressida took a step forward, her hand darting up to cover her mouth.

A golden balloon in the shape of a plus sign was moving into the flight path of the plane.

Adam's blood ran cold. Saul squinted up at the tin shed hanging underneath the balloon.

"No, no. Surely, they can't be thinking . . ." Saul muttered, twisting his thick fingers nervously around his shepherd's crook.

Before he could finish his sentence, the creature leaped from the shed and swept across the sky in a long, graceful arc. With astonishing judgment, it landed on the wing of the plane, seeming almost to stick there. The small plane rocked violently from side to side for a moment until the skillful pilot compensated for the extra weight and got the plane back on straight and level flight. But now the creature pulled at the pilot's door with all its strength. The hinges broke away and the creature threw the door to one side. It spun away, down, down into the valley far below the clouds. The talent thief, cloak flapping fiercely in the wind, crawled inside the cabin.

"They prefer to take a talent when it's in action," Adam said quietly.

Amy looked at him and nodded grimly.

CHAPTER TWENTY
ADAM THE BRAVE

· · · · · · · · · · · · ·

Barely a minute later the creature emerged from the cabin clutching a glowing pale blue sphere. It leaped from the wing of the plane onto the roof of the tin shed as the balloon held and passed by. Adam, Cressida, Amy and Saul all turned their attention to the plane. It was apparent that whoever was flying it was in trouble. The plane was juddering and losing altitude rapidly.

"Hey, it can still land safely," Amy said, her jaw muscles tensing.

Cressida buried her face in her hands. Saul squinted up at the golden balloon now disappearing over a distant peak and muttered all the swearwords he could think of under his breath. Adam watched the plane approach the landing strip. It seemed to him that it was coming in too fast.

With a heavy thud the wheels of the plane hit the

ground. The brakes squealed and powdery snow was thrown up everywhere.

"It's down," Amy sighed with relief.

Cressida looked up and smiled. But Saul could see that there wasn't much room for the plane to stop. Before he could even voice his worries, Adam was running toward it.

"Er, what's he doing?" Amy asked.

"Adam, no!" Cressida called. But her voice was weak and would not have stopped Adam anyway. She coughed and watched her brother with a mixture of exasperation, anger and concern.

The plane was slowing down to almost a running pace. Adam sprinted as hard as he could to get alongside it. It was indeed a four-seater with a low wing and one propeller at the front. The livery was two-tone green and VERDI AIR TOURS was written on the fuselage in swirling white lettering. He could see red-haired Grace, straining on the controls, her hazel eyes screwed up with frustration. A plump gray-haired couple was sitting in the back. They were wearing matching check shirts and khaki shorts and had cameras around their necks. They looked terrified.

"Can you slow it down any more?" Adam called out to Grace.

"Believe me, I'm trying!" she yelled back.

The plane slowed a little and, with a grunt, Adam leaped onto the wing. He pulled himself up, looked ahead and saw that they were rapidly running out of runway. A savage drop lay immediately ahead of them. He went through the hole where the door had been and sat down heavily next to Grace.

"We're not going to stop," Grace muttered under her breath.

In the next moment the plane rumbled off the end of the runway and fell away into the abyss.

Amy gave a little cry and she, Saul and Cressida ran across the landing strip and peered over the edge. Already the plane was a long way down, a green speck disappearing into the low-lying clouds far below.

"What was the kid thinking?" Amy said, her voice hushed with shock.

"He doesn't think. He never . . ." Cressida replied, her voice cracking.

"I think he just thought the pilot needed help," Saul said.

A wave of anger and disbelief washed over Cressida. Why did he always have to be so headstrong? He plowed into things with no thought of the consequences. It wasn't that he wanted to be a hero. Saul was right: he just wanted to help. Her eyes started to sting as tears welled up from somewhere deep inside. Her brother was loud, daft, irritating. But that was better than this. Better than not having him around.

"Wait!" Saul cried suddenly, and he shot a finger out to point at a green speck that had emerged from wispy clouds about a mile away from where they stood. The plane was veering from side to side, but at least it was heading upward. Relief washed over Cressida, followed by more anger—how could Adam put her through this?!

Inside the plane, Adam was looking at the instruments with the bemusement of a novice.

"Looks confusing, doesn't it?" Grace said, raising her voice over the noise of the engine.

"A little," Adam replied.

"I've got us pointing away from the ground, but beyond that I don't think I'm much use," Grace said.

Adam was scanning the dials in front of him, trying to work them out. Altitude, speed, bearing.

"Just try and fly so that none of those needles move too much. Okay?" Grace said. "Now grab the yoke and put your feet on the rudder pedals."

"Um, okay," Adam said. He gripped the handles of the yoke and slipped his feet onto the pedals. Instantly he felt what a difference tiny movements made.

"Hands and feet just alter the way the plane is pointing. The staying in the air part is all about power. I remember that much," Grace said, and with that she opened the throttle further.

Then she took her hands away from the controls, which suddenly seemed so very alien and alarming to her. She glanced sideways at Adam.

"Do you know what happened to me?" she asked.

"A creature took your talent for flying, your unique sphere of special ability," Adam replied in a matter-of-fact voice.

"Hmm. Strange as it is—I believe you. It's hard to explain. I know what everything does, but it's like the controls are all bogged down in quicksand. There's no lightness." Grace shook her head and looked at her hands. They seemed clumsy to her now.

"Can we land somewhere else?" Adam asked.

"Nope. We're low on gas. Takes almost a full tank to get to Altitudo. We can't turn back," Grace replied. "We have to land there."

Adam looked up and sideways at the tiny landing strip and swallowed hard. The couple in the back had kept their silence long enough and the man now leaned forward, his face red and sweaty.

"Is this darn *kid* gonna land the plane?" he asked.

"Let's hope so, Mr. Palmer," Grace replied, her voice cool.

"What was that horrible thing?" Mrs. Palmer asked.

"Please, we're going to need you to be quiet and calm," Grace reassured them. She tapped the fuel gauge. The tank really was almost empty. "We've got one shot at this, kid. There'll be no go-around."

Adam could feel his palms becoming moist on the yoke. He nodded.

"It's gonna be difficult, but it's not impossible. I've

proved that many times. Okay? Now, I'll talk you through it," Grace added.

Adam tried to focus on what he was doing. He recalled what Shaparelli had said about Grace. But *he* wasn't a talented pilot. Come to think of it, he wasn't talented at all, never mind a pilot. His hands started to shake. Grace spoke to him kindly.

"What's your name, boy?"

"Adam, Adam Bloom," he spluttered.

"We're going to do this, Adam," Grace said, her voice level. "Okay. We need to make our approach to the airfield. Little more power so we don't drop out of the sky, and pump that lever there. That's the flaps. It'll give us more lift, lower our stall speed." Grace spoke quickly and Adam did his best to concentrate and follow her instructions. "The undercarriage is already down, so we're good to go."

"And stop," Adam tried to joke.

Grace smiled.

"And stop," she repeated as much for her own morale as his. They could do this. They had to.

Saul, Amy and Cressida watched the plane bank around. The sun gleamed on its shiny green wings.

"Adam must be flying that thing. He's doing well," Saul said.

"And, damn, let's hope the kid can land it," Amy added, her jaw muscles still clenched.

"He's stupid, stupid, stupid," Cressida mumbled, looking up, then looking away, then looking up once more. Every fiber of her being was trembling.

The plane was more or less lined up with the runway now. Adam thought it seemed even shorter from where he was sitting, but he tried to push those thoughts to the back of his mind. With more speed than he would have liked, the beginning of the runway came up to meet them.

"Cut the power!" Grace said calmly.

Adam pulled the throttle lever right back and the plane dropped and bounced onto the grass runway.

"They're down!" Saul cried.

"Drop the anchors, Adam!" Amy said.

The plane was rolling along at great speed as Adam slammed on the brakes.

"Not too much or you'll tip her onto her nose!" Grace warned.

The plane was slowing but it was rapidly running out of runway again.

"We're not going to stop," Adam said, feeling helpless as the edge of the landing strip loomed large in the windshield.

"They're not going to make it," Cressida said to herself. She wrung her hands together as a sick feeling rose and lurched in her stomach.

Adam suddenly had a thought. He turned to Grace. "Can we get the wheels up?" he blurted.

"Not now that we're on the ground," she replied.

"Is there a manual override?" Adam went on.

Grace realized what he was thinking. She swallowed hard and pointed to a handle next to Adam's leg. He grabbed it. The plane was very near the edge now.

"Sorry," he said to Grace before yanking the handle.

Saul, Cressida and Amy all gulped as the wheels buckled under the plane. It collapsed forward so that the propeller dug into the ground, throwing up frozen chunks of mud. With a loud wrenching noise the plane plowed along on its belly, the wings grinding on the frozen ground. But it was stopping. Saul sprinted toward it, his crook held out at arm's length. With a final effort, Adam slammed the rudder fully to one side and the plane spun quickly sideways and slewed to a grumbling halt. It teetered at the very end of the airfield sideways, one of its wings jutting out over the edge, the propeller twisted and mangled. Saul managed to hook one of the damaged wheel struts with the end of his crook, and as he dug his heels into the snow and heaved backward, he provided just enough pressure to finally stop the plane dead and tease it back from the tipping point.

Adam collapsed into his seat. His heart was hammering fit to burst.

Grace smiled at him. "You can be my copilot anytime."

"Um, if it's all the same to you, I think I've had my fill of flying for now," Adam replied.

The two passengers leaned forward, their faces pale and angry.

"We'd like our money back," they said in unison.

Amy and Cressida ran up to Saul as Adam and Grace

clambered carefully out of the plane on the side that was facing the airfield. Adam's hair stood up even more than usual. The two passengers squeezed their way out behind them and Grace slapped some bills into their outstretched, ungrateful hands. With a satisfied grunt they marched off in the direction of the village.

"I can't believe what you did," Saul said to Adam. "It was either incredibly stupid or incredibly brave."

Adam shrugged.

"Let's label him brave, shall we?" Grace said, patting Adam on the shoulder.

Cressida looked at her brother. "Stupid seems more fitting," she mumbled angrily. Adam looked into her eyes. Sometimes he really could not figure her out.

Behind them, with a grinding, slithering noise the plane suddenly collapsed and, expelling an idle sigh, it slid off the edge of the runway, falling silently into the distant valley, spinning end over end.

Grace let out a little groan and leaned over to watch it plummet into the clouds below.

"Burning brake pads! Let's get away from this dizzy-making drop and go grab some hot chocolate," Amy suggested as she slapped Adam heartily on the back. He gave a weak grin.

"Six sugars for me," he mumbled.

CHAPTER TWENTY-ONE
THE NATURE OF TALENT

· · · · · · · · · · · · ·

Shaparelli was overjoyed to see everyone again. When he saw Grace Verdi, he bowed, held his finger to his lips, rummaged in a pocket and produced a small key. He tiptoed his enormous bulk over to a decorative display case and unlocked the door. As if handling the eggs of some endangered species, he took a delicate set of china cups and saucers from the case.

"Only the best for the amazing and beautiful Miss Verdi," he said.

Shaparelli joined everyone at their table. It had been a quiet morning and he relished the prospect of good company. The hot chocolate was in a large silver jug and it smelled wonderful. Next to the jug was a silver plate piled high with glistening chocolate cookies, all shaped like the varied weather vanes of Altitudo. Shaparelli poured the hot chocolate into the china cups with a satisfied huff. Adam and Amy were the first to take sips and they grinned at one another. This was even better than the hot chocolate at the Hotel Peritus.

"How was your flight in, Miss Verdi?" Shaparelli asked as he fed cookie crumbs to Tarloff, who was perched, as always, on his shoulder.

"Interesting," Grace replied.

"Go on," Shaparelli urged, grabbing a chocolate cookie and pushing the whole thing through his mustache into his mouth.

"I lost control of my plane and this extremely brave boy leaped on board just before we shot off the end of the runway. He then brought us in safely," Grace said, patting Adam on the back.

Shaparelli looked at Adam with a newfound respect. He let out a low whistle.

"Tell me, how is your chocolate?" he asked Adam urgently.

"It's great," Adam replied.

Shaparelli nodded and turned back to Grace. "But why did you lose control?"

"That's the hazy part," Grace replied. She looked around at Saul, Amy, Cressida and Adam. They all looked at each other. How could they put this?

"An ancient creature stole her talent for flying," Adam said finally. "It came out of her as a shiny blue sphere."

"There's a villain and his talent thief on the loose in this world of ours," Amy added.

"And we're all victims," Saul said.

Cressida nodded.

"Um, except me," Adam said, "because I have no talent."

Grace glanced at him, her head on one side. But before she could say whatever was on her mind, Shaparelli exclaimed, "A thief of talent? I can scarcely believe it!" He pushed another chocolate cookie into his mouth.

"I can scarcely believe it myself," Grace echoed.

"And yet," Shaparelli continued, licking the crumbs from his mustache, "I heard the clockmaker of Goggo recently lost his superb ability to craft his tiny clocks. That was very odd."

"Yep, that sounds like the work of Fortescue and his creepy chum," Amy said.

"This is all too much for a humble aviator," Grace said, staring at her outstretched fingers. She hadn't touched her delicate china cup of chocolate—she couldn't trust her once-sure hands not to drop it.

"Come with us!" Adam said to Grace, his eyes shining. "We're going to stop them and get back the talents they have taken. You can get yours back too."

"What exactly has been taken?" Grace asked. "What is 'talent,' anyway? Who's to say it won't come back? Who's to say someone can really take it?"

"But they've got all these glowing spheres," Adam said.

"I heard of a bald man once who stole locks of hair.

Think about it," Grace said. And with that, she stood up. "Thank you, Mr. Shaparelli. This was wonderful."

Shaparelli beamed from ear to ear.

"Anytime, anytime," he boomed.

"We should be going too," Amy added.

Shaparelli nodded. "Come back soon. You are always welcome." He lifted his heavy bulk from his chair and looked at Adam, Saul, Cressida and Amy in turn with warm yet worried eyes. "Be careful out there," he added.

Grace Verdi hired a handsome horse from the blacksmith in Altitudo. It was a muscular dapple gray with a thick white mane. She led it out into the middle of the square where Adam, Cressida, Amy and Saul were gathered. Grace kissed Adam on the forehead and ruffled his hair. Then she pulled herself up into the saddle and looked down at them all.

"What will you do now?" she asked.

"Push onward," Adam replied. "There are other possible victims we must try to reach before Fortescue does."

"And I'm not stopping till I get my sphere back," Amy said.

"Wherever you go, I hope all of you find your happiness," Grace said, and with a warm smile, she goaded the horse into action and trotted out of Altitudo.

"We'll find your talent sphere, Grace!" Adam called after her.

"Mail it to me!" she called back, waving as she turned a corner and disappeared from view.

"Shall we take a look at the map in the notebook to see who's next on Fortescue's list?" Saul asked.

Adam and Amy nodded, but Cressida did not look so keen. She followed the others at a distance as they headed back to the Silver Swift, which they had left parked outside Shaparelli's cafe.

Cressida's spirits lifted dramatically when they reached the car and she saw a familiar figure standing next to it. It was someone she admired. Someone who she felt could understand her. The figure looked directly at her with pale blue eyes framed by white eyelashes.

"Fancy seeing you in Altitudo," said Hans Fortissimo.

"Hans! What are you doing here?" Cressida asked, her voice cracking with excitement.

Adam looked at her. This surprise appearance had certainly woken her up.

"I live nearby in a large house," Hans replied. "And I demand that you be my guests. You all look drawn and tired."

"Well, that's mighty good of you, Hans, but we—" Amy began before Cressida interrupted. Her cheeks were glowing pink.

"We'd love to, Hans." Cressida turned to Amy, Saul and Adam. She could sense they needed a little winning over. "It's what we need: a chance to mull things over, plan our next move."

Saul and Amy exchanged glances. It was probably a good idea. They nodded. Adam looked at Hans. He had a niggling feeling in his gut, but everyone else seemed sold on the idea. He gave a weak smile, which Hans took as the deciding vote.

"Then it is settled." Hans raised a hand, clicked his fingers, and a huge black limousine purred up next to him. "Follow my car. It's a long drive but well worth it," Hans instructed, directing his comments to Saul and Amy. Next he switched his attention to Cressida and his attitude became warmer. "Travel with me if you like, Cressida," he said with a curious lilt to his voice.

Cressida's cheeks grew hotter and she gave a quick nod. Hans opened the limo door and Cressida stepped inside. Hans followed her in and closed the door.

Adam rolled his eyes. Just as he was starting to view the four of them as a team, here was his sister letting the side down. But maybe he was overreacting. After all, it was probably good for Cressida to spend time with someone her own age. He just wished he liked Hans more. He seemed like a peacock to Adam, all preening bright colors and not much else. But Saul and Amy seemed content to go along with everything, so Adam shrugged off any worries about going to Hans Fortissimo's house and squeezed himself into the rear seat of the Silver Swift once more. Saul started the car up and followed the black limousine out of Altitudo.

As they drove through the twisting streets, Adam waved

again at the happy children of Altitudo, who were stopping what they were doing to point at the car. When he turned to look back, he saw that the children soon returned to their games. A car was worth a wave, but it could not interrupt their play for long. What a great place to live, Adam thought.

Saul was thinking the same thing. He glanced at Amy. She was staring at his hands on the wheel and her expression surprised him. It was one of gentle envy. He laughed.

"You'll get to drive her again soon, Amy," he said, "and you'll drive her just the way you used to."

Amy glowed with pleasure. Sometimes Saul said exactly the right thing.

The two cars rumbled out of Altitudo and began to speed along curving roads that led eastward again. It was snowing gently, but the roads remained clear, so progress was good. The looming gray- and white-speckled crags of the Kappa-Nage mountain range watched over the two automobiles all the while, their stoic enormity making them seem like scuttling ants.

Inside the limo, Hans leaned forward and opened a polished wooden cabinet that was built into the back of the driver's seat. Inside were bottles of drink and attractive glasses with spiral patterns etched into them.

"Care for some sparkling grape juice, Cressida? It's very good."

"Don't mind if I do," Cressida replied as she unbuttoned her coat.

Hans took out a couple of glasses and opened a small bottle. It gave a refined little hiss. He poured the fizzing green liquid into the glasses. He gave one to Cressida and clinked his own against hers.

"To genius," he said, taking a swig.

"To genius," Cressida agreed, and she took a generous sip. The juice was sweet and refreshing. She watched the chilly, snow-covered landscape pass by and settled down deeper into the warmth of the seat. She liked this. It felt grown-up and easy. Hans watched her. Cressida turned and looked into his eyes. She liked his unusual white lashes. She removed her spectacles and tried to focus on Hans's face with her pale green eyes.

"My talent is gone as well," she whispered.

Hans nodded slowly. The way he understood was attractive to Cressida.

"Then we must stick together," he said, moving closer.

The pale yellow sun was beginning to set into a distant, icy blue haze when Hans's limo turned off the road and headed up a long private drive. The Silver Swift followed, burbling softly. Adam looked at the neatly pruned fir trees that stood at attention on both sides of the drive. Would the house be as impressive as this grand approach?

Finally Adam had his answer as they pulled into a large area of gravel in front of an imposing mansion with pillars on either side of a towering front door. The door was painted in black-and-white stripes so that it resembled a piano keyboard. The cars stopped and everyone got out, their breath foggy in the cold evening air. Saul pulled his trusty shepherd's crook from the car. Adam hung back for a moment. He took Fortescue's notebook from his coat and wedged it down behind the backseat of the Silver Swift. He had a feeling it would be safer there. Then Adam got out of the car and looked around. He let out a low whistle. The Fortissimo house was the kind you saw in movies where elegant ladies in evening gowns pushed men wearing top hats into swimming pools. It was luxurious on a grand scale and the grounds were impressive too. Adam noticed that the far end of the neatly trimmed lawn gave way to a sheer cliff face and the mountain ranges beyond. Only a low hedge stood between the lawn and the awesome drop, so there were spectacular views from practically anywhere in the garden. It was getting late and snowy owls were hooting in the trees.

"You shall be staying in the guest lodge," Hans declared proudly.

"Guest lodge?" Adam asked, looking around and wondering where it could be.

Hans smiled and pointed up in the air. Near the edge of the lawn, at the top of a very tall and very sturdy-looking pine tree, was a large wooden tree house.

Adam raised his eyebrows and looked over at Saul and Amy, who also looked surprised. To Adam, a tree house was little more than a wooden platform balanced on branches or, at best, a shed crammed into a branch fork. However, this was a real house, with a chimney, windows and a front door. A ladder led to it.

"We call it a lodge because it is 'lodged' into our tree." Hans sniggered at his own joke. "All our guests love it! Except the ones with vertigo. But before you scuttle up, let us all go into the main house and eat."

Hans gently took hold of Cressida's elbow and led her into the house.

CHAPTER TWENTY-TWO

THE HOUSE IN THE TREE

• • • • • • • • • • • • •

A banquet was laid out for Hans and his guests in an enormous black-and-white-decorated dining room. Paintings of Hans and other haughty-looking Fortissimos covered the walls. Everyone sat down at the table and gazed with wonder at the huge amounts of mouthwatering food.

"My parents are often away on business," Hans said, pushing a honey-glazed baby carrot into his mouth. "But, as you can see, I am well looked after."

"Will that be all, sir?" asked a tall, thin man standing by the door. He had a mean, pointed face and small watery eyes. His dark suit was pristine but drab.

"Yes, thank you, Gerston. You and the others have not done too badly. You may go now. But tell the cook his carrots are too mushy." The butler gave a little bow, clicked his heels together and left the room. "Gerston is slightly dim-witted but incredibly loyal," Hans said.

"How have you been since the, um, incident?" Cressida asked Hans.

"Well, I have tried not to make a mountain of it too much," he replied. "How about you?"

"Not so great, really," she admitted. "Even my speaking voice is croaky."

"It sounds lovely to me," Hans said with a comforting tone, making Cressida glow.

"But we're going to get it back—Cress's singing voice," Adam said emphatically, running his hands through his sticking-up hair.

"And how do you intend to do that?" Hans asked, pulling a drumstick from a roast chicken and taking a big bite. He barely looked at Adam.

"We're going to track down Fortescue and the creature," Adam replied as he chewed on a sweet-tasting cherry tomato.

"You're *still* talking about 'creatures'? I cannot believe you!" Hans cried.

Adam pointed at Saul and Amy, who were quietly stuffing their faces.

"These two believe the creature exists," Adam said.

"Well, everybody knows adults will believe anything," Hans said with a sly grin. "Cressida, do you believe in this creature?"

"I—I've seen it," Cressida stuttered. "Well, I've seen something."

Adam nodded with satisfaction. "See?" he said, looking at Hans. "We will catch up with it and we will get all the talents back and Cress will sing again and you will play the piano again and Grace will take her plane up again without flying into something and Saul will find his sheep again and Amy will race and win." Adam took a deep breath.

Hans applauded slowly.

"Hooray for positive thinking," he said with a sneer. "The good guys will win." Hans bit down on an asparagus tip. "If there were a creature and it really had the power to take the talents from people, I wouldn't be chasing it, I'd be joining it. Maybe Fortescue is the one with the right idea."

Adam did not know how to respond to this, but he noticed that Cressida was listening intently to Hans.

"Perhaps Hans is right," she said slowly. "Maybe we should be talking to Fortescue about how we could help. Perhaps he's doing something great with the talents he is collecting."

Hans smiled and nodded.

"Cress, are you losing you mind?" Adam blurted out. "He tried to bury us in an avalanche, not to mention attempting to burn us in our beds."

"Listen to Adam, Cress. Kid's got a point," Amy said.

"Yes—do you really think Fortescue's going to be up to something good?" Saul asked Cressida softly.

Cressida looked confused and said nothing. Adam threw his napkin down on the table and pushed his chair back.

"I'm going to bed," he said, and walked out of the dining room.

"Careful climbing up the ladder!" Hans called after him in a singsong voice.

Cressida looked at Hans and gave him sheepish smile. "Sorry about my brother. He can be a little hotheaded."

Hans dismissed this with a wave of his hand.

Amy frowned, pushed her chair back and stood up. "You have no need to apologize for your brother," she said to Cressida frostily.

Saul got up as well. "Been a long day. Think I'll take that terrifying climb up to bed. Thank you for dinner, Hans." And giving a little supportive smile to Cressida, he left, shepherding Amy before him.

Hans waited until Amy and Saul were outside before turning to Cressida. "You know, I believe we think very much alike." He chopped at the table gently with the edge of his hand. "*Very* much alike."

"I do too," Cressida replied.

Hans lowered his voice and leaned toward Cressida. He stared hard into her eyes. "There's something I must share with you."

"What is it?"

"Come with me." Hans took Cressida's hand and led her out of the room, along the hall and into the dark depths of the sprawling house.

Saul looked up at the ladder to the tree house.

"Ladies first," he said to Amy. "I can catch you if you fall."

"Well, I don't know whether to feel charmed or insulted," Amy replied. "But I guess I'd rather land on something big and soft, so I *will* go first."

"Why, thank you," Saul said with a grin. "And I definitely feel insulted."

"A shepherd should have thicker skin," Amy said as she scampered up the first few rungs.

It was a long climb and Amy was relieved to be heaving herself onto the solid wooden step that lay at the base of the dark green front door. She stood up with shaky legs. Saul stepped up behind her, teetering on the ledge.

They both went in and closed the door firmly behind them. It was small inside and busily decorated with wallpaper covered in musical notes and matching black furniture with white cushions. The whole room felt like a piano. Adam was there already, lost in thought, moving rapidly back and forth in a rocking chair which had treble clefs cleverly carved into the sides. In a small fireplace, a fire crackled and gave out a warm glow. On the mantelpiece above it were a number of china plates with Hans's face beaming out from the center of them.

"Phew! What a stomach-churning climb," Saul said, flopping into an armchair and pulling out his pipe.

"It's higher than it looks from the ground," Amy said. "Good thing I liked to climb trees when I was a kid."

"What kind of family expects their guests to climb a tree?" Adam asked. He looked and sounded extremely grumpy.

"You don't like Hans much, do ya, kid?" Amy inquired.

Adam spotted a bed tucked away in a corner of the room, and suddenly feeling very weary, he headed toward it and flopped down without even taking his shoes off.

"Not really," he replied.

"Seemed all right to me," Saul said. "Good food."

"You can't judge someone by their food," Adam said.

"Well, how do you judge people, Adam?" Amy asked.

Adam folded his arms behind his head and gazed up at the ceiling. A spider with a fat stripy body was busy spinning a web in the beams.

"I dunno. I guess you shouldn't judge people at all," Adam answered. "But I get the feeling Hans is bad news."

"You're just being the protective brother. Nothing wrong with that," Amy said, plopping herself down in the rocking chair.

"Well, I believe in looking out for my family," Adam said. "I'd look out for you two. You seem like family now. To me."

Saul and Amy looked at one another with surprise. There was a pause, then Amy took a deep breath. "Look, Adam, sure, we've gathered together in a common cause, but speaking for myself, I just want to get my driving feet back and get on with my life. Alone. Well, me and the Silver Swift. That car is my family."

Adam mulled over this piece of information for a moment, and then Saul spoke cautiously.

"Same goes for me, really. I like you, Adam, but I

was once happy on my own, tending to my sheep, and I'd like to return to that if I can," he said, fiddling with his pipe. "My sheep were *my* family before all this creature nonsense."

A dense, heavy silence filled the tree house for a long while. Saul and Amy both felt a hot wave of guilt wash over them. They did like Adam, but this merry traveling band could only be temporary. Strangely, Amy and Saul found they could not look at one another either. By voicing their desires to be alone, they had thrown up an invisible wall between them all.

"I see," Adam finally said. "Well, good to know. Good night."

Amy and Saul did not know what to say to this. With an awkward cough, Saul put his pipe out and got up from the chair.

"Yes, good night," he mumbled. "It looks like there's a bedroom squashed into the roof. I'll take that one, shall I?"

There was no response. Saul climbed the steep wooden staircase in the corner of the room and pushed through a small door into an oddly triangular bedroom. The door clicked shut behind him.

Amy pushed herself out of the rocking chair and headed for a door at the back of the tree house.

"And I'm hoping this leads to another bedroom and not thin air," Amy tried to joke as she opened the door. There was only silence from Adam, so she said quietly, "Good night, Adam," and went through the door into a tiny bedroom with a small bed in the shape of a concert piano. She closed the door behind her with a dull thud.

Adam tensed at the noise. His mind was racing with the events of the day. As he watched the curtains covered in musical notes flutter slightly in the breeze wafting through an open window, he suddenly missed his parents. He missed their beaming, ruddy, breathless faces when they used to come speeding up to him after another flawless ice-skating routine. Their talent had made them, and others, very happy. Their happiness had given them life. That's what Fortescue was taking. He wished Cressida had come up into the tree house. He did not trust Hans. He tossed and turned and, finally, after what felt like hours, he fell into a shallow, fitful doze.

It was still dark when Adam awoke. Initially he did not know where he was. Then his senses became more alert and he could hear the gentle snoring of Saul and Amy. But there was another sound. A sound that his subconscious had heard and had prodded him awake to take note of properly. It was the sound of someone playing the piano.

CHAPTER TWENTY-THREE
APPLE GREEN
· · · · · · · · · · · · · ·

Adam left the tree house and crept back down the ladder, being careful not to lose his footing in the dark. He walked up the lawn toward the house. The grass looked inky blue in the darkness. Adam crunched quickly across the area where the cars were parked. He went through the front door and followed the sound of the music like he had that time in the corridors under the Hotel Peritus. The tune was mysterious and creepy and seemed to repeat itself again and again. He walked down corridor after corridor. The house was vast. Finally, when the music was at its loudest, he came to a door with a musical note painted on it. He pushed it open and there before him was Hans sitting at a grand piano, his face lit up by a single candle, his hands skillfully sweeping across the keys. Cressida was sitting nearby with a faint smile on her face. Adam stepped into the room.

"How come you can play again, Hans?" Adam asked.

"What are you doing here? Go away. You're disturbing my recital," Hans snapped.

"But back in the hotel you had lost all your talent," Adam went on.

Hans just gave him a curious smile and continued to play the same strange repeating tune.

Adam turned to Cressida. "Cress, aren't you wondering how?"

"I'm just enjoying the music, Adam," Cressida said quietly, with irritation.

Suddenly Hans stopped and turned to face Adam. The haunting tune echoed for a moment around the room. The flickering of the candle made Hans's features look distorted and cruel.

"I made a deal," Hans said.

"What kind of deal?" Adam asked, an anxious feeling stirring in his stomach.

"I had visitors last night, and those visitors offered me a fraction of my talent back if I invited you to my home and kept you here," Hans said. He started to play the same sinister tune again. "I can only play this piece. But it was worth it."

"Who came?" Adam asked, suddenly trying to see into the dark corners of the room.

Hans laughed. "Why, your creature, of course!"

And as though that was a signal, the luminous eyes of the talent thief emerged from the darkness. It stepped into the light and stared at Adam, its red cloak swaying gently, its face still shadowed by the hood. Fortescue stepped from behind the door, cutting off Adam's exit. Cressida stood up and looked uneasily from Hans to the creature to Fortescue.

"It is unfortunate that you heard Hans playing and came here," Fortescue said to Adam. Then he looked at Hans with an irritated expression. "But I suppose the maestro couldn't wait to stretch his fingers."

"When you have to play, you have to play," Hans said with a sickening grin.

"It would have been easier if you'd stayed up in the tree," Fortescue said.

"What would have been easier?" Adam asked.

"Your disposal, of course," Fortescue snarled. "I am tired of being followed. I will allow nothing to get in the way of my plans." Fortescue took a deep breath and calmed himself. "Still, at least that madwoman and the shepherd are being dealt with."

At this, Adam rushed to the window. In the gloom, he could just make out Hans's butler, Gerston, chopping at the trunk below the tree house with a large ax. The ladder up to the tree house was now lying broken and twisted on the lawn.

"As I said, he is *very* loyal," Hans gloated.

"Cress, we have to help them!" Adam cried.

Cressida looked confused. "They gave Hans his talent back," she whispered.

"They gave him one tune, a tune that will slowly drive him mad," Adam said.

Hans reached out and brushed Cressida's arm with a featherlike touch.

"Cressida, join us," Hans said. "Fortescue and his hideous creature are my friends now."

"Don't listen to him, Cress!" Adam implored. "They're not friends!"

Fortescue stepped forward with a curiously blank look on his face, his eyes dull, his mouth slack.

"Adam is right," he said as he plucked a piece of sheet music from the top of the piano. In one rapid movement, he struck a match and set light to it. Fortescue gestured sharply with his head for the creature to guard the door, then he wedged the burning piece of paper into the strings of a harp standing in a corner. Hans let out a little cry of shock. With a withering chatter the gold paint of the harp's wooden frame started to buckle and crack, sending wisps of dark, rancid smoke curling into the air. Fortescue stepped back.

"We're a duo, a select club of two, no further members needed." He pulled a small key from his pocket. "I'm going to lock the three of you in now." Fortescue tugged at his collar. "Phew, is it me or is it getting a bit hot in here?" He let out a dry cackle and almost sauntered to the door, beckoning the creature to follow.

Hans got up from the piano and lurched for Fortescue in sudden panic, his features distraught. "Take me with you! I still have talent! These two have nothing! They *are* nothing!"

"What?!" Cressida cried. "Hans, what are you saying?"

Hans turned on Cressida, his eyes wide and staring, sweat beading on his forehead. "Get away from me!" he bellowed. "Talent is everything! Those without it don't deserve to *live!*"

Smoke was beginning to curl its way across the floor, building in volume, eager to spread. Cressida was staring at Hans with heartbroken amazement.

Fortescue and the creature had taken advantage of Hans and Cressida's argument, and Fortescue was out the door, his talent thief close behind him. Summoning all his courage and energy, Adam lunged for the creature, pulling it back into the room. The talent thief let out a baleful howl. Fortescue spun around, his face cloudy with anger.

"Hold him still!" he barked at his minion. The creature wrapped its long sinewy arms around Adam, one claw enveloping the boy's chest and the other resting on top of his tufty-haired head. Its cloak enveloped Adam and for the first time he could feel the chilled, dry, leathery texture of the creature's skin. Even in the heat of the burning room, under the cloak the creature was surprisingly cool to the touch. Adam tried not to breathe in its unpleasant musty smell.

"You never give up, do you?" Fortescue jeered.

"I'm just trying to save my sister and my friends!" Adam blurted. He struggled to break free with all his strength, and as he did so . . . something astounding started to happen. A bright light began to glow under the creature's claw, the one that was on Adam's head. The creature trilled curiously.

Cressida took a shaky breath. Fortescue stepped closer, his mouth open with sheer amazement.

"What *is* going on?" he said, his eyes widening.

The creature raised its hand and an apple green sphere domed from the top of Adam's head. It had a soft milky sheen to it and tiny sparks of light fired off at random across the surface. Adam felt dizzy. Images were flooding through his mind—chasing the creature in the aviary, pleading with Amy to take them with her, escaping the avalanche, approaching Saul perched on his rock, landing Grace Verdi's plane.

"I thought he had no talent!" Fortescue exclaimed.

The creature let out a confused snarl as it clasped the sublime sphere to its chest and clung on to Adam with its other limb.

"He does *not* have talent," Hans barked. "He is worthless."

"Something quite extraordinary is happening here," Fortescue declared. "We will take the boy and his sphere. This is utterly remarkable and needs further study!"

Adam still felt dizzy, but he reacted quickly nonetheless. He elbowed the creature in the rib cage and wrenched his sphere from its clutches. He scrabbled over to the harp, now burning fiercely along with the carpet under it, and raised the glinting orb above his head.

"Let Cressida go or I throw it into the fire!" he snapped.

The creature yelped with alarm and Cressida's eyes filled with tears.

"You don't know what you're holding there, Adam," she whispered. "It could be dangerous for you if you destroy it."

"I don't care!" Adam exclaimed over the crackles of the fire. "I'm not leaving you locked in this burning room."

Fortescue scowled. The room was now almost entirely filled with acrid smoke and his eyes stung. "Fine, fine, she can go free, but you come with us!"

"Throw the key into the fire!" Adam demanded, holding his sphere closer to the flames and feeling the sweat drip into his eyes.

Fortescue nodded to the creature and then flipped the key into the heart of the fire. The creature bounded over and wrapped its arms around Adam with the force of metal cables being drawn tight. Adam slumped wearily on the spot, like a puppet whose strings had been cut. He was exhausted.

Fortescue grabbed Adam's sphere and slipped it into a pocket. "Let's go!" he yelled, running out of the room. The creature, carrying Adam, loped after him. Hans looked bereft.

"But I want to go with you!" he called to the creature. "I want the power you have!"

The talent thief merely lashed out as it passed Hans,

sending him flying across the room. The boy landed heavily in a large armchair and started to sob. The creature growled. For a fleeting moment its gaze rested on Cressida and she could sense its expression softening slightly. Then it ran out, Adam pinned in its strong arms.

Cressida looked at Hans with a mixture of pity and disgust in her eyes. Was he just going to sit there while his house burned down around him? She rushed over to the door and dragged a giant vase into the room from the corridor. She discarded its unattractive, spiky plant and, with an ungainly swing, she threw the remainder of the contents over the fire. A deluge of water hit what was left of the harp and carpet with a loud, gratifying hiss, dousing the flames.

Then Cressida tore out of the room after the creature. As she turned a corner, she just caught sight of Adam's face through the tattered ends of the creature's cloak.

"You're *not* nothing, Cress! Whatever Hans says. You're fantastic, with or without talent!" Adam yelled. "If only you'd believe it."

Cressida stopped in her tracks. It was the nicest thing anyone had ever said to her. And it was Adam, her kind, dependable, dumped-on brother, who had said it. A sudden despair kicked in—and now he was being taken and there was nothing she could do about it.

"Save Saul and Amy!" Adam added as he was whisked outside through a side door.

Cressida hovered for a moment and then raced back

through the maze of a house until she reached the front door. She ran out onto the lawn.

The tin shed and the balloon in the shape of a plus sign were hidden behind tall trees at the back of the Fortissimo house. The creature carried Adam inside the shed and threw him down.

"Careful. That boy is valuable!" Fortescue ordered.

The creature hissed quietly and grabbed hold of the rudder bar that steered the balloon. Adam noticed that the large sack holding all the talents from Fortescue's latest trip was stored in a corner. A slight glow emanated from it. A grappling iron hooked under a tree root was holding the balloon down. Fortescue unhooked it swiftly, leaped into the shed, and within moments the balloon was rising.

But Adam was not going to be taken without a fight. He stood up and felt only a little light-headed. He had felt very weak after the creature had first removed his sphere (*he* had a sphere!), but aside from that he didn't feel any different—no croaky voice, no lack of coordination, no dulling of the senses. So what had gone from him . . . nothing? And yet, a sphere there was. He pushed these thoughts aside—his strength was returning now and he was desperate to get to his friends to help, whatever hurtful things they had said to him only a few hours earlier.

Adam barged the creature out of the way, and with a screech, it let go of the rudder bar and fell against the wall of the tin shed. Adam wrenched the rudder bar around so that the balloon was heading over the main house toward the tree house.

On the lawn, Cressida was desperately trying to stop Hans's butler from chopping at the base of the tree. But he was strong and determined to get on with the job—the tree was almost ready to be felled.

"I'm just following orders, miss," Gerston said over and over in a stiff manner.

Cressida tried to call up to Saul and Amy, but the effort made her voice crack and splutter.

"Saul, Amy, wake up," she whispered, tears rolling down her cheeks.

Gerston dropped the ax, went around to the other side of the tree and pushed with all his might. The trunk began making a nasty cracking noise.

Above, in the tin shed, Fortescue was getting really angry. Keeping Adam away from the rudder bar was like keeping wasps away from a picnic.

Adam had just one thought in his mind: to steer the balloon over the tree and save his friends. For the third time the creature threw him down and Adam got back up again, wrestled the rudder bar from it and pulled it right around once more. The confined space gave Adam an advantage over the cloaked, gangly creature and Fortescue. Being smaller, he could create a great deal of chaos and out of that chaos he hoped to maneuver the shed where he wanted. The tin shed spun and the balloon slowly spun with it until, sure enough, they were gliding over the tree house. Adam could see it shaking. The tree would fall soon and it was clear that the house would then plummet into the valley far below.

Inside the tree house, Saul and Amy had finally awoken when all the china plates had fallen from the mantelpiece and smashed into bits. They rushed from their rooms to the front door, opened it and realized with horror that the ladder had been taken away and that the whole place was swaying alarmingly. They looked at each other with rising fear. Saul interlaced his fingers with Amy's and squeezed.

CHAPTER TWENTY-FOUR

RETURN OF THE TALENTS

· · · · · · · · · · · · ·

This time Fortescue dragged Adam away from the rudder bar and pushed him over to the other side of the shed. Adam fell hard, but when he put his hand out to break his fall, it landed on a coil of rope, the coil of rope attached to the grappling hook. Adam thought quickly. He kicked away at the latch holding shut the trapdoor in the shed's floor. With a metallic yawn it fell open and Adam could see the roof of the tree house coming into view. Fortescue had no idea what Adam was up to, but he guessed it was not for his benefit.

"It's like being in a barrel going over a waterfall, with this infernal boy in here!" Fortescue yelled.

He lunged at Adam, but Adam ducked and skidded across the floor on his stomach, holding the grappling hook tight in his hand. He dangled it down through the hatch and watched as the roof of the tree house moved across his line of sight. He kicked at Fortescue, who was trying to pull him away, and waited for the right moment. As the tree house chimney became visible, Adam threw the hook with all his might. He had timed it perfectly—the grappling iron fell straight down the chimney.

"Ha! Yes!" Adam exclaimed. He grinned to himself as Fortescue yanked him back roughly from the trapdoor.

Inside the tree house, the hook had fallen down into the grate and then jerked back up and clamped itself onto the metal hood of the fireplace. And at that moment, with a terrific tearing, cracking sound, the tree fell.

Cressida ran clear and watched as it landed heavily across the lawn, its branches and leaves shuddering violently, the top half of it sticking out beyond the cliff at the end of the garden. But the house had not fallen. With astonishment, Cressida looked up. The tree house was suspended from the bottom of the tin shed and spinning slowly.

"Adam . . ." she said under her breath.

Gerston the butler slapped his hands together and headed back into the house as though he had just finished pruning the roses.

The weight of the tree house was pulling the balloon slowly downward. Saul and Amy were both leaning out of the front door and looking up. They could see Adam through the hatch of the tin shed. He was struggling with Fortescue and the cloaked creature, but he was also smiling.

"Everything's going to be fine!" he called down to them as he wriggled in Fortescue's armlock.

The tree house was about twenty feet above the ground now. Fortescue fought to untie the grappling hook's rope. Adam tried to stop him, but with a defiant snarl, Fortescue finally succeeded. The tree house dropped to the ground. It practically whistled as it fell, fast and heavy. All of the windows smashed, the slates fell off the roof and the front door fell forward onto the lawn. But as the noise faded, Saul and Amy stepped out, shaken but safe.

Cressida ran over to them and they all looked up to see Adam far above, waving down. Saul flicked his crook by way of thanks. Then Adam was wrenched from view and the balloon started to rise more rapidly.

Adam was relieved that Saul and Amy were safe. Perhaps he should sit quietly now and conserve his energy. But a thought struck him. A very good thought. One that could help everyone. As quick as lightning, he skidded over to the other side of the shed and grabbed the sack full of talents. Fortescue's eyes went wide with horror.

"No!" he cried.

"Yes," Adam said firmly. He scooted over to the open trapdoor again and dropped the sack of talents through it. The sack fell down into the darkness. Fortescue let out a long, dismal wail. Adam felt a wave of satisfaction wash over him.

Saul, Amy and Cressida saw the sack fall from the tin shed. It was weighty and it fell quickly, down and down, and just when they thought it was going to plummet into the valley below, it snagged on the upper branches of the fallen tree, whose branches now jutted far out into thin air. They all looked at each other with excitement.

"Does that sack contain what I think it contains?" Saul asked, his eyes shining.

"Boy, does that kid fire on all cylinders!" Amy said.

"Yes, he does," Cressida said quietly, watching the balloon in the shape of a plus sign drifting away into the distance.

With a grunt, Saul climbed up onto the tree trunk and walked carefully along it. He swallowed hard and looked down at the jagged rocks nestled in the dark mist far, far below. He tapped on the trunk with the butt of his crook, the rhythm fast and skittish like his heart.

"Want me to go?" Amy called.

"No, it's fine. Better my thick ugly neck gets broken than your slim, graceful one!" he called back.

Amy smiled to herself in the darkness and watched anxiously as Saul edged out into thin air. The sack was dangling from a branch right at the very tip of the tree. Saul went down on all fours as the trunk started to shake. He inched out farther and farther. It was a big tree, so he hoped that his weight would not be enough to tip it over the cliff edge. But the thinner branches near the top were beginning to complain. He lowered himself onto his belly and tried to ignore the sharp little cracking noises the tree was emitting around him. Amy and Cressida could just make out Saul's silhouette. He was holding his crook at arm's length.

"Be careful!" Amy called.

"I'm not returning without the sack!" Saul yelled back from the gloom.

But then there was a ground-shaking thud as the last remaining splinters attaching the tree trunk to its stump snapped. With a low, earthen cry, the whole tree rolled sideways. Saul slipped off the trunk, but he grabbed quickly at a nearby branch as his legs fell away into the blackness. He let out a frightened yelp. Then, hanging on as tightly as he could, focusing all his strength on his arms, he pulled himself back up, his heart hammering.

"You still there?" Amy called out into the darkness.

"Er, yeah. Still here," Saul called in return. "Just," he added under his breath.

When the tree had settled once more, he moved slowly and carefully on toward the sack until, finally, he managed to hook it up and pull it toward him. Saul crawled back in quick, careful movements. He was just beginning to think he was safe when, without warning, the whole tree began to tip over the cliff edge with a deafening rumble. Saul leaped to his feet, and as the tree slid in slow motion off the cliff, he sprinted along the trunk as fast as he could and jumped back onto the lawn just as the tree tumbled, with a leafy roar, into the chasm below.

Saul knelt on the ground, breathing hard, his face sweaty. Then he held up the sack, a broad smile breaking out on his face.

"If this is full of artichokes or something, I am *not* going to be happy!" he said.

As Saul emptied the sack right there on the lawn, the talent spheres rolled out, alive with a vibrant and wonderful energy. The sun was starting to rise and the spheres glowed eerily in the pale light of dawn. There were about eighty or so and each one was different from the next. They were all roughly the size of an orange, but they varied in color and texture and they were all hypnotically beautiful in their own way, except for one, which seemed bruised and dull and apparently had a wedge missing.

"How do we find our own?" Amy asked.

Saul shrugged. "Perhaps we call them. What's yours called?" he joked.

Amy rolled her eyes and started to sort through the spheres. They felt warm and tingly to the touch. She picked one up and stepped back. It was yellow, with darting red oval shapes under the surface.

"This one looks pretty good. Now, do you reckon I have to eat it?" she asked.

"The creature takes them from the top of the head," Cressida replied.

Amy held the sphere over her head and pushed it down. But it stopped against her skull and would not go any farther, no matter how hard she pushed.

Saul also started to sift through the glowing orbs. He picked each one up and looked closely at it. Finally he gave a triumphant whoop. "I can see my face reflected in this one!" The sphere was white and waxy with black speckles. "Couldn't see anything in the others."

Saul raised the sphere above his head, closed his eyes and slowly and carefully pushed it down onto his tight blond curls. The sphere glided into them and disappeared. Saul's eyes flicked open and he fell to his knees with a groan. He clamped his hands over his ears and clenched his teeth in a pained grimace.

"Saul, are you all right?" Amy asked, stepping toward him, her face a picture of concern.

"It's too much," he cried. "I can hear everything, smell everything, feel everything, see everything. It's as though someone has turned the volume of the world up. I can hear the slugs crawling."

"It's bound to be a shock to the system," Cressida said gently. "Take your time."

Gradually Saul became calmer. He took a few deep breaths, looked around and stood up.

"I'm all right," he said. "My tracking senses are back. Hans is approaching."

Sure enough, Hans stepped from the shadows and ran over to the spheres. He rummaged through them roughly.

"Hey, careful!" Amy said.

"You have to see your own face? Is that right?" Hans said as he picked up each sphere and peered into it.

"If you can bear to," Cressida muttered. As she observed the careless way Hans handled the talent spheres, a fury took hold. "I don't know what I saw in you, Hans. Beneath your talent and self-confidence is a truly despicable person. If only you were more like my brother. Adam may not have talent, and he may get on my nerves, but he's a good person who cares about people. But you only care about yourself!"

"Oh, please, will you stop with the whining and preaching, Cressida," Hans sneered. "I'm not weak. I am ruthless, and that's what you have to be to get by in this world. Now where is my stupid sphere?"

Hans had been avoiding one sphere as he searched, but finally he was forced to pick it up. It was the bruised-looking one with the wedge missing. Hans looked into it and his distorted features stared back at him. Saul, Cressida and Amy exchanged troubled looks as Hans rammed the sphere down inside his head. Then, with a strange, victorious laugh, Hans ran back to the house. Cressida was glad to see him go. She and Amy continued to sort through the spheres, looking for their own.

In the next moment a horrible clanging noise drifted from the house. It was followed by Hans screaming at the top of his lungs—a mad, hollow cry full of frustration and anger. There followed the sounds of someone smashing to

213

bits everything they could lay their hands on. Cressida stared back at the house.

"I assume when they broke his sphere apart and gave him a small piece back, they ruined the whole thing," she whispered.

Saul nodded. "A corrupt talent. Come on, find yours. Let's get out of here."

"Yes, of course," Cressida rasped.

But Amy was the next to find her sphere.

"Aha!" she cried as she held the glowing orb aloft. It was silver with dashing flashes of azure blue pulsing through it in figure-eight patterns. She pushed it down easily into the top of her head and immediately began to wriggle her fingers and tap her toes.

"Steaming hubcaps! Somebody get me to a racetrack! I can feel the joy of racing flooding back into my veins!" she exclaimed.

Saul nudged her and she turned to see Cressida holding a delicate-looking pale pink sphere. Her eyes and cheeks glowed in its light. Cressida swallowed hard and raised the sphere higher. She pushed it gently down and it disappeared inside her head.

"Yes?" Saul asked.

"I think so," replied Cressida. Her voice was no longer a whisper. It sounded strong and firm. And then Cressida breathed in deeply, closed her eyes and began to sing. The song had a powerful beauty, and it spread outward from the garden like a warm breeze, rising up and caressing the very mountaintops. Amy and Saul both had to catch their breath as Cressida's voice sent shivers of pleasure down their spines.

"Now that's a talent worth hanging on to," Saul said, looking at Cressida with respect.

CHAPTER TWENTY-FIVE
CRESSIDA'S PEP TALK

· · · · · · · · · · · ·

Cressida bundled the remaining spheres into the sack and walked up the garden toward the Silver Swift. Amy was already at the wheel, a huge grin on her face. The engine was running with its deep, familiar throb. As the golden glow of dawn spread its stealthy fingers across the Fortissimo estate, Cressida could still hear Hans inside the house, venting his rage on any breakable object he could get his hands on. Her thoughts turned painfully to Adam.

She knew they had not been getting along well recently, and she had to accept that much of that was her fault. She had not given him enough credit; she didn't care whether he had talent or not, he was brave, thoughtful, selfless—the kind of brother anyone would be proud to have, irritating though he could be. Their parents were gone but they had each other. That was the important thing. She simply hadn't appreciated it. And now he was gone too.

Saul stood by the car, looking around, listening to the birds and animals, smelling the mountain air. He was obviously relishing having his highly tuned senses back. Amy turned when she saw Cressida approaching and wound down the window.

"Where can I drop you?" she asked. "I'm going to take Saul home on my way back."

Cressida could hardly believe her ears. "Where can you drop me?!" she echoed.

Amy looked a little sheepish. Her smile faded for a moment, but she recovered it quickly.

"The Dashwood Grand Prix starts in only three days, so I'm going to have to scoot if I want to get there on time. Me and the old girl are gonna wipe the floor with the opposition now that I've gotten my racing feet back an' all," she said.

"And have you forgotten why you have your racing feet back?" Cressida fumed.

Amy's smile faded completely this time. "No," she mumbled.

"Adam has been whisked away to who knows where for who knows what reason and you're wittering about car races!" Cressida exclaimed.

"Adam has proved he is a very brave and resourceful kid. He'll soon escape from Fortescue and the creature. He doesn't need us cramping his style," Amy said. She turned to look at Saul. "Saul, am I right or am I right?"

Saul took a deep breath. He remembered their last conversation with Adam, in the tree house.

"We should go after him," he said. "He won't escape on his own."

Amy snorted and narrowed her eyes at the shepherd.

"How many more years of racing do you have in you, Amy?" Cressida asked.

Amy looked blank. "I don't know. I haven't thought about it."

"Okay, let's be generous and say five," Cressida said. "When those five years are up, you'll have plenty of time to sit back and look at your trophies and think what an amazing woman you are. But in ten years' time, when your looks have gone and nobody comes knocking on your door anymore and you've polished all the chrome off those trophies, a niggling question will keep popping into your head. Know what that question is?" Cressida asked.

"No, but I got a feeling you're gonna tell me," Amy said, chewing her lip.

"'I wonder if he's okay, that kid?'" Cressida said. "'I wonder if he made it home.'"

Amy clenched her jaw muscles for a long while, and then she looked up at Cressida.

"Damn! Get in! And you, Saul," she spluttered. "Heck, I wasn't really going to leave the kid. There'll be other races. Not as swanky as the Dashwood Grand Prix . . . but I guess an old gal who's losing her looks ain't got much choice!"

Cressida gave a sigh of relief and swallowed hard. She hated confrontations, but this one had been all too necessary. She went around to the passenger door and squeezed her way into the back, laying the sack full of talent spheres gently on the floor next to her. Saul climbed in too. He looked over at Amy quietly fuming and tried to suppress a smirk.

"If it makes you feel any better, I reckon you got a good fifteen years before you lose your looks," he said.

"Silence!" Amy barked. "I want silence while I drive. I've taken enough lip for one day. Now, that balloon was heading east, so let's toe it eastward and see if we can catch sight of it. Hold on to your magnetos!"

So saying, Amy flung the car into first gear and let in the clutch. With a screech and a cloud of smoke, the wheels spun and the car shot off down the drive.

Cressida settled back and watched the fir trees fly past in a blur. Amy really was an excellent driver, fast and sure. Cressida closed her eyes and thought about Adam again. Though she hated to admit it, he had been right. Her talent *had* been worth chasing after. She had only truly realized how precious it was when she had picked it out from all the others and seen how unique and beautiful it was. But fragile too. Talent does not make one great the way Hans thought it did. In fact, like Shaparelli had said in the café, happiness comes out of respecting yourself and others. Talent is a bonus to be shared—the way her parents had done.

Cressida opened her eyes and looked at the road ahead. They were heading east into the morning sun and the warmth was pleasant on her face. Saul and Amy were quiet, but Cressida could tell that Amy was happy to be driving again, even if it wasn't in some fancy grand prix. Her leather gauntlets gripped the wheel with relish. Saul was searching the sky with eager eyes for any sign of a balloon in the shape of a plus sign and a dangling shed.

"Why did Fortescue take Adam?" Saul asked now.

"They pulled a sphere from him," Cressida replied.

Amy let out a low whistle. "It doesn't surprise me—of course the little dynamo is talented. Though I can't quite put my finger on how. Can you, Saul?"

"Hmm. No—but since there was nothing there the first time that dratted talent thief tried him, it will certainly give our man Fortescue something to think about. I suspect Adam's talent sphere is quite different from those he's come across before."

Cressida felt a knot of fear for her brother deep in the pit of her stomach. She hoped that the three of them were equipped to free Adam. The creature surely would not harm him, but then again, it was fiercely loyal to Fortescue and that madman was capable of anything.

She tried to relax and shifted sideways, resting one arm on the back of the seat. Her fingers brushed against something hard and square, and she shot upright again as she plucked Fortescue's notebook from behind the seat. Adam must have put it there for safekeeping, she thought. Well done! She hadn't really looked at it before; Adam had more or less kept it to himself, but now she realized she had a chance to learn a bit more about the ruthlessly driven

Fortescue. She opened the notebook at random and found Fortescue's list of items needed for the trip to the Marscopian jungle with Saul. Cressida scanned down.

INVENTORY FOR EXPEDITION TO MARSCOPIA WITH SHAFER

- 1 deluxe Wonder-Nite camp bed (for me)
- 1 standard wafer-thin sleeping mat (for Shafer)
- 1 "Storm-defiant" tent with ground-anchor technology (for me)
- 1 "April Shower" picnic tent (for Shafer)
- 16 large tubes of Balcony-Brite toothpaste
- 1 toothbrush (Shafer can bring his own or use his finger)
- 1 Marscopian phrasebook (revised edition)
- 1 spare pair of sunglasses
- 1 "Real Man" mustache trimmer
- 10 pairs anti-odor socks (keep hidden)
- 1 can of wasp repellant (Marscopian-wasp version)

- 14 packs of sugar-coated lemon bunnies (keep hidden)
- 1 can of Summerdaze whipped cream
- 20 cans of Summerdaze peach slices (in syrup NOT peach sweat)
- 30 cans of Pixie-pillow ravioli
- 3 jars of Jangla coffee
- 1 tub of Bonlacto milk powder
- 2 crates of Turnip Soup, Turnip Soup, Turnip Soup (oh how I despise it, but it is the cheap option)
- 1 mini-bottle of champagne for one (for when I find the creature, keep hidden)
- 1 Gloom-Busta lantern
- 1 pouch of Hacking Haze tobacco (for bribing Shafer if he gets fed up)
- 1 large suitcase full of determination!

I will find you, creature!

Cressida switched her gaze from the notebook to Saul, who was still fiercely scanning the skies.

"Fortescue had a secret supply of sugar-coated lemon bunnies in his tent," she said.

Saul kept his gaze skyward. "I knew it," he muttered. "Explains why he got through so much toothpaste too. A man as vain as Fortescue wouldn't be able to bear the thought of rotten teeth."

Cressida laughed and read down the page again. There was something in the list that caught her attention. It niggled at her, but she didn't know exactly why. A moment later Saul jabbed at the windshield.

"There!" he exclaimed.

Amy slowed the car and strained to see. Cressida leaned forward and peered up through the windshield too. Neither of them could spot anything.

"Where?" Amy asked.

"To the left of that cloud that looks like a newborn lamb," Saul said.

"You have a woolly mind, Saul Shafer," Amy joked with a smile.

Amy and Cressida both followed Saul's finger and saw a tiny speck high up in the distance.

"Is that it?" Cressida asked.

"That's it," Saul confirmed, and there was no trace of doubt in his voice.

Amy instantly became a blur of furious movement, gear selected, foot down, hands gripping the wheel. The Silver Swift roared into life again, her hearty bellow echoing around the mountains. Even though the balloon in the shape of a plus sign was merely a dot on the horizon, Amy was convinced that they could catch it. But she would have to drive flat out. As the car approached a nasty hairpin bend, she dipped the clutch, threw the gearshift into neutral, applied the brake with her toe and blipped the accelerator with her heel. Then she threw the gearshift into a lower gear, let the car roar around the hairpin bend, losing hardly any speed, and accelerated away again.

"Whoa, you really know how to drive this!" Saul said. The hairs were standing up on the back of his neck.

"Yeah, I do," Amy agreed, her voice a mixture of pleasure and defiance. "You still got your peepers on the balloon?"

"Yes, it's heading pretty much due east still. I can just smell that strange musty scent the creature gives off. That could help if they disappear from view," Saul said.

"I hope Adam's all right," Cressida said, straining to see the balloon in the distance. "I haven't been very nice to him recently. The truth is, I've always been, I don't know, a bit jealous of him, I suppose."

"Why?" Saul said, turning around to look at Cressida.

"I don't know. He's braver than me," Cressida said. "I'm used to hiding behind my singing—whether I'm showing off with it or complaining about it—but he is what he is. He's happy to be himself. Does that make sense?"

"Yes, kind of," Saul replied.

"I want him to know he's great," Cressida said. "Really annoying but great."

"When we reach him, you can tell him," Amy said as she flung the car skillfully around another bend.

CHAPTER TWENTY-SIX
PAINTED SMILES

· · · · · · · · · · · · ·

Inside the tin shed, Adam was lying down facing the wall. He was looking through a rusty hole and could see the sun glinting on something far away. It was tearing around bend after bend and heading in the same direction as the balloon. He smiled to himself. Amy must have her racing feet back, which meant that Saul and Cressida probably had their talents back as well. He was pleased. Adam rolled over and looked at the cloaked creature hunched at the rudder bar. What a peculiar thing it was, a talent thief, older than history, unique and—in coalition with this madman, Fortescue—a terrible force. Adam switched his gaze to Fortescue himself. He was sitting quietly on a wooden box next to the creature, the light glinting off his sunglasses.

"How come the creature removed a talent sphere from *me*?" Adam asked.

"Interesting, isn't it?" Fortescue said, batting the question away.

"Where are you taking me?"

"I want you to be my guest at my home," Fortescue replied. "It is a great honor because, apart from my friend here"—Fortescue nodded in the creature's direction—"you are the only person ever to have received such an invitation."

"And if I don't want to be your 'guest'?" Adam asked.

"Like I said, it is an honor and you will accept it as such," Fortescue repeated. His tone suggested that there would be no further discussion on the matter.

Adam moved to the front of the shed and peered through a grimy window. The snow-covered mountains were giving way to gently rolling hills as they traveled farther east. Adam could see small farms dotted all over the landscape below. He could just make out two horses pulling a plow across a sloping field, with a tiny figure guiding them. Adam's gaze moved on. Up on the crests of the hills were clusters of lush green trees that seemed alive with verdant secrets. All so beautiful, but Adam found it hard to enjoy the journey as he worried about his unknown destiny. He lay down again and looked through the rusty hole. The Silver Swift was still there in the distance, but it did not seem any closer. He closed his eyes and tried to use the shed's gentle rocking motion to send him to sleep.

When Adam awoke from his shallow doze, he immediately peered back through the rusty hole and tried to spot the Silver Swift. He could just see a shiny dot on the horizon. They had obviously fallen behind. Adam felt a nervous twinge in his gut. Despite Amy's superior driving, it was faster to travel in a straight line by air than it was to follow twisting roads. Adam thought briefly of trying to get control of the rudder again. But he dismissed this thought almost straightaway. He would only be able to grab the bar for a few brief moments before the creature and Fortescue overpowered him eventually. He had noticed another grappling hook attached to a coil of rope tucked behind a stack of paint tins, but he decided it would make a clumsy weapon. It was better to conserve his energy. When the balloon finally came down, Amy would get a chance to catch up. That is, if she and the others didn't lose track of the balloon in the meantime.

Adam got to his feet and went over to the window at the front of the shed once again. A winding ribbon of road below led up to a pair of enormous wrought-iron gates set into a hulking redbrick wall. Ivy clung to the expanse of brickwork, lending it a distinguished yet neglected air. The wall seemed to encompass a vast area that, at this moment, was lost in a strange, heavy, ashlike dust that hung thickly in the atmosphere. The area outside the wall consisted of dry, windswept plains ranging in color from rust red to sandy yellow.

"What a desolate hole," Adam muttered.

"Also known as my home," Fortescue said sharply.

Adam winced. "I'm sure it's really top-notch inside."

The shed sailed over the top of the wall, then Fortescue reached through one of the windows to turn a valve on the outside. The balloon in the shape of a plus sign started to descend.

The shed touched down with a dull, dusty thud and Fortescue nodded to the creature, who picked Adam up in a strong, incapacitating bear hug. Adam tried not to gag on its overwhelming rancid smell.

Fortescue stepped out of the shed and his minion followed with their captive. Adam, locked in the creature's embrace, half smothered by its cloak, looked around as best he could and took in the bizarre and disturbing surroundings. There was a great expanse of dry, dusty land enclosed by the wall, and wandering everywhere were muscular men wearing gray overalls and masks made of tin. Painted onto the masks in red paint were crude faces with creepy smiles. Adam shuddered.

"W-who are they?" he asked shakily.

"My groundsmen," Fortescue replied.

"What do they do?"

But Fortescue ignored him and gestured instead to an imposing building at the other end of the compound. Also made of red brick, it loomed out of the dust, bruised and tired looking despite its impressiveness.

"Let's get down to the business of the day," Fortescue said, striding off toward it.

Adam glanced from side to side as the creature carried him after Fortescue. The "groundsmen" were carrying heavy, crude-looking spears. Adam noticed, as he watched carefully, that each one was patrolling a fixed route between the building and the perimeter wall. Adam guessed that the groundsmen were the security for every inch of this arid wasteland.

Finally, Fortescue reached the massive double doors of the building. Their metal was rusty, but the combination lock to one side of a small door built into the double doors looked new. Fortescue turned the dial quickly backward and forward, being careful to shield the sequence from Adam, and the door sprang open. They stepped through and Adam gasped at the sight that lay before him within the cavernous building.

It was raining inside, but instead of water dropping from the ceiling it was . . . molten metal. Just in front of Adam, searing syrupy sheets of yellow and orange fell from pots high in the ceiling, streamed across the floor in a river of fire and disappeared into huge charred drains. It was like some twisted homemade volcano. And it felt just as hot. Adam tried to wiggle his hands free so that he could wipe away the sweat that was building rapidly on his brow, but the creature pinned him tighter. Instead Adam watched the glow of the falling melted metal reflected in Fortescue's sunglasses. He had a satisfied half smile on his face. All was well in his domain.

Fortescue went over to a small box on the wall in the shadows. He opened it with a key, which he pulled from his pocket, to reveal another combination lock. He twirled the dial a few times and, after a flurry of thick spattering noises, the metal stopped falling. At such close range Adam couldn't help noticing that the creature's ears seemed to twitch in time to the clicking of the combination lock.

The river of hot metal was draining away quickly now, and Fortescue set off through the building, his footsteps echoing loudly on the still-steaming floor grilles. The creature loped after him with Adam.

"I'm guessing this is an art gallery and you specialize in very weird, very . . . dangerous modern art?" Adam said, trying to make light of the dreadful place.

"This used to be a factory," Fortescue said. "I had it converted."

"Into *what*?" Adam asked.

"A warning to unwelcome visitors," Fortescue replied.

They had safely reached the end of the building and now Fortescue opened another box hidden in the shadows and, like before, turned the dial on the lock back and forth. A rising, bubbling noise followed and within moments the deadly, sticky rain was falling once again, making an impassable barrier.

"All this to get rid of door-to-door salesmen!" Adam muttered in a bid to cheer himself up. But it was no good.

His spirits sank. How would Amy, Saul and Cress ever get through?

"And now it has the added bonus of keeping you from going astray," Fortescue said. And with that, he headed over to a small door and spun yet another combination lock on the wall next to it. He pushed open the door and strode forward into a forbidding darkness.

"Come along. Glory is a reward for the driven, not a trinket for the day-tripper," Fortescue said, removing his sunglasses and slipping them into a pocket.

Adam did not like the way things were going. Fortescue seemed even more unhinged than usual. And all this protection and secrecy—it had to be about a grander plan than just the "collecting" of spheres? The terrible second phase of the plan that the notebook hinted at, perhaps? Adam's mouth felt dry and he noticed he was shivering as the creature carried him onward.

As Adam's eyes became used to the darkness, he worked out that they were traveling along a series of narrow corridors. The odd lightbulb here and there provided just enough illumination to see the way. The corridors were leading downward. After what seemed like hours, Fortescue came to the end of a slightly wider corridor, pushed open a wooden door and stepped through.

The room beyond was vast. The creature, holding Adam, followed and kicked the door closed behind it. As it put him down, Adam looked around with awe. Compared to the grim dustiness outside and the crude defense mechanism above, this place had a charming splendor. The room was lined with enormous circular panels of colored glass and looked like a gigantic library—but there were no books, only hundreds and hundreds of shelves. Wooden ladders with green leather steps led up to higher walkways with brass handrails and yet more shelves. Most of the shelves above were empty, but the ones at ground level were full with . . . glowing talent spheres. The creature was transfixed by them—lost in a joyous trance as it loped from one to the next, caressing them gently hello again.

Adam went across to one of the shelves that had on it a small, bright red sphere with yellow speckles. Underneath it was a plaque which read, "Prof. Ernst Applebaum— Genius Scientist and Philosopher." Adam moved to the next shelf, which held a heavy-looking blue sphere with purple swirls moving on its surface. Underneath this one was a plaque that read, "Simone Florentino—Award-Winning Opera Singer." The next shelf was empty—but then the plaque below it caught Adam's eye. "Saul Shafer— Tracker Extraordinaire." Adam spun around to face Fortescue, who, following Adam's gaze, shrugged.

"Between Golden Harvest expeditions I bring the talent spheres I've collected back here for safekeeping. Saul's was the first!"

"But where is it?" Adam demanded.

"You should know." Fortescue flared his nostrils. "It was in the sack with the other spheres you so kindly redistributed. We took to taking Saul's sphere with us on our collecting trips. I thought it might be . . . useful, if any tracking of our next victim was required."

Adam was puzzled. *How* would they use it?

But before he could ask, Fortescue continued, "As you can see, I still have a long way to go." He stretched his arms up to indicate the seemingly endless empty shelves above. "And it's going to take even longer now, thanks to the spheres you just lost me." He was amused by Adam's horror-struck expression.

"You're going to fill this whole place with people's talent spheres?" Adam queried.

"That's part of my dream," Fortescue said mysteriously.

The creature had moved over to a large chair now and was perched on the back of it, staring at Adam with its hypnotic eyes.

"But . . ." Adam tried to collect his thoughts, tried to make sense of what he was seeing, "Why? And what then?"

"Come, let us talk over dinner," Fortescue said in his most charming manner.

CHAPTER TWENTY-SEVEN
TABLE MANNERS
. . . .

Argh, I've lost sight of it," Saul said as he peered into the distance. "The balloon must have landed somewhere behind that range of hills."

Amy banged the heels of her hands on the steering wheel with frustration. "Saul!" she said.

"Hey, I have the vision of a hawk, but even a hawk can't see *through* hills," Saul said.

"Well, ain't you a disappointment," Amy said, gently mocking.

"But the scent of the creature is still strong," Saul added. "I reckon if we turn left at this fork in the road, we'll still be heading in the right direction."

Amy floored the accelerator and swung the car off toward the distant shimmering hills that Saul was squinting at.

"Don't lose the scent, Saul. Keep sniffing," Cressida urged, leaning forward and patting Saul's shoulder.

After another couple of hours, the Silver Swift slowed to a halt and the cloud of dust the wheels had been kicking up settled. Ahead lay the towering redbrick wall and huge black iron gates.

"End of the line," Amy said, switching the mighty engine off. "But, you know, I'd be willing to bet that this is the kind of crummy joint Fortescue would call home."

Amy, Saul and Cressida peered through the massive iron gates. The air was thick with dust, which glowed gold in the fading light of the evening. They could see the tin shed and the balloon in the shape of a plus sign and the old factory building at the far end of the compound, but their attention was focused on the dozens of marching men in masks with painted smiles. Cressida noticed the spears they were carrying. The show of force made her blood run cold. Her brother was in there!

"What's all this for?" Cressida asked, her voice cracking with emotion.

"I guess it's Fortescue protecting his assets," Saul said. "He must keep the spheres he's collected so far here."

"How do we get to Adam?" Cressida wailed.

"Hey, let's not be getting any colorful ideas," Amy said. "Knowing Fortescue, those guards will be well paid to slice any intruders into a million pieces. I say we stay out here where the air is fresh and people have all their limbs."

Cressida turned on Amy suddenly, her eyes white-hot behind her spectacles.

"I've got a news flash for you, Amy: not everyone in

life can just swan about doing as they please without a thought for anyone else. My brother is in there and I'm not going to wait out here a moment longer than necessary! But you can go if you want."

Amy looked completely taken aback at this outburst, and Saul stepped in quickly, his hands raised as if to soothe Cressida.

"Hey, Cress, maybe these guards go home at the end of the day and we can sneak in then somehow," he said.

As if in response to Saul's suggestion, a bell rang and the guards stopped patrolling and filed away toward a small gate built into the wall on one side of the compound. Cressida felt a spark of hope, but it soon faded when another gate near the first one sprang open and dozens of identical guards stomped out into the compound and took up the same pa-trol patterns. Pale yellow lamps dotted around the top of the brick wall flickered into life and cast an eerie glow. Cressida gave a desperate sigh of frustration.

"The night shift," Saul said, resting a comforting hand on Cressida's shoulder.

Cressida watched the guards and thought hard. They all looked so similar and their vision was probably hindered by the crude masks.

"I'll be one of them," she said finally. Both Saul and Amy raised their eyebrows with surprise. Cressida turned to them, her eyes shining. "It's what Adam would do. Amy, I'm sure I saw some racing overalls in the Silver

Swift's trunk. They look a bit like the ones those guards are wearing."

Amy nodded.

"I'll do it," Saul said.

"Amy's overalls really wouldn't fit you, Saul," Cressida said with a smile.

She had a point. Amy went over to the trunk of the car and opened it. She pulled out a pair of overalls that *were* very much like the guards', except they were a slightly lighter gray. Amy ripped her name off the front and then tore the large number seven from the back. She gave them to Cressida, who took off her coat and stepped into the overalls, pulling them up over her trousers and sweater.

"You're smaller than they are. You'll stand out," Saul worried.

"So, I'll have to be a weedy guard. I can't think of a better plan. I have to get in there and find Adam," Cressida said. "Anyway, it's getting dark, which will help. Now, what to do about a mask?"

"The only metal we have is here," Saul said, pointing at the Silver Swift.

Amy scowled at Saul. Then she heaved a sigh, dropped to the ground and pulled herself under the car.

"Forgive me, baby," she muttered. There followed a metallic ripping noise. Amy emerged with a thin metal panel about the size of a large envelope. "Gift from the selfish lady," she said as she held it out to Cressida.

"Sorry, Amy, you know . . . for talking to you like that," Cressida said, taking the piece of metal with a bashful smile. "And thanks for this."

"Hey, it's only fitting that the Silver Swift's sump guard should be used as a guard disguise," Amy said with a shrug.

Cressida was grateful. She knew it had been a difficult thing for Amy to do. "Now, where can I get some paint around here?" Cressida asked.

Amy pulled a lipstick from her pocket. "Always gotta be prepared for those podium photo shoots."

By the time the mask was finished and tied around Cressida's head, she did resemble a Fortescue guard, though smaller, in a lighter uniform and with a lopsided mask. Amy reached into the trunk once again and pulled out a large monkey wrench. She gave it to Cressida.

"It's good and heavy. Crack a skull like a walnut," Amy said.

Saul frowned. He was watching all this with a growing feeling of helplessness. He was used to being the searcher, the fixer, the rescuer.

Cressida went over to the wall and started to haul herself up the ivy covering the crumbly brickwork.

"Tell me when it's clear to go over," she hissed back at Amy and Saul. She could hear the quiet fizzing of a lamp just above her. Her temples were buzzing with apprehension and her palms were sticky with fear. But she thought of Adam and her resolve returned. She would find him.

Through the gates, Amy and Saul watched the guards striding this way and that, and when they were sure there was nobody looking at Cressida's part of the wall, they nodded at her. Cressida heaved herself over and dropped down into the compound. Instantly, she started to march like the guards, taking a zigzag approach to the factory building. Amy and Saul watched her go, trying hard not to imagine what might happen should Cressida be discovered.

"That is one plucky girl," Saul said.

"Yep, she's a real eye-opener," Amy replied, her face reflecting a new solemn respect.

Fortescue, Adam and the creature had moved to a small but beautiful room off the library. The walls were covered in a dark green floral wallpaper, and copper vases full of dried flowers sat on low wooden shelves. Fortescue and Adam were seated at either end of a white cloth-covered rectangular table, and the creature sat rather uncomfortably midway between them. The soft glow of candlelight glittered off heavy silver cutlery. Adam noticed how strange the creature looked. Perhaps it felt safer or just more comfortable in Fortescue's domain, for now its hood and cloak were removed and Adam could see the creature clearly. It was such a mix of mismatching features. He marveled at its battle scars, peered at its peculiar blue leathery skin and shuddered at its fearsome teeth. It was far too big for the chair it was sitting on and it loomed over the table so that the candles lit it from underneath, giving it a terrible but somehow noble aspect. Its eyes shone with confusion as it peered at the cutlery on either side of its plate.

"Do your best," Fortescue said to the creature. "I've grown tired of you eating off my carpets."

Fortescue ladled some thick soup from a tureen into his bowl and then passed the ladle to the creature, who took it as though it were an item of abject mystery. With a clumsy movement it managed to slosh some soup into its dish, though most went over the tablecloth. Then, with a watchful eye on Fortescue, the creature picked up its spoon. Adam ladled himself some soup too, and he and Fortescue started to eat while the creature slurped, gargled and slopped.

"What did the factory make before you had it converted?" Adam asked. He felt uneasy being in this place, at this deranged dinner party, but his curiosity remained.

"Funnily enough, this," Fortescue replied, jabbing his spoon in the direction of his soup. "The Fortescue family grew turnips out there on the land we just walked across, and then they turned the turnips into turnip soup. In the factory they made tin cans to put it in. They called it Turnip Soup, Turnip Soup, Turnip Soup, because apparently it's 'three times as tasty,' whatever that means. Utterly disgusting, isn't it? So bland. Yet there are still several thousand cans to get through—don't want it going to waste."

The creature's spoon clattered against its fanglike teeth while Adam mulled this over.

"So, you didn't want to carry on the family business?" Adam asked.

"No, I didn't!" Fortescue barked ferociously. "I wanted a life of greatness."

The creature suddenly bit the end off its spoon and spat it into its bowl, sending a wave of soup onto the table. It pushed the bowl away and stared up at the ceiling. Adam watched it with fascination and then turned his attention back to Fortescue.

"And are those really your guards out there?" Adam asked.

"Such an ugly word." Fortescue winced.

"Why the masks with the painted smiles?"

"I like to know I'm surrounded by happy and admiring employees."

"Even if they're not?" Adam snapped.

Fortescue ignored this and pushed his own soup bowl to one side. He lifted a silver cover off a platter to reveal a huge chunk of meat loaf. Gingerly, he gave a large knife and fork to the creature. "Would you do us the honor of carving?"

The creature stood and leaned over the meat loaf. For a moment it was still and quiet, but then it attacked it like a lunatic. A few short seconds later it sat back down on its chair and dropped the carving knife and fork on the floor. Adam and Fortescue looked at the meat loaf, or what was left of it. It lay in tiny ribbons all over the table.

"Thank you," Fortescue said with a stiff cough. He lifted the ladle again and scooped up some meat loaf for Adam, then some for his talent thief and some for himself.

The creature, watching Fortescue for guidance, picked up the knife and fork that were on either side of its plate at the same time as Fortescue did. Copying Fortescue, it stabbed a piece of meat loaf with its fork and began to eat. Fortescue nodded with satisfaction.

"So . . . why are you two taking the talent spheres?" Adam asked.

Fortescue gave a satisfied smirk and wiped his mouth with a napkin. "Because I want to own all of the talent in the entire world."

"Yes, but *why*?" Adam tried again.

Fortescue let out a sigh. "You know at school there are bright children and children who are good at sports or art and even some that are good at everything?" Fortescue asked.

"Of course," Adam replied.

"Well, I was never good at anything," Fortescue said.

"My life story." Adam shrugged.

"But more than that, I was terrible at everything. I was small and plain. I had no grace or wit or skill. I did everything wrong. My classmates laughed at me and picked on me or, worse, simply ignored me. I was rich, blast it, they should have at least respected me," Fortescue growled, anger building in his voice. "And all I had to look forward to was a lifetime running a ridiculous soup factory! Until I found an old book of legends in my father's library. Now, soon," Fortescue went on, his eyes shining with a terrible glint, "I shall rob all the outstanding people. They shall be as dull and underwhelming as I was! And I will have the most beautiful, superior, coveted collection the world has ever known! Ha ha haaa . . ." The creature's ears twitched slightly and Fortescue quickly added, "Er, that is, *we* shall. My wonderful friend and I."

"But that's not all, is it?" Adam probed. The plan was already crazed and barbaric enough, but Adam knew that there was more to come. "In your notebook you said there was another phase, something to do with how the creature got out of the legendary crater . . ."

Fortescue let out a twisted, gloating laugh that echoed around the room. "And wouldn't you like to know the answer?"

How *did* the creature get out of the crater? Think! Adam told himself urgently. As he did so, a tiny spider dropped down in front of him and scurried across a landscape of shredded meat loaf before shooting over the edge of the table out of sight. Adam and the talent thief watched it go. There was something about the look in the creature's eye, something about the way the spider moved that made Adam think. He remembered the talent thief bolting from him on the roof of the Hotel Peritus . . . What if it was not the drainpipe it had climbed with such ease, but the wall itself . . . ? The truth hit Adam like a thunderbolt!

"Your pet doesn't just take talent spheres from others, it can use them itself, can't it?" Adam blurted. "What were the names of the other ancient creatures that got stuck in the crater? There was some sort of reptile and a . . . a lesser-bearded blue-all-over monkey—that's why Saul couldn't see the talent thief at first, in the jungle, because it took that monkey's sphere, and then somehow it made that talent its own."

It explained the talent thief's curious, disparate appearance too, its blue beard mismatched with lizardlike skin and claws, then a strong but gangly frame and limbs—the only thing that seemed to make sense about it were its glowing, hypnotic eyes and trilling sounds.

"And that's the answer to the question of how it got out of the crater," Adam went on. "There were bugs and spiders down there. Somehow, it must have used a spider's climbing talent to escape."

"Clever, clever, clever!" Fortescue cried, applauding with gusto. "Bravo! Top of the class! Yes!" Fortescue sniggered. "Nowadays my clever little creature has dozens of fine, tiny hooks on its palms, just like a spider."

Adam remembered the talent thief's almost sticky grip.

"You know, I believe at first it thought the spheres might serve as food, so it ate them. But instead, it found itself taking on the talents that the spheres represented." Fortescue lowered his voice. "I don't think it ever fully understood the implications of that. After it escaped the crater, it seems it preferred merely to collect them instead. More fool it . . ."

Suddenly, the second phase of Fortescue's plans unfolded in Adam's mind like a map being opened out to show strange far-flung places.

"You plan to take on the spheres you're stealing yourself!" he gasped.

"And I will become the most talented person the world has ever known. People will idolize me! I will hold this world in my hands the way the creature holds a talent sphere, fascinated by it but ultimately the master of it." Fortescue laughed hysterically. Then he stopped abruptly. "My experiments are already under way. It is not proving as easy as I had hoped, I admit. It seems we humans cannot simply eat a sphere in order to absorb its talent power. But I am confident I will get there, and I am prepared to keep trying until I succeed, whatever the consequences."

Adam felt sick.

The creature was only half listening to the conversation around it; most of its concentration was focused on trying to gather up the small ribbons of food with its clunky fork and knife. It growled to itself with frustration and jabbed at its plate. Adam watched it for a moment and then turned back to Fortescue again.

"You're ruining lives," he finally said.

"Funny thing is, I really don't care," Fortescue replied.

"And what about me?" Adam asked. His voice sounded small and lost.

"Well, you are an enigma. Talentless to talented,"

Fortescue replied, his brow now creased with bemusement. "We intend to find out how."

Adam suddenly felt very afraid and lonely. "You're not going to let me go, are you?" he asked.

Fortescue shook his head slowly. "And there are no irritating friends to save you now."

The creature let out a sudden cry of frustration and threw its fork across the room, where it stuck in the wall and quivered.

Adam gulped.

Fortescue turned to the creature. "For that, you get no ice cream."

CHAPTER TWENTY-EIGHT
A WHIRLWIND
OF ACTION

· · · · · · · · · · · · ·

After dinner, Adam was taken to a small, white-tiled room somewhere underneath the sphere library. To one side of the room he saw a large cage with matted straw in the bottom. Adam figured it must be the creature's bed when they were at home. Around the cage were dozens of glinting trophies and trinkets. The creature loped over to caress them, watching spellbound as the light reflected off the shiny metal surfaces. "Special gifts from one friend to another, aren't I good to you, Nipso?" Fortesecue said almost absently as he bustled about the lab.

In another corner of the room was a bench and a very odd-looking piece of apparatus abundant in brass fittings and masses of wires. And on the wall farthest from the door, what looked like a periscope hung down from the ceiling.

Fortescue beckoned the creature to him with a twitching finger. The creature put down the glittering necklace it was absorbed in and loped across the laboratory. "See if he's generated another sphere," Fortescue ordered. "If he's done it once, he might do it again."

Adam stepped back, but the creature was fast. It leaped toward him and held his shoulder with one claw while it hovered the other over Adam's head. Adam smelled the familiar musty smell, heard the gurgle and began to feel faint. But no sphere emerged. Fortescue's face dropped with disappointment.

"Hmm, I suppose we must work with what we have, then," Fortescue said. He turned to the bench where something was covered with a silk cloth. He removed the cloth to reveal a dimly glowing green sphere.

"Is that mine?" Adam asked.

"It *was* yours," Fortescue replied.

Adam sat down quietly and watched Fortescue examine his sphere under an old, rusty-looking microscope. The creature sat on the other side of the room, swinging between watching Adam with curiosity and gazing at the sphere protectively.

"Yes, this definitely doesn't seem to be the same as the other spheres," Fortescue said eventually.

"Well, I like to be different," Adam replied.

Fortescue sat back and pondered for a moment.

"Actually, all spheres are different, unique in their own way," he said. "In the past we have even taken lots of small spheres from the same person in one go. Those are the jackof-all-trades-type people, multitalented but not in a particularly thrilling way. Those spheres are of no use to me. But yours is different again. It's less flashy but it's robust. I like it." Fortescue looked at the creature. "Come here," he said, and the talent thief stood and strode over to Fortescue. Fortescue lifted the sphere and gave it to his minion. "What do you think?" he asked.

The creature wrapped its long claws around the sphere and closed its eyes. It let out a few swift grunts followed by a low howl. Fortescue cocked his head at the creature's ululations.

"It says it has strong energy," Fortescue said to Adam, "but it's made like a cloak, not buried like a diamond." Fortescue frowned. "Let me get this straight. The boy put together his own talent sphere. But how?" he asked, leaping to his feet and snatching back the sphere.

"Hey, careful," Adam urged.

Fortescue ignored him and took the sphere over to the bizarre device in the corner of the room. A small metal cage sat suspended in front of a complex diagram of the human brain. Wires ran from all the different chambers of the brain pictured to sockets on the cage. Fortescue placed the sphere into the cage.

"Most talent spheres operate on the same wavelength as the part of the brain that governs inspiration," Fortescue said. Adam got up and went over to the machine. "Let's see about yours," Fortescue added as he flipped a switch. With a droning noise the cage started to spin on its axis, and after a few seconds a part of the brain diagram lit up. Fortescue looked puzzled as he turned the machine off.

"What is it?" Adam asked with concern. "Am I some kind of weirdo?"

"Your sphere originates from the 'intention' part of your brain," Fortescue replied.

"Don't get it," Adam said.

Suddenly Fortescue slammed his fist down on a desk. Adam jumped and the creature flinched. "Then why don't *I* make talent spheres! I am a whirlwind of action!" Fortescue shot a finger at the creature. "Tell me!"

The creature slunk back from Fortescue's anger.

"Tell me!" Fortescue yelled.

The creature hesitated and, with reluctance, let out a series of timid mewing noises.

"What?" Fortescue barked. He thought hard. "My intentions are usually directed toward myself, not others? Is that what you are saying? Whereas this boy is always outward-looking and . . . noble?" Fortescue exclaimed. "Oh, please!"

The talent thief gave an apologetic little yelp.

"Be quiet. You talk too much," Fortescue snapped as he began to pace the room.

The creature fell silent and hung its head. But as Fortescue paced up and down, it seemed to Adam that, moment by moment, the madman's mood was shifting from disbelieving fury to sheer glee.

"Perhaps the boy has the greatest talent of all!" Fortescue finally announced with a triumphant tone. "He will be my most crucial acquisition yet!" He turned to Adam, his breathing becoming rapid. "When I find the way, I will take on *your* talent sphere first! I want the sheer determination you have, boy!" Fortescue clamped two fists to his own head and then fanned his fingers out wide. "It will make me unstoppable!" He started to laugh hysterically, then stopped suddenly. "Now, if your talent is governed by intent, rather than innate, I want to see if we can get you to produce another sphere for my collection in the meantime. Or two! Or three! Or four! Or five hundred! The more determination the better."

Adam did not like the sound of this. Fortesecue was babbling virtually incoherently now. Adam looked at the creature. It was sad and subdued. Maybe he was imagining it, but the creature seemed to be looking at Fortescue with a flurry of questions forming in its ancient eyes.

"There's much to do!" Fortescue exclaimed suddenly. He glanced at his watch. "But first I want to check all is ticking along quietly topside."

Fortescue went over to the periscope and pulled it down from the ceiling. He looked into the viewfinder and could see his guards marching as they should. He moved the periscope around, and something stopped him.

"What do we have here?" Fortescue said, concern creeping into his voice. He pushed the periscope back up out of the way. "Take the boy to a secure room and lock him in," Fortescue said to the creature. "I'll be back shortly."

With that, Fortescue almost ran out of the laboratory. He was going to see why there was a short guard in a non-standard uniform patrolling his grounds.

Cressida was doing her best to stride like a guard, but her knees felt weak and wobbly with fear. What would they do to her if her cover was blown? Her breathing sounded heavy and anxious inside the mask. And yet despite the trepidation she felt, her thoughts played on the strange journey her life had taken recently. What a long way she had traveled, both geographically and in experience. From a luxurious yet sad and dull life in Riverfork City to walking through dozens of dangerous-looking armed men in a bid to save her brother. She felt very unsure and afraid, and yet there was a spark of new life that had ignited within her. For once she was doing something positive, something with purpose. Going after Adam was waking her from a long and miserable trance, a trance she had fallen into the moment she heard her parents had fallen through the ice.

Despite feeling as though she stood out like a kitten in a snake pit, Cressida finally reached the factory building undiscovered. She saw the combination lock next to the door and cursed under her breath. There was no way she could stand here all night trying out different combinations. Suddenly Cressida heard someone on the other side of the door. Panic fluttered in her stomach. She looked around for somewhere to hide and decided her only chance was to duck down on the side of the building that lay in dark shadow.

Just as she disappeared from view, Fortescue stepped out of the door and scanned the compound. He scowled with annoyance. Perhaps he was being too jumpy. Security had become his main priority since he had started the Golden Harvest project. He knew only too well that, as he took more and more valuable talents, there was a greater risk that people might work out what he was doing and hunt him down. A scraping noise made him turn. He walked quietly along the front of the factory building, turned the corner with a sharp movement and peered into the shadows.

There were stacks of wooden crates piled up against the side of the building. They stretched away into the gloom. Fortescue made a mental note to put up more lights around the area as he crept between the crates, glancing this way and that. He heard a creak and turned to look at a larger crate nestled in the darkness. Cressida looked back at him from inside it, through a knothole. Her heart started to race. Do not come over here, she was thinking, please do not come over here! Fortescue approached the crate with stealthy footsteps. He put his fingers under the lid . . . but just as he was about to lift it, a rat scuttled out from behind the crate and chattered at him. Fortescue jumped back and let out a shuddery yelp. The rat must have made the noise. He hated rats. He spun on his heels to head back in. He had much to do. The short guard must have been employed by mistake. He would track him down in the morning and fire him. Fortescue marched away and turned the corner.

After a few seconds the crate lid moved to one side and Cressida stood up. She pushed her mask onto the top of her head and gave a sigh of relief. That had been close. Good thing Fortescue was such a coward! She looked down at the rat.

"Thanks," she said. The rat sniffed the bottom of the crate. "But you can go now. Go on. Shoo."

The rat scurried away, pausing for a moment to twitch its nose at a huge iron ring set in what looked like a very large wooden trapdoor. Cressida could see its massive iron hinges glinting in the gloom. But she had no time to ponder on this; instead she looked down at the contents of the crate she was standing in. It was half full with cans of soup. She picked one up and read the label.

Cressida put the can down and looked around at all the crates. Every one had the same labeling. She thought back to Fortescue's list in his notebook; for a moment there was definitely something niggling in her mind. But she couldn't sit and muse on it. She had to try to find a way into the building. She looked up and saw that crates were stacked all the way to the tiny windows high up on the forbidding structure at one end.

With quick, decisive moves Cressida heaved herself onto crate after crate. Eventually she reached the windows and she peered into the factory. The first thing that struck her was how huge it was—and then she noticed a tiny figure striding across the enormous floor space. It was Fortescue. She followed his progress all the way to the door at the far end and watched as he fiddled with something on the wall. Must be another lock, thought Cressida. Adam will be through there. Fortescue disappeared from view and then Cressida felt a deep rumbling course through the entire building. A sinister bubbling noise hit her ears, and with mounting horror she watched as vast amounts of glowing molten metal began to drop from the ceiling and flow across the factory floor. In the dark of night it blazed bright and hot.

Cressida tried to catch her breath. It was a terrifying sight. But, more important, it meant that there was no safe way to get to that door at the far end of the factory. Her spirits sank. She could think of nothing else to do but lay low for a while before returning to Amy and Saul and telling them of her grim discovery.

CHAPTER TWENTY-NINE
PREPARING THE SWIFT
· · · · · · · · · · ·

The creature held Adam close as it strode downward through dimly lit corridors. Adam was trying his hardest to get used to its unpleasant musty smell, but it was no good—he still wanted to gag. The creature was gurgling. It was a strange noise, throaty and wet. It was almost as though it was trying to comfort itself. A moment later, it pushed Adam into a small room.

"You do know what you're doing is wrong, don't you?" Adam asked Fortescue's minion.

The creature thought for a moment, a wave of conflicting emotions flowing across its face. But then its features hardened off and it closed the door and locked Adam in.

And so Adam waited. And waited. The room was basic with a bare stone floor, a table, a chair, a bed and one candle, which threw strange, juddering shadows up the walls.

There was no window. This room must be far underground, thought Adam. He lay down on the bed and tried to sleep, but a million thoughts were spinning through his head. He could also hear distant noises—clanging, scraping, raised voices. Fortescue and his beastly accomplice were certainly busy with some project.

Adam thought about the talent sphere that had emerged from him. So he wasn't so average after all! He had his own kind of talent, if not in the usual way. He had somehow made himself special. He liked this idea. It meant he could choose his own way through life, knowing that if he stuck to what he thought was the right thing to do, he would have what he needed to get by.

But none of this changed the fact that, right now, he was imprisoned in a small room in an old factory defended by boiling metal—with a loony on a terrible power trip and his accomplice. He thought of his sister and Saul and Amy. Would they try to rescue him and put a stop to Fortescue's evil plan? He hoped they would, but then, as he thought about how impossible it would be to do so, he decided it might be better if they just left him behind and went safely home. He felt no shame when tears came. His sobs echoed back at him from the gray walls.

Adam awoke with a start. He had fallen into a deep but troubled sleep, and now Fortescue and the creature were leaning over him. He could not tell how long he had been dozing. He stood up blearily.

"Check for talent," Fortescue said excitedly to his sidekick.

The creature hovered its hand over Adam's head and Adam felt momentarily woozy. But no sphere emerged. The creature hissed and shook its head.

"Right. Let's see if we can't *make* you generate more talent," Fortescue said. "If my little experiment works, we'll soon be extracting spheres from you by the dozen. . . ."

With that, Fortescue blindfolded Adam and pushed him out of the room. Adam was led along more winding passages until suddenly he got the feeling that he had entered a large space. The blindfold was taken off. Adam found himself alone and surrounded by the most complete darkness he had ever experienced. It was like floating in outer space—but there were no stars or planets here.

"Hello!" he called, and his voice echoed back at him, sharp and loud. He took a few steps forward and bumped into something like a cool, glass wall. What was going on? He felt along the wall and came to a corner. He turned and felt his way along another wall and then another and another. He seemed to be in a box made entirely of glass. Then, without warning, the darkness was replaced by a bright light. Adam staggered back. Moving pictures were starting to play on the surfaces all around him. Vivid and real, they overwhelmed his senses.

The cool light of dawn was spreading across the compound as Cressida drew near to the main gates and used the changeover of the guards as a chance to sneak back over the wall. With the fear of discovery still licking at her heels, Saul and Amy helped her to safety from the other side.

"Falling liquid metal?" Saul said with disbelief in his voice. "Are you kidding?"

Cressida shook her head, wincing slightly at the memory of it.

Saul and Amy grimaced at one another. Amy gazed through the gate at the factory building. She narrowed her eyes as if weighing something up. Cressida's bravery had triggered something inside Amy. "We'll punch through in the Silver Swift," Amy declared in a defiant tone. Saul and Cressida looked at her with surprise.

"Hey, let's not be getting any colorful ideas," Saul said.

Amy rewarded Saul's mockery with a dry smile. "I think we all know it's the only way."

Cressida took a deep breath and nodded. Saul glanced over at the car. It was strong and powerful. It could work. Possibly. He also gave a little nod.

"We're gonna have to put the snow chains on the tires. I'm guessing rubber and molten metal ain't exactly a winning combo," Amy said.

Moments later, Amy, Saul and Cressida were crouching in the dust, carefully fixing the chains to the tires. Amy and Cressida worked on the driver's side of the car while Saul did the other. Amy called across to him.

"How you doing over there, Saul, honey?"

"Okay, except I think my chains were made for much smaller wheels."

"Well, you'll just have to use those strong shepherding arms to stretch them, then, won't you?"

Saul grinned broadly. He thought about Amy as he worked. He had never met anyone like her. She was stubborn and strong-willed and sometimes very selfish. But she was a breath of fresh air too, and Saul knew only too well that there was nothing a shepherd liked more than fresh air. And she had called him "honey." Nobody had ever called him that before. Whatever was about to happen in the hours to come, he was glad he had met her.

Amy felt sadness as she attached the chains to her car. It was ironic that they had just driven across hundreds of miles of icy, snowy landscape and had not once needed the snow chains, and now they were putting them on to drive across hot, molten metal. She admitted to herself that the Silver Swift was not really built for this, but her mind was now made up to help Adam.

"I thought about what you said," Amy remarked, looking across at Cressida. "Sad old lady surrounded by nothing but trophies and stale memories."

Cressida was embarrassed. She felt her cheeks grow warm. "I only said that so you would help—"

"No, you were right," Amy interrupted. "It happened to my ma. She was a star rodeo rider. She left my pappy and me to go touring for years with some half-baked show.

Seems she was happier entertaining kids she didn't know than looking after me. When she finally came home, my pappy told her he didn't want her. And she seemed like a stranger to me as well. So she went away again. Got herself a lonely little shack on some windswept cliff somewhere. I don't want to be like her."

"You're not." Cressida smiled. "My mother and father were always away a lot too," she added. "But when they *were* home, they were lots of fun."

"Were?" Amy asked.

"They passed away. It was an accident," Cressida said quietly.

Amy shuffled awkwardly. She was not used to dealing with the knotted tumble of other people's emotions.

"I'm, er, sorry to hear that," she said eventually, and was surprised to notice the depth of sympathy she felt.

When the tires were prepared, Amy, Saul and Cressida took refuge from the baking midday sun inside the car. Saul and Amy sat together in the front while Cressida lounged sideways in the back.

"We'll go in tonight. When the guards change," Amy said, sharing some candies (in official Silver Swift wrappers) around.

The three of them tried to keep their spirits up by singing silly songs. But so wonderful was Cressida's voice that even the most frivolous song sounded like a concerto performance, and Saul and Amy were soon stunned into a blissful silence, listening and allowing their thoughts to drift into dreamy places far removed from the reality of the near-impossible task before them. But then the sun was retreating behind far-flung hills, and like a theater spotlight being switched off, Cressida saw it as her cue to cease singing. A charged silence swept over them all.

CHAPTER THIRTY

THE EMOTION OF MOTION

· · · · · · · · · · · · · ·

Adam was surrounded by moving pictures. And the pictures were so vibrant and looked so real that before long he had totally forgotten he was inside a glass box. An elderly man with a long gray beard, wearing a thick woolen explorer's coat, was walking backward in front of Adam with a look of sheer terror on his face. Adam turned to see on the screen behind him a tiger approaching, its eyes gleaming, fangs wet with saliva. The old man tripped on a tree root and fell with a dusty thud. The tiger moved in closer.

"Get up!" Adam called.

But the old man just pushed himself away weakly on his elbows. The tiger licked its lips and crept closer still. Adam's heart was pounding.

"Shoo! Go away!" Adam waved at the big cat—though, of course, it could not see him. Adam did not know what to do. Was it better to pretend you were dead? No, that was bears. With tigers it was just better to get away.

"Please get up," Adam pleaded with the old man.

But with a deep, satisfied growl the tiger lunged first. Adam threw himself between the man and the tiger and . . . the pictures froze, then faded to black. Adam lay on the floor, out of breath and bewildered.

"What's going on?" he called into the darkness.

"You enjoying my little home movies?" Fortescue's voice boomed out of nowhere. "That was the beginning of phase two of my grand plan—we tried putting a brilliant young runner's talent sphere into an old man. We could not get it into his head, so we tucked it into his coat pocket, and as you can see . . . it didn't work. We have come some way since then, though, and I will succeed with a human one day, and when I do, every talent in the world will be my own. MINE!"

Adam ran forward, slammed into the glass wall and crumpled to the floor.

"Let me out," he cried as he scrambled to his feet.

"I'm afraid not. We have other delights to show you."

Adam watched as the moving pictures began playing again. This time two trapeze artists were flying through thin air. The red and white stripes of a fairground tent were dimly visible behind them. Adam felt a bit queasy: the surrounding darkness made him feel as if he were hovering alongside the acrobats in the air.

"This was one of my greatest extractions!" Fortescue's voice boomed again.

Then another voice called out, and it seemed to come from far below Adam. It must be the ringmaster, Adam thought.

"And now, the most talented trapeze artist ever, the Great Paulo Zorgana, will attempt the triple somersault with a twist! Can it be done? Should it even be attempted? Why, I tried to talk Zorgana out of it, but he demanded to be allowed to try! Can he succeed where countless others have tried and failed? Let us find out, ladies and gentlemen! Watch if you dare!"

Adam told himself this was just a recording—it had already happened, there was nothing he could do, he should just look away—but it was so real all around him, he found himself swept up in the excitement instead as he watched the two trapeze artists swing to and fro. The catcher was hanging down from his bar by his legs, muscled arms outstretched, loose and supple. The Great Paulo Zorgana was swinging back and forth, faster and faster, his strong arms easily supporting his weight, his stomach muscles tense.

But then Adam noticed something familiar moving up above. It was sliding down one of Zorgana's trapeze ropes at tremendous speed. Adam stepped forward.

"No!" he called. His fingers clutched in vain at the images in front of him.

The creature stopped just above Zorgana and its long

claws extended. In a matter of moments Zorgana's copper-colored talent sphere was in the talent thief's caressing grasp. It scuttled back up the rope just as Zorgana let go of the trapeze.

There were no somersaults. Just an ugly, twisted fall down into darkness. Adam leaped forward once more, trying to reach for the man's hands . . . and the pictures faded away. Adam covered his eyes.

"Why are you doing this?" he whispered. He tried to peer into the darkness but could see nothing.

"Every time you reach out to help these people, you are generating talent energy," Fortescue replied. "A few more of my movies and we should have another sphere for my collection."

Fortescue's monstrous behavior lit a sudden fireball of fury in Adam's belly.

"This is wrong!" Adam cried. "Everything you do is wrong!"

"Silence!" Fortescue shouted. "Life isn't about 'right' and 'wrong.' "

"That's exactly what it's about," Adam muttered to himself, "if you can tell the difference."

Far above, in the makeshift control room that Fortescue had had built for his glass box of moving pictures, the creature stood silently next to Fortescue, looking down at Adam. The boy seemed very small and scared. He was trapped and alone. And yet he still stood his ground. In the jungle, he would be respected. The creature turned to Fortescue. The veins were standing out on the man's neck, his usually groomed red and gray hair fell about his face wildly and his white mustache bristled over a trembling sneer. He seemed to be enjoying himself. The creature did not know what its own feelings were exactly, but they did not feel good. It shuffled uneasily and, for a tiny measure of comfort, clutched at the favorite glittering necklace it had put on only an hour or so before.

It was pouring with rain, and deep, bone-shaking thunder was rumbling across the sky. The playful shower that had started ten minutes earlier had quickly turned into a brooding torrent of noise and downpour. Cressida turned up the collar on her coat and lowered the sack full of talent spheres down into the hole she had dug. Quickly she pushed the loose earth back into the hole before it turned to mud. They had all decided it was a good idea to leave the talents here, to be collected when they had rescued Adam. *When* they rescued Adam, not *if*.

Stabbing rain lashed down violently into the large puddles that had already formed around the Silver Swift. The dark, swirling clouds were reflected eerily in her shiny paintwork. Amy and Saul were on either side of the car, tying blankets to the roof with string.

"The rain is a stroke of luck, you know," Amy called across to Saul. "Wet blankets will give us greater protection."

Cressida splashed her way back to the car. "Last chance,

Amy. I really don't want you to feel like you have to do this," Cressida said, wiping water droplets from her spectacles.

"What kind of competitor would I be if I turned down a challenge like this?" Amy replied.

Cressida switched her gaze to Saul. Her questioning expression offered him a guilt-free get-out clause too.

"Get in," Saul said, by way of answer.

Cressida stooped and clambered into the backseat. Amy and Saul looked at each other over the now-soaking wet blankets.

"This your idea of showing a lady a good time?" Amy asked, raising her voice over a long and booming thunderclap.

"I didn't think you'd go for moonlight and dancing."

Amy laughed as they both got into the car. She tied her sopping-wet hair back into a ponytail and pulled on her racing gauntlets. Saul wiped his sticky palms on his woolen trousers and tried to ignore the uneasy fluttering that was building in his gut. Cressida attempted to block out thoughts of all the myriad things that could go wrong with this shaky plan and focused on Adam.

"We just wait for the green light now," Amy said, rattling her fingertips impatiently on the steering wheel.

The main gates were a mere dozen car lengths away. The only noises were their breathing, the rain pattering sharply on the hood of the car and the odd grumbling bellow from the broiling, tempestuous clouds above.

Then it came. The distant bell that signaled the guards

to swap. Amy waited a few seconds for the sinister men to begin their march over toward the exit on the far side of the compound, and then she fired up the engine. The Silver Swift growled into life.

"Hold on to your magnetos," Amy said quietly.

With a vengeful snarl the car leaped forward, throwing up mud as the wheels fought for meaningful traction. It hit the double gates with such force that they flew open, one of the gates actually breaking free from its rusty hinges and landing heavily on the wet ground. Amy increased speed as they crossed the compound. Guards, hearing the roar of the car, turned from their positions in line to exit the compound and started to race back toward the Silver Swift.

"We've got a fan club," Saul said, glancing sideways at the hordes of painted smiles rushing at them.

Amy grunted in reply and flipped the overdrive switch. The car wailed with raw power and Saul, Cressida and Amy were thrown back in their seats by the force of the acceleration.

"We need the extra juice to bust through those doors, anyway," Amy said.

The guards were throwing their spears now. A couple glanced off the car door and left large dents. Cressida jumped at the noise of the impact. Amy winced. But she had no time to dwell on the decorative state of her car because they were fast approaching the factory doors. Amy pushed her foot down harder on the accelerator. Her mouth felt dry, but her reflexes were sharp. Being totally absorbed in the task ahead was keeping fear at bay. Then the Silver Swift hit the doors with the force of a runaway train.

The doors splintered under the impact and the car shot through into the cavernous space beyond. And in that moment, Amy realized the full enormity of Fortescue's defenses—they were faced with falling sheets of boiling-hot metal and a ponderous shifting river of flame. Amy felt her foot lifting from the accelerator. Was there still time to stop? But she rapidly quashed this momentary dalliance with failure. In all the races she had taken part in, she had never once tap-danced on the brake pedal to the tune of fear. It was doubtful they would get through, but her courage and resolve were absolute. She rammed her foot down on the accelerator again. The car careered headlong into the searing hot rain and fiery river of molten metal.

CHAPTER THIRTY-ONE
SEARING HEAT
· · · · · · · · · · · · ·

The speed of the Silver Swift was so great that it thundered halfway across the gluey orange and red liquid metal with little trouble. The snow chains did their job well, separating the tires from the hot substance beneath them. But then the treacle-like consistency of the glutinous metal began to take hold of the tires and the car was soon losing speed with a spine-chilling finality. Eventually, with a sickening squelching noise, the Silver Swift ground to a juddering halt.

It was then that Saul, Amy and Cressida really began to feel the cruel fingers of fear grip their hearts. A steady stream of hot gloop fell onto the car. Where it struck the wet blankets with an angry hiss it solidified into random splatters of dull gray metal. But the scalding rain kept falling. Amy, Cressida and Saul watched it hit the hood and start to burn slowly through it. They were all painfully aware that the same thing was happening on the roof above them. Amy changed into first gear and revved the engine, but the wheels churned on the spot, throwing up fountains of white sparks.

"Well, this wasn't the plan, now was it?" Amy said, her eyes glistening and her voice catching in her throat. She applied her foot to the gas once more and twisted her hands on the steering wheel with sheer frustration.

Saul looked at her with tenderness. It touched him to see her falter and reveal a soft vulnerability beneath her brash and glossy surface.

"Maybe there's still a way through this," he said. But he didn't really believe it.

The chains on the tires were melting to nothing, and now the rubber was beginning to blister and pop. Cressida looked up—the inside of the roof was red-hot, and little drops of scalding metal were dropping down inside the car. She scooted to one side as a piece the size of a golf ball fell and burned through the seat.

"It's coming in," she said quietly, her heart thumping.

The heat inside the Silver Swift was rapidly becoming unbearable. Saul let out a yelp and quickly shrugged out of his coat as a few drops of melted metal went through it. Suddenly Amy sat bolt upright, as though hope itself had rapped her firmly on the knuckles.

"Hot apple pie! There *may* be a way through," she said, and she stared at the dashboard—at a small red button under a hinged glass panel with the word DANGER above it.

"Sorensen's folly is only to be used in the most crazy, hazardous, no-other-option, toe-curling type event," Amy said as she flipped the glass panel up and hovered her hand over the button.

"I think we can safely say we're there," Cressida said, scooting to one side again to dodge another falling molten blob.

"Hank Sorensen built a gas-propellant system into the chassis for the ultimate high-speed thrill," Amy said.

"Hit it! Let's get out of here!" Saul said.

"It's really not stable, you know, not at all," Amy replied.

"Who cares?!" Saul said, beads of sweat rolling down his forehead and dripping into his eyes.

"Once I hit this button, I'll have no control over the car. It'll take off like a box of fireworks," Amy said.

Saul looked at her with a tender patience as the white-hot roof drooped down to within a hairsbreadth of his head.

"Press the button, Amy," he said.

Amy hit the red button.

The car shot ahead with a blistering surge of speed. Long, flickering flames emerged from the exhaust pipe. The force was so great that the wheels barely touched the searing gloop beneath them. The Silver Swift swept across the remainder of the deadly floor space with an earsplitting whine, shuddering and flicking from side to side as it went. Amy, Saul and Cressida were being shaken like beans in a can.

And then, with a gut-wrenching thud and a jarring twisting of metal, the car slammed into the far wall.

Saul opened his eyes with a groan. His knee was throbbing and he felt decidedly dizzy. He sat up and looked around. They were well clear of the gluey metal. In fact, half of the car was buried in the end wall, pieces of red brick scattered all around. Cressida sat up and rubbed her shoulder.

"I think my innards are all upside down," she spluttered.

"Me too," Saul replied. He looked down to see that his favorite shepherd's crook was broken in two. He felt a momentary twinge of sadness, but then he glanced across at Amy, who was lying still and quiet. A cut on her forehead was bleeding. A bolt of panic shot through Saul's chest.

"Amy?" he said, touching her shoulder. "Amy?" he repeated. How much damage would this madman and his strange aide be responsible for before they could put a stop to him? Suddenly Saul's fury knew no bounds.

"Amy?" he urged for the third time, his fingers digging into her shoulder.

With a soft grunt, Amy moved. Slowly she pushed herself upright and opened her eyes.

"Well, whaddya know, the red button actually works." She put a hand to the cut on her forehead and winced.

Relief swept over Saul like a tidal wave.

Cressida let out a long tremulous breath. "You had us worried."

"Ah, just taking a nap," Amy replied, with a well-intended flourish of her hand that ended in a twinge of pain and a plaintive yelp.

The three of them kicked their way clear of the car and Amy surveyed the wreckage. Her car hardly looked like a car anymore. The trunk was peppered with holes, the roof had caved in, the wheels were buckled, the tires ripped to shreds and the chassis was bent into an S shape. What lay buried in the wall looked even worse.

"She ain't gonna be patched up this time," Amy acknowledged, dusting herself down.

"You all right?" Saul asked.

"Yep, actually," Amy said, sounding surprisingly bright. "It was only a machine. A *great* machine, but a machine nonetheless. Let's get on, find Adam."

"Argh, there's another combination lock," Cressida said, smacking the palm of her hand next to the dial beside the door. But just as she finished speaking, a large section of wall that had been shattered by the impact of the Silver Swift fell away, revealing a corridor beyond. The car slumped down on its chassis a fraction farther as though it were pointing the way.

"Looks as though the Silver Swift wants us to gate-crash," Saul said, pushing his way through the hole in the wall. Amy and Cressida followed.

"Is it just me or do you two feel hopelessly lost as well?" Amy asked as they wandered down yet another dimly lit corridor. Her voice echoed along the metal walls. Thick iron girders crossed the ceiling at regular intervals, giving the corridors a tunnel-like feeling.

"Now that you mention it, I think I've seen that girder before," Saul said, squinting into the gloom above. "There's a good chance we're going around in circles."

Amy rolled her eyes and Cressida sighed with frustration.

"Some rescue party," Cressida mumbled. Her face looked tired and drawn. The longer it took to find Adam, the more worried about him she became. The wild and deadly defense system had convinced her, beyond any shadow of a doubt, that Fortescue was completely deranged.

"Could you track Adam like a sheep, maybe?" Amy asked Saul.

"Not easily. He's not woolly enough."

Amy and Cressida both shot Saul a look that told him to leave out the lame jokes. He gave an apologetic grimace, then closed his eyes and started to sniff the air.

"There are so many strange odors down here," he said. "The creature's scent is strong, and there's the smell of wet earth and Fortescue's rather pungent aftershave." Saul opened his eyes and looked at Amy and Cressida. He shrugged. "Maybe if I had something of Adam's I'd fair better, but . . ."

A thought struck Cressida. She put her hand in her trouser pocket and pulled out a handkerchief.

"Any good?" Cressida asked in a hopeful tone. "This belongs to him."

Saul took it and breathed in the aroma. He handed the handkerchief back to Cressida and then sniffed the air again, his nostrils twitching.

"Hmm, there's the faintest hint," he whispered and turned. "This way."

Saul's expert tracking took them on a tour of Adam's journey through Fortescue's underground world. They marveled at the huge library.

"Some of these spheres are achingly beautiful," Cressida said as she peered at Ernst Applebaum's talent sphere.

But when they came to the tiny room that Adam had been kept in, the tangled bedclothes and general squalor were too much for Cressida.

"Adam!" she called, turning on the spot, the tears starting to roll down her cheeks. "Can you hear me?"

"Hey, hey," Saul said. "I can still smell him. He's here, alive. Somewhere."

Amy grasped Cressida's hand and led her swiftly out of the room, following Saul, who had now quickened his pace.

He led Amy and Cressida down dark, steeply sloping corridors until finally they came to a pair of large metal double doors. Cressida pressed her ear to one of them.

"I can hear something—music maybe," she said quietly, stepping back from the door.

"Okay, so what's the plan, folks?" Amy asked.

Saul took a deep breath. Plans were all very well. Sometimes they were even useful. But in all his years of pulling sheep from ditches and hedges, he had never needed anything other than the strong desire to rescue what needed rescuing. He took another deep breath. The boy was definitely on the other side of these doors.

"Let's just get him out," he said.

Amy and Cressida were surprised at this direct approach, but they were too tired to object. In fact, as they watched Saul step back and kick the doors open, they warmed to the idea. All three of them barged through.

It was dark in the room beyond, but as their eyes became used to it, they could see Fortescue in a booth high up on the far side. The room was vast and sprawling and most of it was lost in gloom. However, in the center Saul, Amy and Cressida could just make out a number of film projectors surrounding a glass box—and inside the box was Adam. Squatting on top of it, claw extending down through a hole, was the creature, a pile of shimmering green spheres similar to the one that had been taken from Adam in the Fortissimo house beside it. Cressida gasped, her hand shooting up to her mouth with horror—poor Adam.

Moving pictures of a ballet dancer were flickering across the four glass walls and music was playing. From Cressida's perspective, the pictures were stretched and distorted, but she was sure that for Adam they looked very real.

He was waving frantically at the dancer, trying to warn her of the celluloid creature that was approaching slowly behind her. Cressida could not bear to see her brother trapped and confused like this.

"Stop it!" she shouted.

Adam stopped in his tracks and turned to try to locate the source of the voice.

His senses were filled with the vibrant sights and sounds of the ballet and fear for the ballerina. He had to reach her . . . he knew he was too late . . . but so many people were being hurt and attacked; he couldn't help feeling despair for them, he couldn't stop trying to help . . . he was so tired, so dizzy and drained, but he could not rest . . .

But now, above and beyond that, he could have sworn he heard his sister.

"Cress?" he muttered. "Is that you?"

Fortescue swore under his breath and flipped a speaker switch on the control panel.

"This is a private screening," he said with a grimace. "Don't be forming any outlandish ideas. The glass box is unbreakable. Full marks for getting in here, though. Let's hope my defense adviser knows how to defend himself."

"Cress, you shouldn't have come," Adam yelled. He could not see Cressida, but now he knew for sure she was there.

"My motivational vignettes are working so well, I'm really not in the market for interruptions," Fortescue snarled with irritation. He twisted a dial and a spotlight came on and swiveled to light up the creature. It shrunk back at the glare. "Round those three up and lock them up," he barked, "and eat the key."

The creature hesitated momentarily.

"Do it!" Fortescue yelled.

The cowed talent thief leaped off the glass box and loped across the shadowy floor toward Cressida, Amy and Saul. With the flicker of the projector light illuminating its curious blue skin and long, sinewy limbs, it looked even more eerie and strange than usual. But then it stopped in its tracks.

Cressida had started to sing.

CHAPTER THIRTY-TWO
PITCH-PERFECT
· · · · · · · · · · · · ·

Her voice sounded powerful yet tender, and the song was one of freedom and joy. Adam could not see her and he wondered what she was doing, but he welcomed the sound of her singing voice. It swirled around him and infused hope back into his heart.

The creature turned and looked up at Fortescue, whose teeth were gritted underneath his neat white mustache. He gestured violently for the creature to move in on Cressida, but it stood still, its ears twitching in time with her song.

Then, with amazing control, Cressida pushed the song up an octave. Fortescue, irate now, barged his way out of the control booth and descended the stairs rapidly.

"I'm really not in the mood for a musical interlude. Take her sphere!" he snapped, but the creature continued to ignore him.

And Cressida pushed her voice higher again. Saul and

Amy had to cover their ears even as they gazed at Cressida—admiring but bemused. As Cressida sang higher still, Adam, inside the glass box, also covered his ears. Then Fortescue and even the creature shrank back, and the creature wrapped its arms around its head. Breathing deeply, Cressida pushed her voice even higher so the sound she was producing was as loud and as shrill and as piercing as she could make it. Just as she was about to run out of breath, the very thing she had hoped for happened . . .

The glass box shattered into a million pieces. Tiny shards of glass exploded outward, pattering down onto the black floor with a sharp sustained tinkling. Adam stood stunned, but free.

Saul and Amy lowered their hands in unison and gawped with amazement.

"Boy, can that girl sing," Amy said.

"And I used to think music was boring," Saul added, hoping the ringing in his ears would stop soon.

"No, no, no!" Fortescue howled.

Adam picked his way carefully through the broken glass toward Cressida.

"So you got your talent back, then," he said.

Cressida hugged him. Adam raised his eyebrows with surprise but returned the hug.

"And I'm glad to have it back," Cressida said, her voice thick with emotion. She paused. "I'm sorry I wasn't nicer, but I'm better now."

"Enough! Family reunions fill me with such revulsion,"

Fortescue said, stepping closer to the creature. He had the uneasy feeling that his thunder was being stolen. He had to take back control. "Lock all four of them up until we can rebuild the glass box," he snapped. The creature hovered. "Now! I am not in the mood for negotiation! *I* am your friend, am I not? You must do as I ask . . . Nipso."

At the sound of its name, the creature gave a low growl of recognition and loped menacingly closer to Cressida, Adam, Saul and Amy. They all knew that although there were four of them and only one creature, it could easily overpower them and steal their spheres again. Saul and Amy swapped melancholy glances. They had come so far. Were they really going to rot away in a small underground room? Saul got ready to challenge the creature anyway.

"No, don't hurt it!" Cressida put her hand on a stunned Saul's arm. Something had sparked again in Cressida's mind like a match striking. "That name, did Fortescue give you that?" She spoke directly to the creature. It seemed to nod.

"See," Fortescue leered smugly, "I am its one true friend—I am even the one that named it."

"And what an effort you went to, Fortescue," Cressida snapped back. "Now, let me see, my guess is that soon after you found the talent thief, it looked at you and Saul talking, calling each other by name, and it thought: I wonder what my name is, who I am. It's understandable that after hundreds of years on its own it wanted a friend and a name." Cressida glanced kindly at the creature as she spoke. "But instead of honoring this need with anything resembling an effort, you lit on the first thing you saw and made that its name—Nipso. It's not even a proper word, never mind a name. In fact, it's off one of your soup crates, isn't it?! The end of *turnip* and the beginning of *soup*."

"A soup you find disgusting," Adam added.

The creature's ears twitched—it took a confused step back toward Fortescue.

"But what about all the wonderful presents I've given you, Ni . . . er, dear friend," Fortescue yelped. "Don't listen to them, listen to me!"

Even as the creature stopped again and turned back toward Adam and Cressida and their two friends, something it was wearing around its neck gave Cressida another idea. It was her silver necklace!

Gently, she reached out and plucked at the charm, resting incongruously against the talent thief's blue body. "Was this a present from your *friend* Fortescue?" she asked. "Is that what all your glittery trinkets and trophies are?"

The creature paused, touching a tentative claw to the necklace and, momentarily, Cressida's hand, still resting there.

"I'm sorry. None of those were picked especially for you either. Fortescue didn't even pay for them; he stole them—off the people you took talent spheres from when you were on the road."

Fortescue bristled uncomfortably at this revelation.

"You love beautiful things, don't you?" Cressida went on, looking deep into the talent thief's ancient eyes and smiling. "And Fortescue has exploited that."

Fortescue glowered at Cressida, one brown eye, one blue, as the creature turned his way with hurt and confusion evident in its wild features.

"What are you trying to do?" he asked simply.

"I just want to get us all safely out of here," Cressida replied.

"I'm not letting the boy go," Fortescue said. Now he flicked his attention back to the creature. "The world is a cruel place. Other people would put you in a cage, or on a stage, even kill you to find out what makes you tick. That's why I gave you your beautiful cloak, to keep you safe from prying eyes. Can't you see how fortunate you are to be with me, protected yet given every opportunity to collect the spheres you love so much?"

The creature turned again and took a hesitant step back in Cressida's direction.

"You gave it that cloak so you could keep the creature's existence secret—nothing more," Cressida almost shouted. "It's so essential to your evil plans, what else could you do? You've been misleading it all along. There are good people in the world who wouldn't dream of trapping such a wise and wonderful being, whatever you say." Saul found himself looking sheepishly at the floor as Cressida said this. "The simple fact is, the creature has a respect for life that you do not." Cressida glared at Fortescue. "Something so moved by beauty, so in tune with the life around it and so longing for friendship must have that, at least. And that is the wedge that will drive you apart."

"That's why it felt guilty when it took Cressida's talent," Adam piped up. "I'm sure it did."

"And it warned Cressida about the burning of my house," Saul added.

Fortescue shot a furious look at the creature as it squatted down and began to make a low, anxious burbling sound. It flicked its troubled, muddled gaze from Cressida to Fortescue and back.

"It's probably figuring out for itself right now that you are a rather ghastly little man with very poorly judged facial hair," Amy said, happy to have her own opportunity to put this obnoxious person in his place.

Fortescue scowled at the confused creature. He was growing tired of this stalemate. He took a deep breath.

"Enough!" he said firmly. "I won't ask again—capture these dangerous people. They are threatening our wonderful Golden Harvest plans! We are the same, you and I; we want the same things. You must stay with me." But there was a hollow ring of desperation in his voice.

"The irony is that once your plan is truly complete, Fortescue," Adam said, stepping up beside his sister, "your talent-sphere collection won't be there for the creature to enjoy anymore, anyway. It will be inside an all-powerful you instead. What are you going to do with the talent thief then?"

Nobody missed the guilty expression that flashed across Fortescue's face before he had a chance to hide it.

Cressida spoke quickly to the creature now. "You two

aren't the same, you're not! The beautiful talent spheres that you care for so much mean nothing to Fortescue beyond the power that they represent. The same goes for your friendship. I know what it's like to feel lonely and different. But a real friend doesn't lie to you, doesn't try to label or change you, or use you, or even expect anything from you." She glanced at Adam with a smile before looking back at the creature. "Fortescue is only pretending to be your friend so that you'll do what he needs you to do—what he isn't capable of doing himself."

The creature gave a loud, throaty growl and rose suddenly to its full height once more. Cressida's words had finally convinced it—Fortescue was no friend!

Fortescue shrank back as the towering talent thief turned toward him, but Cressida stepped in front of it mid-stride. The others watched her with surprise.

"Will you help us get out of here?" she asked simply.

The creature stared at Cressida—in its dark universe, it seemed another spark of light had appeared. There was a truth that hung, newly recognized, in the space between them. After only a moment, the talent thief murmured a deep, resounding consent. And just like that, it spun on its heels, fanning out its long arms in a protective way, and loped toward the doors. Saul, Amy, Cressida and Adam walked ahead of it.

Fortescue took a few angry steps forward. "Stop! You belong to me! Hear me!" There was panic in his voice.

But the talent thief only growled as it ushered Cressida,

Adam, Saul and Amy into the corridor and began the long, twisting journey up to ground level.

"Even if it wants to help you escape, it can't," Fortescue yelled up the corridor after them. "How will it get you past my defenses, eh?!"

As soon as they were out of sight, Fortescue flung himself at the wall and flipped a switch on a speaker box. A public-address system let out a high-pitched whine in the compound above. The guards, who had been in a state of confusion since trying to stop the Silver Swift, turned their painted smiles to the speakers mounted on the walls of the old factory building.

Fortescue's voice boomed out. "Would all groundsmen watch the factory doors. If anyone tries to escape, use whatever force necessary to detain them."

The creature's helping them was a surprise to everyone except Cressida. They had thought it was cruel and ruthless, a savage thief, a clone of Fortescue. But now they could see that the creature, who seemed wise in some ways yet naive in others, had been hoodwinked by Fortescue. Adam felt proud of Cressida for realizing this. It just might save them.

Adam, Cressida, Saul and Amy stepped through the hole in the wall and took in the shimmering, blazing gloop again. The Silver Swift still lay there, broken yet heroic. Saul and Amy swapped despairing glances.

"Looks like we're stuck in the pits," Amy said.

But the creature ducked through the hole and walked straight over to the box containing the combination lock to turn the defense system off. It ripped the box open and put its long fingers on the combination dial. Adam remembered back to how the creature's ears had twitched in time to the clicking and clacking of the dial. Sure enough, it spun the dial deftly backward and forward. Within moments the folds of silken death had stopped falling and drained away.

The creature picked up Cressida and Adam and began to sprint across the factory floor.

"Well, this is unusual. I haven't been carried since I was three," Cressida said, trying to ignore the overpowering smell.

"Actually, I'm getting used to it," Adam replied.

The creature's bare feet made rapid slapping noises on the vast metal floor. Saul and Amy did their best to keep up.

Ahead, dozens of sinister painted smiles were waiting for them, hovering like ghouls by the shattered double doors. Adam shuddered. How would the creature deal with them?

CHAPTER THIRTY-THREE
THE ENAMEL ABYSS

· · · · · · · · · · · · ·

The creature hit the gathered guards like a battering ram, with a fearsome, earsplitting, gargle-like yell. Some of the guards backed away just in time, while others were physically scattered left and right, landing with winded grunts on wet mud. As Saul and Amy emerged from the factory close behind the talent thief, the full scale of the problem hit them.

The other shift had also emerged, doubling the number of guards in the compound. Now a sea of painted smiles jostled and shoved at the five fighting for their freedom. The storm was still raging in the night sky and the frequent flashes of lightning lit up the guards' masks like sinister mirrors.

By now Fortescue had also reached the broken outer factory doors and grimly he took in the chaos that the creature was causing. The gathered throng of guards was being tossed asunder, left and right, like a frantic parting of waves. The creature was headed for the golden plus-shaped balloon in the center of the compound and nobody was going to stop it.

A long-suppressed feeling of failure awoke once more in Fortescue. It spread through his body as if a cold tap had been turned on, sending icy shivers of defeat along his veins. The creature would not leave him. It would not. He had spent most of his life tracking it down, had invested so much time and money in its training and his plans. He would not fail! He bellowed out across the compound, his voice sharp and desperate:

"I will double the pay of anyone who stops them!"

A new resolve swept through the gathered guards like a shot of electricity. Suddenly the creature was finding it more difficult to make headway, slowing as the crush moved in. Cold hard cash was at stake and these henchmen would do anything to get it.

Squashed tight against it, Cressida almost felt the creature search deep inside itself for a final boost of energy. With the tin shed almost within reach, it barged once more left and right, toppling the guards like dominoes. At last it opened the shed door and shoved Cressida and Adam inside. It was panting with the exertion. It looked first at Adam and then deep into Cressida's eyes.

"Cave safe," it said in a faltering, guttural voice.

"Thank you," Adam replied, moved by the sound of the creature's first words.

"Come with us," Cressida urged.

The creature faltered. . . . It stepped back, then changed its mind, reaching, to Cressida's delight, to pull itself through the doorway. Too late! It was torn away by the baying guards. Cressida reached out for it. Hand and claw touched momentarily. Then the creature disappeared into the heaving mass of brainwashed guards. Tears welled in Cressida's eyes.

Suddenly Saul broke through to the shed and leaped inside.

"Let's get this thing up in the air!" he gasped, kicking away two guards who were trying to follow him in.

Adam was already reaching out of one of the windows and turning the valve to inflate the balloon. It started to rise and the shed shifted slightly.

"Where's Amy?" Cressida asked with urgency.

"She's right behind me," Saul replied.

But then he leaned out of the shed, and to his horror, he saw Amy's pale, frightened face, small and distant among an ocean of nasty, grinning masks. He could not hear her, but he could see that she was saying, "Go, go."

"Get out of here! *Now!*" Saul yelled at Adam and Cressida as he flung himself back into the angry mob.

The tin shed started to rise rapidly, giving Adam and Cressida a bird's-eye view of the pandemonium below. Half of the guards were herding the now-weary creature back toward the factory and Fortescue, jabbing at it with their spears. The other half were swirling around Amy, keeping her in place, awaiting further orders. Saul was punching his way through them like a hare leaping through a wheat field.

"We can't leave them," Cressida shouted.

Adam was thinking the same thing. He grabbed the rudder bar and twisted it around so that the balloon tracked Saul's progress from the air.

"Pass me that, Cress," Adam asked, his brown eyes twinkling as he pointed behind a stack of paint tins at the coil of rope and grappling hook he had noticed before.

Down below, Saul elbowed and shouldered and fought his way through the guards, and with his heart hammering, his breath ragged, he finally reached Amy. She was a point of glittering light in all this grimy chaos—the best reason he would ever have to go down fighting.

"I told you to go," she said weakly.

She let him hold her while the guards massed around them, crushing and jeering. The rain continued to lash down and Saul and Amy were soon soaked and shivering.

"What will happen to us?" Amy asked, her voice soft.

"We're just two lonely, selfish people with no rhyme or reason. Does it really matter?" Saul said, looking deep into Amy's blue eyes.

Fortunately, what became of Saul and Amy mattered very much to Adam and Cressida. Just then a grappling hook plummeted out of the sky and knocked out the five guards around Saul and Amy. The shepherd and the race car driver looked up to see Adam leaning out of the trapdoor in the bottom of the shed.

"Grab hold, you two!" he yelled down.

Shaken from their gloomy mood by the exuberant boy above them, Saul and Amy caught hold of the hook and in a few seconds they were lifted clear.

The stormy winds buffeted the balloon and it was soon sailing high, leaving the empty-handed guards behind far below.

Fortescue watched the splendid balloon go with a grim and pained expression. They knew so much. They could bring the world to his doorstep. And who was it that had helped them to get away . . . ? He screamed across at the guards who had failed to hold Saul and Amy.

"If that creature escapes, all of you will suffer the consequences!"

The other guards ran across the compound to join the cajoling mob already poking and jabbing the creature into the dark space beside the old factory building. Fortescue followed quickly and climbed up the stack of crates so he could look down on the creature and supervise the action.

"That's it," he called over the noise of the thunder that still boomed across the sky. "Operation Bathtub—in case of emergencies. We've rehearsed it enough times."

The guards were herding the creature somewhere specific, in the direction of a large wooden trapdoor half hidden under a crate. The creature looked up at Fortescue with anger, confusion and hurt playing across its face. But Fortescue only laughed cruelly.

And then, as the creature thudded out across the wooden trapdoor, it sensed something was very wrong. The guards all fell back suddenly. The creature looked around at the masks that surrounded it, and all its fight left it. It barely noticed as Fortescue bounded down off the crates and searched out a lever near the wall. Without hesitation, Fortescue pulled.

The trapdoor fell away and the creature dropped, for what seemed like an age, down into the darkness, flailing for something to grab hold of. A number of crates fell with it and they broke open as they hit the bottom, spilling cans of turnip soup across the floor. A squeaking rat plummeted in after them.

The creature landed heavily, but it was back on its feet almost instantly, staring up at the familiar silhouette of Fortescue far, far above.

"This pit is lined with enamel," Fortescue called down. "For all your talents, you are trapped like a spider in a bathtub!"

The creature pressed a long claw against the wall of the pit. It felt cool and smooth to the touch. Then the talent thief howled. It was back in the crater. But this time a spider could not save it.

"I hope yours is a slow and hungry death, you traitor!" Fortescue hissed. "Thanks to you and your oh-so-worthy, talented friends, I must dismiss my guards, destroy the factory and find somewhere to lie low. But be warned—Fortescue is not finished. I still have some spheres—and one day this world will lie quivering before me—fearful and humble in the shadow of my all-powerful greatness!"

Then he stalked away, leaving the creature whimpering to itself softly in the dark.

The balloon in the shape of a plus sign finally bobbed free from the frenzied clutches of the storm. As the clouds dispersed, a calming full yellow moon cast its light down on the tin shed and its occupants. The stars shone brightly too, the familiar constellations comforting the weary travelers. A shining river wove its way like a silver ribbon through hazy valleys below.

Adam had just finished filling them in on the finer details of Fortescue's terrible plans.

"Now there's a few entries for your journal, Mr. Shafer, on top of the boiling rain and exploding glass boxes," Amy said, pushing her hair from her eyes. Her body ached but she felt light of spirit.

"Not sure pen and paper would do it justice," Saul replied.

Adam stood at the front of the shed. He could see the Kappa-Nage mountain range in the distance, lofty and noble. Its peaks seemed like old friends. He shifted his attention inside.

"Shame about your car, Amy," Adam said.

"Hey, I may have lost a car, but I've gained so much more," Amy replied, her voice soft. "I was a dynamic woman traveling at great speed but ultimately going nowhere. For the first time in my life I've made meaningful human contact." She laughed. "And it took some flaky nonhuman creature thing to get me there."

Cressida moved to the rear of the shed and watched Fortescue's old factory recede into the distance. She was so grateful to the creature for what it, along with Adam, had taught her.

"We should rescue it, get it away from Fortescue," Cressida said, her tone clear and definite.

Adam looked over at her as he settled down on some paint cans and took hold of the rudder bar. His sister had changed. And for the better. She was warmer, kinder—but more important to Adam, she seemed happy.

"I agree. It could be tricky, though," he said. "Fortescue will probably be on the move again soon, expecting us to come after him."

"Well, I've tracked and saved many a sheep from a pack of wolves," Saul said. "It's no different."

"And there's the talent spheres we buried," Cressida suddenly remembered. "We need to fetch them. We should try to get the rest back as well."

Amy yawned. She couldn't help herself. "That sounds like a real combustion chamber of a mission," she said.

"But let's grab a few days of rest first, eh?" Then she glanced at Saul, the man who had saved her, the man who had filled her heart. "What do you say, shepherd?" she asked.

"Whatever we do, I think we should stay together," he said with a smile.

Amy turned her gaze to Adam and Cressida. With a depth of feeling she had never known before, she said, "Seems like a good plan."

And in that moment, floating over a strange land in a tin shed, Adam and Cressida felt they had found home.

EPILOGUE

· · · · · · · · · · · · · ·

And so the creature sat at the bottom of the deep pit, staring through the gloom at the smooth enamel walls. It had tried to climb out, but its spider talents really were of no use when faced with such a sheer slippery surface.

Day after day, the creature peered at the pieces of crate that had fallen down with it. It could not read, but it knew now that its so-called name, "Nipso," was written again and again all over them. How could Fortescue really have been the creature's friend when he thought no more highly of it than he did a horrible can of soup? Even worse, the creature realized, he had had this terrible trap ready all along.

One night, the rat that had also fallen down into the pit scuttled out from a dark corner, squeaking with hunger. The talent thief opened a can with a sharp claw and let the rat drink.

The creature watched the rat as it filled its belly, and as it did so, it sensed another presence in the fur of the rat. A tiny hopping thing—a flea. With gleaming eyes and quick, stealthy movements, the creature plucked the flea from the rat and began its peculiar trilling song. While doing so, it had a twinge of guilt. It had never felt that in the Marscopian jungle. Being with humans had certainly complicated things. But it had brought an extra dimension to the creature's world too. A minuscule glowing black sphere hovered up out of the flea. The creature marveled at the beautiful, barely visible speck of matter. Then it flicked it into its mouth and swallowed instantly, absorbing the astounding jumping talent that the flea possessed.

Now the creature fell into a long sleep. Its body chemistry altered gradually as the sun and moon wheeled across the sky. Layers of muscle began to build on its once thin and sinewy legs.

It was nighttime when it awoke again, and the creature felt immediately the surging power in its newly meaty thighs and calves. It scooped up the rat and its now earthbound flea and, with an incredible burst of power, leaped free from the pit.

It landed gently and put the rat on the ground. The charred remains of the factory building loomed nearby.

The creature wanted to leave, to get as far away as possible from Fortescue's old home and his lies. Maybe it would return to the beautiful Marscopian jungle. Maybe it would seek out a true friend—the singing girl. Someone who could help it grow and understand where its place was in the world. It squatted down and then leaped high into the night sky. Within moments it was far away.

One stormy night the talent thief crept into a dream **Alex Williams** was having in his home in deepest Cornwall. He demanded that Alex write this book, or whatever genius he had for storytelling would be taken from him. The result lies within. Alex hopes the talent thief is satisfied and will now leave him to his quiet life of movie watching, mountain biking and painting pictures (not of that scary talent thief).

After completing a foundation diploma in art and design at Falmouth School of Art, Alex went on to study film at Plymouth College of Art and Design. He is now a Best Writer BAFTA-award-winning children's TV and film screenwriter and author, living in Cornwall, England.

The Talent Thief was first published in the UK in October 2006 and was immediately optioned for a major motion picture. Alex is also the author of *The Deep Freeze of Bartholomew Tullock.*